"Why do I frighten you, Lily?"

She shook her head vehemently, appalled at her cowardice. "You don't!"

He was her husband, after all. It wasn't as though he would hurt her in any way. It was herself she feared, what she might become if she let herself respond fully. "I told you I'm not afraid of you."

His chuckle was wry. "Well, darling, you scare the hell out of me."

Surprised, her train of thought lost, she turned to face him. "I do?"

He nodded, one side of his mouth kicking up in a half smile. "Indeed. You are so different from any woman I have ever known." He trailed one finger up her arm to her shoulder. "So very different."

Lily closed her eyes and sighed. "I don't know what you want."

"Yes, you do. I want all of you, Lily. Everything within you. Everything you are!"

* * *

The Viscount
Harlequin Historical #747—April 2005

Praise for Lyn Stone's recent titles

The Scot
"A delightful tale of a young woman determined to have freedom within her marriage, if not under the law."
—*Romantic Times*

The Highland Wife
"Laced with lovable characters, witty dialogue, humor and poignancy, this is a tale to savor."
—*Romantic Times*

Bride of Trouville
"I could not stop reading this one....
Don't miss this winner!"
—*Affaire de Coeur*

The Knight's Bride
"Stone has done herself proud with this delightful story...a cast of endearing characters and a fresh, innovative plot."
—*Publishers Weekly*

LYN STONE

THE VISCOUNT

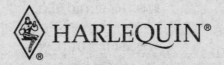

HARLEQUIN®

TORONTO • NEW YORK • LONDON
AMSTERDAM • PARIS • SYDNEY • HAMBURG
STOCKHOLM • ATHENS • TOKYO • MILAN • MADRID
PRAGUE • WARSAW • BUDAPEST • AUCKLAND

ISBN 0-373-29347-X

THE VISCOUNT

Copyright © 2005 by Lynda Stone

This edition published by arrangement with Harlequin Books S.A.

® and TM are trademarks of the publisher. Trademarks indicated with
® are registered in the United States Patent and Trademark Office, the
Canadian Trade Marks Office and in other countries.

www.eHarlequin.com

Printed in U.S.A.

Please address questions and book requests to:
Harlequin Reader Service
U.S.: 3010 Walden Ave., P.O. Box 1325, Buffalo, NY 14269
Canadian: P.O. Box 609, Fort Erie, Ont. L2A 5X3

This book is for Mary Ann Caissie, a friend I treasure.
Thanks for sharing good times and bad, kiddo.
Your smile and optimism are priceless.

Chapter One

London—April 1859

Lily Bradshaw quickly rolled off the bed and bunched up the heavy blanket so it would appear that she lay there sleeping if anyone looked in. Then she crept over and huddled beside the locked door. There was no other place to hide. And then, not for long.

"Has she awakened?" a voice rasped. Though obviously intended as a whisper, it almost boomed within the near silence.

"I expect it will be a while, considering," came the smooth, untroubled reply, hardly even muted below a normal conversational tone.

Lily had been awake for nearly an hour by her reckoning. She had lain, clutching at the scratchy blanket, frozen with fear as her eyes grew accustomed to the meager light from the small barred window set high in the door. The cell reeked of urine and despair. And it was cold. Very cold. She shivered now and deliberately slowed her breathing, knowing she could not afford panic.

"Is she in there alone?" A shadow blocked light for a few seconds as if someone peered inside, gave up the attempt to see anything and then moved away.

"Yes. We isolate new arrivals here until they can be examined and placed in the proper ward. No time for that yet, of course, since her admittance was an emergency of sorts. Would you care to see her?" Silky and dark, the tone was more frightening than that of the one growling the questions.

"Not necessary. You know what to do next?"

"Of course." A short pause, then Silky Voice spoke again. "I will give her more of this laudanum tonight before she wakes completely. That will ensure she remains tractable. Then I will give her something stimulating to put her in top form for her examination. You have notified the proper authorities?"

"Word will be sent in the morning once I hear from you that all is in order here."

"Excellent."

Lily shivered and covered her mouth to stifle a whimper of terror. She was not precisely sure who her examiners were supposed to be, but from the howls and screams echoing through the walls and floors this past hour, she could make a ready guess. Someone had locked her in a madhouse and was planning to prove her insane.

Her next thought was of Beau. What had they done with her son? Surely he still remained safe at Sylvana Hall. Safe with his nurse, playing with his toys, reading his primer and doing his sums. No one had any reason whatsoever to harm a small lad of seven. But then, no one had reason to put her in an asylum, either. Or had they?

Suddenly as that, common sense caught up with her and she realized precisely who would benefit. With her declared insane, her husband's brother Clive would gain control of both her son and his inheritance. And, as his uncle and only male relative, nothing would stand between Clive and the title. Except for the little boy who held it now.

Jonathan had died two years ago. Had Clive been waiting for enough time to pass after Jonathan's death so that he wouldn't rouse suspicion? Perhaps his own funds had run out. Or maybe greed had simply overcame him.

She could not say for certain whether the man with that growling whisper was her brother-in-law, but it was possible…even probable. Who else could it be?

No sooner had she thought it than she heard the voice again. "Suppose she is lucid when they arrive. In their view, two brief episodes of hysteria might not qualify as insanity and warrant…this."

"Not to worry. She will convince them." Lily could hear a smile in the other man's assurance. "But we should move her immediately to Plympton's after you obtain the writ for her committal."

"Why not simply leave her here in London?"

She was in London? How in the world had she gotten here?

"Plympton is privately run, of course," said Silky Voice, "and it will be easier to manage her care there than here in London. Safer, and certainly more convenient for me. I shall have the earl to deal with, as well, if all goes as planned."

A nasty scoff. "That old lunatic? Duquesne should have put him away years ago instead of keeping him at home. So you're to be one of his attendants?"

Silky Voice again. "Assuming Lord Duquesne hires me, which I'm certain he will. I hear he's desperate for another caretaker. My interview with the viscount takes place tomorrow at nine and I have letters of referral. I shouldn't think he'd be too particular, and even if he is, I am well qualified."

"Just be certain you're here when she is examined. I warn you, muck this up and you will not be working anywhere, Brinks. Do I make myself clear? I want her taken care of."

Silence.

Then one set of footsteps moved away until they became inaudible.

Lily's heart drummed so loudly, she was afraid the man remaining—Brinks, was it?—on the other side of the portal could hear it thumping.

She had to get out. Now. Before her greedy brother-in-law arranged for her permanent incarceration. But where could she go? She hated London and never came here if she could avoid it. She knew virtually no one here.

But you do, a small voice whispered inside her head. *And he helped you once before.*

Lily shook her head at the ridiculous thought. The only reason he even came to mind was the mention of his name just now. Viscount Duquesne had his own troubles. Why should he do anything for her?

Though they hailed from the same county, Lily had not seen the man in years, not since she was a child. Dark rumors concerning his shadowy dealings with so-

ciety's dregs, his apparent willingness to do anything—
no matter how dangerous or outrageous—for a price,
had rendered him a social pariah.

Even if that were not the case, his lack of fortune and
his father's illness would have put him beyond the pale.
Not someone a lady approached for help. Duquesne
was an outcast, so she had heard, living in an eyesore
of a once-grand mansion on the fringe of Mayfair.

Even if she had firm promise of his assistance, how
in the world could she escape this place? Though she
was five feet, seven inches, tall for a woman, she
doubted she possessed enough physical strength to
overpower a man.

She shifted nervously and her boot heel scraped
against the floor. Her breath hissed inward at the sound
as she froze.

She remembered returning to the library at Sylvana
Hall following her afternoon ride, removing her hat, ac-
cepting a sherry from Clive and sipping it. She disliked
sherry, but his politeness had been so out of the ordinary, she had taken it. Thank God she had dashed most
of it into the potted plant when he was looking out the
window or she might still be unconscious. The cad must
have drugged her.

If, indeed, it *was* Clive. The voice she'd heard was
somewhat muted and teemed with an excitement Clive
rarely exhibited. She simply could not be certain.
Though they were far from close, she had always gotten on well enough with him, or so she thought.

Had she been brought here this afternoon? Yesterday? The day before? There were no windows opening
to the outside, so there was no way to judge the time of
day or night. She guessed night, since lamplight flick-

ered through the bars in her door. But if there were no windows in that outer room, either, then it could be midday for all she knew. The bare cell was furnished with only a bed that was bolted to the wall and a small tin chamberpot. She glanced at the item now and decided it would be useless as a weapon.

Thank God they had not undressed her or removed her riding boots. One of those might work. The heels were substantial with their metal crescents tacked on to prevent wearing down of the heavy leather. She slipped the boots off, hefting one in her hand to test its weight.

She heard the footsteps of the second man. He was leaving, too! "Brinks? Oh, Mr. Brinks!" she called, drawing out his name, trying to sound distraught. Not much acting was required for that. "Could you come in?" Hopefully he would be curious as to how she had learned his name.

The sound of his departure halted immediately. Lily sensed him just on the other side of the door, listening.

She turned her face away when she spoke so he would not know she waited near it. She slurred her words. "I am so thirsty. I would do anything for a drink. Anything," she added with a loud sigh. "I feel so tired. So…weak. Mmm."

Long minutes passed. He hadn't gone away. He must be considering the advisability of entering, or perhaps of administering more of the mixture that had rendered her unconscious. *Come in. Come in. Now, before I lose my courage.*

Her silent pleas were answered when she heard the rattle and snick of the key in the lock.

A head poked inside cautiously, then a shoulder. A hand holding a lamp.

Desperate, knowing he would soon discover that tangled blanket on the bed was not her person, Lily reached out, grabbed his hair and yanked him inside before he thought to resist. She kicked at his feet. They flew out from under him and he fell, sprawling forward with a loud grunt as he hit the floor. She struck immediately. The heavy heel of her boot cracked soundly against his temple and he lay still.

His lamp had crashed to the floor and fire leaped from the small puddle of fuel. She grabbed the blanket off the bed and tossed it over the blaze, relieved when it extinguished the flame. However, she was now in the dark again with only faint light emanating from the crack of the door that stood ajar and the small window in it.

She hurriedly ripped at the buttons on the front of her riding habit and shrugged off the jacket. Then she slipped out of her shirtwaist, skirt and petticoat. Might as well go the whole way, she thought, pulling off her chemise. Naked save for her stockings and garters, Lily began to strip the attendant of his clothing. Every stitch.

In what seemed ages and yet the blink of an eye, she managed to redress herself. His clothes fit her a bit loosely, but well enough. He was slight of build for a man, heavier than she was, though not significantly taller. His boots were too large, but she would have to make do with them since hers were obviously those of a woman. She stuffed her own silk stockings in the toes and pulled them on.

He began to stir then and she lifted her own boot, striking hard a second time before conscience could stop her. Why should she care if she hurt the wretch? Look what he'd had in mind for her!

Lily found his money and two letters. Those missives gave her an idea how she might approach Duquesne. Assuming she was successful in getting out of here.

Also, there were two small, stoppered bottles in his pocket. The elixirs that were meant for her? Neither was labeled. One smelled like laudanum. She parted his lips, firmly pinched his nose shut and poured the liquid from that one down his throat. All of it.

He swallowed, coughed and moaned only once. She looked at the other container, recalled what he had mentioned about it putting her in top form, and tucked it into a vest pocket.

After cursory notice of the money she discovered— scarcely enough to hire a hackney across town—she slipped his flat leather folder back into the inner pocket of the coat.

Searching hastily, she found the pocketknife that had clunked to the floor when she had undressed him. Anyone seeing her on the way out or later on the streets would instantly recognize her as a woman. She opened the blade of his knife and began to hack away her long locks without a thought to their loss other than relief.

When she felt her hair was short enough to augment her disguise, Lily gathered up the loose hair, bundled up her own clothing and then spread everything flat beneath the thin mattress so he wouldn't find it immediately when he awoke. Left naked, he would probably hesitate for a while before calling for help.

She opened the door a bit more so that she could see better and located the ring of keys that had dropped when he fell. She stuck those in her pocket.

With a mighty effort, she grasped the fellow beneath his arms and dragged him. The struggle to get him off the floor and onto the bed exhausted her, but she finally managed.

A quick glance around the small chamber assured her that it would pass a cursory inspection if anyone peeked through the door window or opened the door to look.

There was nothing substantial to use to tie him so a gag would be useless. Her only recourse was to get out of the building and away from here before he came around again and made a fuss. She prayed that the liquid she had poured down his throat would be powerful enough to keep him asleep for a while.

After locking him in, Lily pocketed the keys again and strode down the dimly lit corridor to her right. This was the direction the sound of the other man's footsteps had taken. Was it not?

There were windows to one side of it, closed doors to rooms on the other. She saw it was, indeed, already dark outside.

The odors in the asylum were atrocious and the intermittent sounds of human misery, heartbreaking. Lily assiduously ignored both, trying not to wonder how many were locked away in here unlawfully, as she had been.

She continued, walking purposefully, practicing what she considered the gait of a man. A sort of swagger. Longer strides, toes more out than in, since she knew that toeing in caused the hips to sway. She tugged her cuffs as she had often seen her father do and pulled back her shoulders. That thrust out her bosom, she realized when the shirtfront tightened across it. She hunched a bit to make that less obvious.

The corridor opened into a larger chamber. Lily

strode right past a sleeping attendant and traversed yet another wide passageway that she found led to the cavernous entrance hall.

Two men sat conversing on the far side, well away from the main doors. One called out a good-night and she threw up a hand in acknowledgment without looking directly at them or speaking. But when she tried the door, her last obstacle before reaching freedom, she found it securely locked.

Terror gripped her, sucking the breath right out of her lungs. Then she remembered the keys. She fished them out of her pocket and isolated the largest one, hoping her guess was correct. Quickly she inserted it in the door and twisted it right, then left.

Thank God. Again she tried the door handle and, miraculously, the door opened smoothly on its hinges without so much as a squeak of protest.

With a shudder of heartfelt relief mixed with apprehension, Lily strode out, down the stone steps to the street and disappeared into the night.

Only after she crossed the Thames from Southwark, and knew she had escaped her immediate nightmare, did she pause to think about where she was going next. Her knowledge of London was rudimentary at best.

Did she dare turn to Duquesne? Did she have a choice?

Would he or anyone else help her if Clive had already put it about that she was insane? She had made a scene at the Danson's soiree, there was no escaping that.

Was that one of the *incidents of hysteria* he would use to convince people? To tell the truth, she had not felt at all herself that evening and could scarcely remember much of what she had said and done. How long had he been planning to spirit her away and lock her up? Had he even drugged her that night to make her seem mad?

She leaned against the solid brick wall of a deserted haberdasher's shop and shuddered like a leaf in a fierce wind. Tears covered her face and filled her throat and chest. Her breath came in gasps, her head ached to perdition and her knees felt weak as water.

No matter how hard she tried, Lily could not decide what she should do next. What a sheltered existence she had led before her marriage and even after Jonathan had died. No one would protect her now that she needed it. Her father, gone. Her husband, gone. Her son, too young. Her brother-in-law, dangerous. Suddenly furious that no one had given her any preparation in fending for herself, Lily cursed. Right out loud.

All she had wanted thus far was to live a quiet life in the country and to raise her beloved son to shoulder his responsibilities and be a kind and loving man like his father. Since she was twelve or so, her own father had drummed into her that's what she should aspire to. A lot of good that had done.

Anger was a stranger to her, this horrid, all-consuming rage she felt now. And yet she was thankful for it. At least her fury had lent her the impetus to act and kept her from being paralyzed by her fear. She would not give in to the fear now that she had come this far.

Dare she trust Duquesne not to send her directly back to Clive once she related what had happened? Or should she follow through with the outrageous idea prompted by the letters she had found in Brinks's pocket?

That she would even consider seeking out such a

dangerous man brought an even more troubling question to mind. Was it possible Clive was justified? Could she truly *be* insane?

Guy watched his ancient butler, Bodkins, shuffle just inside the doorway. The poor old bloke should be in bed, but he'd be up and around even after Guy retired for the night. How Bodkins managed at his age was indeed a mystery.

It was nigh on nine o'clock. One more entry to make in the accounts and he would have them up to date. A first. He picked a bit of lint off the point of his pen and frowned at the stain on his thumbnail. "Yes, what is it, Boddy?"

"A young gent's arrived, milord. A Mr. Pinks."

"Brinks?" That appointment was scheduled for tomorrow morning. Unless Boddy had forgotten to mention it had been changed. The old fellow's hearing had all but deserted him and his memory was not what it should be.

Ah, well, Brinks was here, might as well have done with it. He would either do for the position or he wouldn't. Shouldn't take long to discover which. "Very well. Send him in." When Bodkins remained where he was, Guy repeated, louder this time.

Bodkins made a slow turn and retraced his steps. Guy shook his head sadly, wondering how much longer he could afford to allow the old dear to keep working. Putting him out to pasture would surely kill him, but if he stayed on here…

"Lord Duquesne," Bodkins announced, his ancient voice cracking. He cleared his throat noisily. "Mr. Pinks to see you."

Guy looked up and smiled. Charm never hurt and often helped where employees were concerned. "Mr. Brinks. Good of you to come."

He reached over to adjust the flame in the lamp. The lighting was insufficient even then. The dark walls of the house seemed to drink up light like thirsty sponges.

Guy regarded his visitor, trying not to do so through narrowed eyes. Damn, he'd be needing spectacles one of these days if he didn't spring for more lamps.

Economizing had become too ingrained a habit when it had been necessary. Even though he wished to keep up the appearance of penury, he might have to adjust spending for a few of his private needs.

He studied Brinks. The bloke was too slightly built for the employment Guy had in mind. And too young, obviously. But perhaps he might work as an assistant to Mimms, someone to fetch and carry things. Taking care of the earl was a time-consuming and physically demanding task, and the valet was aging. Guy had decided that two attendants would be better than one. He almost winced at the thought of the added expense. Habits died hard.

He forced a pleasant expression. "I thought we were to meet tomorrow morning."

"There…there was a sudden change of plan," Brinks said hesitantly. "I am most eager for the job and free to leave immediately. Now. Tonight. If you'll furnish transportation, I could go on ahead, sir."

His voice was rather high-pitched. And he seemed frightened, ducking his head that way. This would never do. If he feared a sane man, he would surely quail in the presence of one as unstable as the earl.

"Well, I haven't exactly hired you yet, now have I? Were you sacked?" Guy asked directly.

"No, my lord. I have two letters of recommendation."

"May I see them?"

"Of course." Hesitantly the lad crossed the room, his steps tentative, his head still bowed.

"Come, come, let's have them," Guy ordered, beckoning impatiently.

As Brinks complied, Guy noted the softness of the ungloved hand that offered the envelopes. The well-tended nails were slightly dirty. Guy would have preferred some indication the bloke could work, and failing that, that he would at least be conscientious about cleanliness.

Quickly he took out the pages and gave them a perfunctory read. One was from a Sir Alexander Morison who had been physician to Hoxton's hospital for the insane three years before. The other from the chief administrator who worked there now. By all reports, Mr. John Brinks was a dedicated employee who was never late and always conscientious in the performance of his assigned duties.

Guy laid the letters aside and spread his palms flat on his desk, regarding his visitor with some amusement. "Do you think I might see something other than the top of your head? You aren't afraid of me, are you, Mr. Brinks?"

The face appeared then, limned with warm light from the lamp that sat just to one side of the applicant. Guy's breath caught at the sight.

Small wonder the boy had kept his head down. Any fellow that pretty would have a damned difficult time obtaining employment anywhere other than on a stage playing female roles. Or perhaps in an institution where his unusual looks would probably go unremarked by his charges.

However, something was wrong here. Brinks hardly looked old enough to have worked three years anywhere other than as a student at school.

"What is your age?" Guy asked, his interested gaze traveling the length of the slender, graceful frame and back to the youthful face.

"Twenty-six, my lord. Nearly twenty-seven."

"The devil you say." Guy scoffed and shook his head. "Well, even so, I regret I can't hire you. You won't suit."

"Why not?" The words were a mere whisper.

"Because you are too small, for one thing. This will require someone with greater strength than yours. Sorry."

Brinks didn't move.

"Oh." Guy realized he still had the reference letters spread out on the desk. He quickly replaced them in the envelopes and handed them back. "I wish you luck in securing another position, Mr. Brinks. And again, thank you for responding."

Even with that obvious a dismissal, Brinks still didn't leave. He seemed unable to stir.

"Is there something else?" Guy asked, steepling his fingers beneath his chin.

"You *must* hire me, my lord. Please. Indeed, I must leave London immediately. The sooner, the better."

Guy studied the unique features carefully. Apprehension lit the earnest dark blue eyes framed with long lashes. Color heightened the cheekbones any woman would kill to possess. Lips, naturally full and red a moment earlier, were now firmed to a pale tight line of desperation.

"Why so eager to get away, Mr. Brinks? Explain and I might be inclined to help you."

Confusion reigned for a full minute, then a sigh rent the air. "A patient, my lord. He's been released from the hospital and has come after me. I dare not even return to my rooms to collect my things. This man is dangerous. He has threatened my life!"

A lie, of course. Easily detected, too. Guy wondered whether Brinks realized the girlish pitch that ensued with the pleading. Interesting. "How is it that this dangerous individual was released?"

"A…mistake, my lord."

Guy crossed his arms and ran a finger over his lips thoughtfully. "I thought all of the criminals at Bedlam had been removed to Broadmoor some time ago."

"This man has committed no crime that I know of. Yet. In his confused state, he blames me for his confinement in hospital because I was the one to…to take care of him."

"Ah. And how has he threatened your life? How? Be specific, please," Guy ordered.

"Well, uh, he's been following me." Brinks swallowed hard, obviously struggling to control the fidgets. Unused to lying this way, Guy figured.

"Following you, eh?" he asked, encouraging further elaboration.

"Yes, and going about Town claiming to *be* me on occasion. He has even charged some things to my accounts at several shops! I dare not even show myself about the city for fear some will take *me* as the imposter."

"My word, what a dastardly thing for him to do!" Guy exclaimed, becoming more fascinated by the minute with this Banbury tale. "Do tell, what else has he done?"

"I fear to guess, my lord. Please, could you furnish me with transportation of some sort and send me on to Edgefield this very night?"

"I see. And if I should do this, you feel you would be safe?"

The nod was almost frantic. "I believe so. I would be most beholden to you if you would arrange it. I promise I would work hard and care for your father as if he were my own." A slight pause ensued. "For as long as I am there."

Guy straightened in his chair and leaned forward. "You know of Edgefield? How is that? The place of employment was never mentioned in my query to your director."

Brinks hesitated, then took a deep breath. "That is where your father resides, is it not?"

"I prefer my father's place of residence to remain undisclosed. Most people believe he is at our family seat in Northumberland and I prefer they continue to believe that. You will tell no one of this, do you hear?"

"Of course not, my lord." Brinks shifted, either unable or unwilling to fabricate any further explanation.

Guy meant to find how this bit of information had got out. "You obviously know more of my circumstances than is warranted. Are you from Kent yourself?"

"Uh…I hail from nearby Maidstone. I suppose I must have overheard someone say…" The explanation drifted away to an uncomfortable silence.

Guy knew it was useless to continue in that vein. He would have to be more direct. There was definitely something peculiar here and he needed to find out what it was.

This application was no jest, he was sure of that now. Desperation and fear ran deep in those troubled eyes that were avoiding his.

Playing at this no longer proved amusing and it was time to end it.

Guy stood. "The interview is now concluded. I do believe you need help," he said with all honesty.

"Then you will hire me? I may leave London now?" Relief softened the face to the point where it was no longer merely pretty.

Guy frowned at the realization. With the worst edge of terror alleviated, Brinks had transformed into an exquisite beauty.

"No, you are not hired," he answered emphatically as he leaned forward over his desk, resting his weight on his palms, his face scarcely two feet distant from the frightened applicant.

"Please, sir! You must!"

Guy shook his head slowly. "I believe it's time for you to abandon this farce and tell me why a young woman would hack off her hair, don a cheap suit of clothes and seek out employment as a man. It is a dangerous charade, dear girl, whatever your reasons. Are you mad?"

Chapter Two

Lily ran, her last hope fleeing faster than her feet. She flung open the door, dashed out into the hallway and ran headlong into the old butler.

With a cry and a grunt, they fell sprawling, a tangle of arms and legs. Before she could scramble to her feet, a large hand manacled her wrist.

"Be still!" Duquesne thundered, crouching over her like a fiend from hell. His tawny hair tumbled across his brow. His piercing eyes, the gray of deadly steel, devoid now of former pleasantness, dared her to move. His jaw clenched and his full lips firmed in a grimace.

Lily cringed. The vise of his fingers loosened, but he did not release her as his attention turned to the elderly servant.

"Boddy? Easy now. Don't try to rise too soon. Is anything broken?" He spoke loudly, but with what seemed tender concern.

She watched, amazed at the way he handled his servant, encouraging him to tentatively test his neck, back and each limb. Then Duquesne stood and assisted the old man to his feet, dragging Lily upright much less carefully with his other hand.

"None the worse, m'lord," croaked the old man who was frowning at her.

"Thank God for that," Duquesne said with a gust of relief. He raised his voice again, but not in anger. "Even so, I believe you'd best go and lie down. Lean on me and we'll make for your room."

The butler straightened and stood away, jutting out his pointy chin and adjusting his waistcoat. One palsied hand patted down the long strands of gray that had previously covered his shiny bald dome.

His squinty gaze focused on Lily's wrist, still caught fast in Duquesne's grip. "I shall summon the night watch."

"No, that won't be necessary," Duquesne declared. "Off to bed with you, and that's an order." His firm words echoed in the cavernous hallway.

"As you wish, m'lord." The butler shot a threatening look at Lily and shuffled off into the shadows mumbling to himself.

Duquesne forced her back into his study and over to one of the high-backed leather chairs. "Sit," he ordered, letting go of her arm and turning to close the door.

He looked fierce. And terribly handsome, a tall, broad-shouldered figure of a man with strong classic features and a supremely self-confident air.

That had been the first thing she had noticed about him, how handsome he was. She had known handsome men before, several of them. Bounders, the lot. For instance, Clive was handsome. Her husband Jonathan had not been. Consequently, the attribute of good looks did absolutely nothing in the way of recommending trust in this man.

The concern he had shown to his servant obviously did not extend to her.

He drew up to his full, considerable height, his hands on his hips. "Now either you will explain yourself or I shall haul you to the magistrate and have *him* determine why you applied for employment with false references."

Lily could not think of any lie that might elicit his aid any better than the truth would do. Earlier she had considered simply laying the situation before him and pleading for help. She wished she had done that at the outset. Her chances might have been better. Now she had no choice.

All she had wanted was the means to reach home, to make certain her son was safe and not in Clive's clutches. Since she had already been dressed for the part and no one—not the men at the hospital, the hack driver or the old butler himself—had paused to question her gender this evening, Lily had believed playing out her charade as Brinks might work. Unfortunately she had not anticipated the keen eye of Lord Duquesne.

She had elected not to trust a man about whom she knew nothing. Well, hardly anything past one brief encounter when she was a child and current rumors of his rough existence. Lily was aware, of course, that Edgemont, one of his father's estates, lay adjacent to that of her son. She had heard that Duquesne's father, the earl, was sequestered there and that Duquesne had chosen some years ago to reside permanently in London.

If Brinks had not mentioned his name tonight, she would never have thought to come here. The problem was, Lily knew more about Duquesne—little as that was—than she did about anyone else in London.

This house declared more about the current state of

his finances than she might have guessed. There was little furniture in evidence, at least in the foyer, hallway and his study. No paintings, sculptures or any other trappings of wealth. Except for this room, what she had seen of the place thus far made it look abandoned and uninhabited.

The chair in which she sat badly needed repair and the ancient velvet draperies at the window appeared threadbare even in the low light cast by the lamp. For the first time she noticed that the bookshelves lining three walls of the chamber were almost completely bare.

A fragile hope bloomed. Perhaps, if she could not appeal to Duquesne's honor, he could be bought. Everyone knew he needed money. Why else would he do what he did? But he was a solitary soul and that was evident, too. Perhaps he liked his circumstances just as they were. Then again, perhaps not. She must take the chance, Lily decided. She would purchase his protection, whatever the cost.

His clothing gave her pause. It was not cheap, by any means. The nankeen trousers were obviously tailor-made for his form. The linen shirt, though wrinkled, was, also. Over that he wore a long open robe of cut velvet that must have come dear, though it was old and somewhat out of style.

She noted his feet were bare. Long, narrow and pale, they imparted just a note of vulnerability that made him seem human.

He now leaned against the front of the scarred old desk, arms folded over his massive chest, ankles crossed, and waited for her confession. "Well?"

Lily cleared her throat and sat forward, hands clasped

on her knees. She looked up at him, feeling like a penitent and hating it. "I must throw myself upon your mercy, my lord, and hope that you will afford me protection."

He raised one eyebrow and quirked his head as if to encourage her to go on. Not so much as a flicker of sympathy.

She sighed, looked down at the faded carpet, glanced at his feet again, then back at the fearsome countenance. "I am Baroness Bradshaw." She hesitated, waiting for him to challenge her claim. When he did not, she continued. "I believe my husband's younger brother drugged me yesterday—or perhaps the day previous... What day is this?"

"Saturday," he replied succinctly.

"Yesterday, then. I had been riding, came into my library and was offered a glass of wine. I only drank half. The next thing I knew, I awakened, locked in a cell in Bedlam. Of course, I didn't know that until I escaped, but—"

He smiled slightly and bit his bottom lip, but still did not comment. Now both eyebrows rose in a silent question.

"After I awoke, I overheard two men conversing outside the door. When one left and the other entered, I knocked him on the head with the heel of my riding boot, dosed him with the vial of whatever he meant for me. These." She reached into a pocket and produced the two small bottles. "Then I escaped in his clothes." She looked down at her attire and back at him.

He glanced away from her, shook his head and chuckled.

Lily jumped up, tears springing to her eyes. "How dare you laugh!"

Suddenly as that, he sobered, unfolding his arms and resting his hands on his hips. "You may tell whatever jokester sent you that I am no fool. This has been a colossal waste of my time as well as yours."

"No one sent me!"

"Then I cannot imagine why you are here concocting this elaborate ruse. I happen to know that Bradshaw died of heart failure two years ago. Now I'll have the truth from you, or else."

Exasperated, Lily clenched her eyes, wrung her hands and heaved a sigh. "I am Jonathan's widow. Mother to Beaumont, the current Lord Bradshaw."

"Ah," Duquesne said with a scoff. "You must not be aware I once met the person John Bradshaw wed and she most assuredly is not you."

"You knew my father, Vicar Upchurch. Surely you recall his daughter marrying above her station eight years ago? It was the news of the county at the time. Even here in Town, tongues were wagging, I expect."

He bent, examining her features. Muttering an epithet, he shook his head, snatched up her right arm and roughly pushed up her sleeve. "We'll see if that's so," he snapped, holding her arm to the light. The jagged scar in the middle of her forearm shone white in the glare of the flame.

At once, his features clouded with confusion and his eyes met hers. "But…but the child I saw was—"

"*Skinny* is the word you must be seeking," Lily snapped. "Skinny and short for my age. I so regret I do not clearly recall our meeting, my lord. I'm certain we would have gotten on famously."

But she did remember that tall, gangly youth with the kind eyes and a frown of concern for her pain. A fellow more than willing to rescue a child. He had barked orders at her father, whom no one ever dared to command. Then he had lifted her in his strong arms and carried her, murmuring comforting things near her ear. She dearly hoped a vestige of that kindness and willingness to help remained.

He grimaced, his gaze casting about as if searching for details of the incident. "The vicar interrupted my afternoon on the green and commandeered my phaeton to rush you to Dr. Ephriam. You had fallen from a tree and broken your arm. The bone was…never mind." Again, he peered down at her scar. "A poor job he made of the repair. Did it heal without incident?"

Lily jerked her arm away and tugged down the fabric to hide the scar. "So you believe me now?"

He gently smoothed her sleeve with his palm and nodded, his lips pressed together as if pained at having sought proof of her identity. "Yes. I believe you are who you claim to be."

"Then will you help me? My son could be in danger. If you would but furnish me a mount to ride home, I would be most grateful."

"In danger? Why?"

She rolled her eyes, exasperated. "Because my child is the only thing standing between Jonathan's brother and the title, of course."

"The boy is now at Sylvana Hall?"

Lily pressed her fingers to her lips for a moment before answering. "In the care of his nurse…I hope." She fought tears and managed to keep them from falling. God above, how frightened she was for Beau.

Again, Duquesne raised his hand, this time giving

her shoulder a bracing squeeze of reassurance. "I'll make arrangements immediately. Have a spot of that brandy while you wait."

"I'll come with you," she declared.

Duquesne shook his head and offered her a smile. "Please, trust me… I'm sorry, but I cannot recall your name."

For a long moment she studied his eyes. They were clear, a clear, gentle gray now, their expression beseeching and somewhat regretful. She also noted a lack of deceit. "I am Lillian," she replied.

His smile widened, perfectly open and guileless, the smile of a friend happily reunited with a friend. "*Lily*, of course. Your father called you Lily."

And just like that, he was gone. Out the door with all speed, bound for she knew not where. Perhaps to summon the Watch or to send word to Clive to come here and collect her. But Lily thought not.

That was not quite true. She *knew* not. Duquesne would have said outright that that was what he intended if he'd meant to turn her over. Somehow, Lily felt she could afford to put her life in his hands. How strange for her to trust on such short acquaintance when she had been betrayed the way she had.

But Lily saw something in Duquesne that touched her. He was so alone and yet not bitter about it. There was also a wariness about him with regard to her, and she realized it was due to instant attraction. Though she knew she was not a great beauty, Lily was no fool.

He attracted her, too, in a very physical way. Allowed to progress, Lily knew that would seriously complicate matters. She would never trade her body for a man's assistance.

Or would she? No, that sort of dishonorable arrangement would never do.

But she had no money left after hiring the hack to get here, and there did not appear to be any coin here in this poor place to steal. Walking to Sylvana Hall would take entirely too long to be of any use. Besides, that was precisely what Clive would expect her to do and he would surely catch her along the way.

Her best chance now lay with Duquesne's providing her means to arrive home quickly before Brinks awoke, raised a cry and notified Clive that she was missing.

Lily spent some time deciding what she might do once she arrived at the Hall, how she would spirit Beau away from there to safety and where they might go. But where could they go? Sylvana Hall was their home. She had responsibilities there that she had no intention of turning over to Clive. Unless she could prove what she thought he had done, he would remain a threat. What she and Beau needed was a permanent guard. Then an outrageous plan occurred to her.

A headache formed directly between her eyes, a megrim she could not afford at present considering all she had to accomplish before morning.

She took up the half-empty bottle of brandy from the desk and looked for a glass. Finding none, she upended the bottle to her lips and allowed herself two sips for courage.

That was how he found her when he returned.

Guy stifled a laugh at the picture she presented, one hand propped rakishly on the edge of his desk, her hips cocked to one side and her head leaning back to drink his liquor.

The light caught on the ragged wisps of her red-gold curls, furnishing a halo effect. Gilding Lily, the rowdy angel, he thought with an inner smile.

He felt damned glad she was not what he had first thought her to be, some charlatan's whore sent round to ply a scam or worse. Or perhaps a spy. He was ever alert for those since he did a bit of work now and again for the war department and had accrued a few enemies due to that. Fortunately, with peace breaking out, those chores were mostly behind him now and—profits aside—he was relieved.

Lily's story seemed too bizarre for a fiction. While Guy did not know Clive Bradshaw personally, he knew there were men who would do damn near anything to acquire a title and whatever went with it. She was right to worry about the boy. And, judging by what she had suffered at Bradshaw's hands, she should be more worried than she was about herself. Damned if he didn't admire her spirit.

She lowered the bottle to the desk with a solid thunk and faced him as directly as a man might have done. "Is my mount ready?"

Guy crossed to the desk, reached around her to snag the bottle and took a healthy swig himself. He offered it to her again and watched her shake her head impatiently.

He set the decanter aside for the moment. "I've sent for someone reliable, a man I trust with my life. When he arrives, I shall have him go and fetch your son and his nurse. Safer if you wait here."

The blue eyes went wide. "I cannot stay here!"

"Better than in the madhouse," he quipped, looking around him, "though not by much, I'm afraid."

She began to pace, rubbing her arms with her palms

in a gesture that betrayed more consternation than he had seen yet from her. "Mrs. Prine will likely die of apoplexy if a perfect stranger demands they leave the Hall and go with him to London. And besides, she doesn't ride," Lily said, flinging the words over her shoulder as she paused at the window.

"By hook, crook or pony cart, she'll arrive with her charge no later than midafternoon, I promise. And you need not worry for their safety."

Her hands flared helplessly. "I cannot simply sit and wait!"

"Of course not. You must go upstairs and have a good sleep. Your son will be shocked enough at your appearance. If you look done-in, as well, he'll be frightened out of his wits."

She scoffed. "You don't know my Beau!"

Guy smiled. "Has your grit, does he? How old is the scamp?"

He proffered the bottle again and she took it, downed a delicate sip and handed it back, resuming her pacing as she did so.

"He turned seven last month."

"Ah, well, I wager he'll relish the adventure."

She collapsed into the chair and buried her face in her hands. Guy watched her sob twice, then go still. She sniffed heavily once and brushed the tears from her face with a determined swipe of both palms. "Botheration!" Then she shrugged and looked up at him. "Forgive me. I know how men despise tears."

"Don't be an idiot," he said gently, raking the disheveled curls off her brow with his finger.

"I *would* like to avoid being treated as one," she quipped with a self-conscious laugh and another sniff.

Indeed. "Why don't you begin from the beginning and tell me again how it happened in detail? No matter how insignificant you think something might be, include it. I might be able to use it."

"Use it? For what?"

"I don't know yet, but you may rest assured this is not over, Lily. Not by a long mark. Bradshaw made a bold move and has gone too far to simply let it lie. Now begin, and leave out nothing."

He watched her carefully as she related her story.

"So you recognized Bradshaw's voice?" he asked her when she'd finished.

"No, but who else could it have been? I assumed it was Clive because he is the only one who would gain anything by such a deed. He would assume control of my widow's portion—the usual third of the estate—and also the remainder that is being held in trust for Beau. Not to mention Beau himself." She swallowed hard, fighting to maintain control of her emotions. "If he would imprison me the way he intended, I shudder to think what he might do to a defenseless child who stands between him and what he wants."

What had been done to Lily frightened her, Guy could see, but not nearly so much as what Bradshaw might be planning for her son. She was right about one thing. Being the nearest male relative, Bradshaw would acquire the title himself if the boy were out of his way.

"Who might be assisting him in this plot aside from Brinks? That's what worries me," Guy admitted. "He would have to prove your insanity in order to obtain a paper of committal to an institution."

Guy watched her gaze slide away as she worried her

lips with her teeth. "What is it? What are you not telling me, Lily?"

She sighed and sat back in the chair, looking almost defeated. "I rarely go out in Society, but I did attend a small soiree the Dansons held at Livsby Grange a week ago. I attended at Clive's insistence. Apparently, I...I caused something of a scene there."

Guy's attention keened. "Of what sort?"

She busily pleated the hem of her coat as she made the admission. "Well, we partook of the buffet provided. Clive brought me a small plate and a cup of punch. All went well at first. I knew most of the neighbors who attended and the conversation was pleasant enough. Soon after we finished our refreshment, we took seats for the entertainment." She halted.

"Go on. What happened?"

"The lights were lowered. A short while later... everyone began swaying as if to a song I couldn't hear. There was a loud buzzing in the chamber. The noises within it grew terribly keen. Frightening. Then...everyone changed into..."

"Into what, Lily?" Guy asked, keeping his voice low and nonthreatening.

She blinked rapidly and her breathing came in fits and starts. "Horrible...things," she whispered, obviously lost in the memory. "I must have screamed. I can't remember. Clive whisked me out and the last I recall was being tossed into his carriage."

"And later? What did you do?"

She raised her hands, palms up, then let them collapse on the arms of the chair. "Nightmares. I dreamt for the longest time, thinking I would never wake. You see, I knew I was sleeping, that none of it was real. But still it terrified me. The next day I decided I must have consumed something wholly disagreeable to my digestion. I was ill all morning. Other than an occasional bout of palpitations and a lack of appetite, I seemed well over it by that evening."

"Nothing of a similar nature has occurred since then?" Guy asked.

"No. He must have drugged me." She looked up at him, her gaze extremely worried. "Suppose some of those present believed me mad? Could Clive employ their testimony against me, do you think?"

No doubt in Guy's mind that was precisely what was intended, but he held those thoughts to himself for the moment. She was upset enough as it was. Instead he said, "We must find a way to put you out of his reach for a while until we decide what must be done."

"Clive is the only one with the right to have me confined, is he not?"

Guy nodded. "Since your husband is dead and your son too young to make that sort of determination, Bradshaw would be the one."

"Then God help me," she whispered. "I should have left off mourning at half a year and married Jeremy Longchamps when he asked."

Guy laughed out loud, surprising both of them. "You can *not* be serious! He would give you about as much protection as a broken flyswatter. He fights like a girl."

She smiled at that. "You obviously know Jeremy."

"All too well," Guy admitted, glad for the lighter topic. "We were at school together. How is it that you know him?"

"He was a great friend of Jonathan's. We entertained him often. I quite like the fellow, odd quirks and all."

"But not enough to marry him, obviously." Thank heaven for that spot of good sense.

"No, not enough for that. I would have felt more like a sister to him than a wife, though he entertains Beau and thinks the world of him." She sighed. "But marrying Jeremy might have prevented this problem. However, I don't regret my decision, really. He deserves someone who would really care for him in a way I never could."

"I shouldn't think Jeremy would notice, he's so full of himself," Guy quipped. Though Longchamps had used to prove amusing at times, Guy had seldom encountered a fellow more feather-brained and oblivious to the goings-on around him.

"You do not seem to be that way," she said. When Guy looked at her, she narrowed her eyes and regarded him as a cat might do a mouse. "You have been very kind in your treatment of me tonight. Are you always so gentle with those weaker than you?"

Guy smiled. "There is certainly no honor in throwing one's strength around."

"Yes, you do seem accommodating and I appreciate that. Tell me, Lord Duquesne—"

"It's *Guy*, if you please."

"Very well. Guy. Tell me, how do you feel about a marriage of convenience?" her expression looked pensive and even a bit sly.

"That depends. Whom do you have in mind?"

"You, of course." She gestured toward him with one hand.

"Me? Ye gods and little fishes, I'm appalled at the very thought," he answered with real conviction. "You don't mean—"

"But I do." She looked around her as if assessing his

study. "It appears you could use…an infusion of wealth. I could provide that."

"This is ridiculous!" But was it?

Arrangements such as she proposed happened all the time. Only not to *him.* Never once had he entertained the idea of marrying for money.

He frowned at her impudence. His paucity of funds had become a well-known fact in recent years. The up-keep and taxes on the estates at Marksdon, Perrins Close and Edgefield, as well as the town house here, were out-rageous.

When one added the expense of providing the best of care for his father, Guy had stretched even his im-proved resources near their limits. Though he had over-come the threat of ruin some time ago, he kept to his frugal ways.

There were worse things than being regarded as poor. That state offered a certain freedom that being wealthy did not. It certainly whittled down his social obligations, which suited him just fine. Aside from the Kendales and the Hammersleys, damned few of his so-called peers bothered to give him so much as a nod.

Keeping his distance had become a way of life. A safer way, especially where women were concerned. Caring too much was not wise. Loving was bloody well stupid.

He answered Lily as gently as he could. "It's kind of you to offer for me, and you do me great honor, Lily, but I must decline. You see, I'll never marry. I cannot."

"Of course you can," she argued in as near a plain-tive tone as he'd yet heard her utter. "Whyever not?"

He leaned closer to her as if to impart a secret. "Because, dear heart, there is bonafide insanity in my bloodline, as you must know. Everyone who is anyone is certainly well aware of it, no matter how carefully they tiptoe around the subject in my presence."

Her eyes softened with sympathy. "Oh, Guy, I do regret your father's indisposition and that you feel you need warn me of it, but his condition has no bearing on this at all. I am not the least concerned about that. All I would ask is that you provide the safety of your name for me and my son. In return, I shall give you my widow's portion. A fair trade in anyone's estimation. What do you say?"

"That you'd be irresponsible to disregard such a drawback, Lily. My father is out of his mind and has been for years. I absolutely refuse to make anyone heir to that."

"Well then, we should be perfectly suited since I am unable to bear any more children." Though she smiled, her eyes said too much of what that admission cost her.

He did not remark on it for fear of causing her to dwell on the sad fact. At least she had one son, one more than he could ever risk having.

Bravely, she went on. "It would solve any financial woes that might plague you. Beau could use a man's guidance, if you felt inclined to bother with him. Jonathan has been gone for two years now, and I must admit that I do miss married life." She smiled sincerely then, ducked her gaze for a second and blushed.

Guy could not help being shocked and a bit amused. "My, my, you are outspoken for a lady. Donning those trousers must have gone straight to your head."

"Spoken frankly as any man, you mean? I was only thinking that this is no time to mince words. I truly do miss being a wife."

He considered the magnitude of what she had just confessed. A woman of quality never allowed she had any interest in the matter of bedding. If he wasn't mistaken, that was precisely what she had just declared. He pretended to take another meaning from her words, one more acceptable for discussion. "So you loved your husband that dearly, did you?"

She grinned back at him, as if to say she knew that he knew exactly what she had meant. "Oh, Jonathan was a brick. He and I got on like the best of mates even though he was much older. I adored him above anything."

Guy smiled, happy for her good fortune for as long as it had lasted. "How excellent for the both of you. In general, there are damned few marriages that recommend the institution. Though I have witnessed a rare exception or two, I, for one, have little faith in the state of wedded bliss." He shook his head and sighed, thinking that would surely end this strange conversation.

Instead of the disappointment he expected, her face brightened with delight. "There you are, then! You shan't be disappointed if we aren't deliriously engaged. Shall we have a go?"

"No!" he exclaimed, amazed by her continued tenacity. "We shan't *have a go!* I never said—"

She batted a hand at him and rolled her eyes with obvious impatience. "Oh, come now, Duquesne. You cannot tell me you have no use for my money, even if you don't particularly like me."

"Of course I *like* you, Lily! It's only that…" But for

the life of him, he could not list a single reason to refuse her. She had shot all of them down like bottles on a fence.

"And we could be friends," she persisted.

"Friends, eh?" It wasn't as if anyone else would ever have him for a husband, given his family history. Or the reputation he'd made all on his own. And as for Lily, apparently she had already experienced the love of her life. Twice that luck would be too much for any woman—anyone at all, in fact—to expect.

If he agreed, he could certainly put the dowry to good use, invest it and see that the original capital remained hers while the interest went to support the estates and tenants for which they both would be responsible. His holdings would become hers in entirety when he passed on and eventually become her son's since Guy would leave no progeny of his own.

This could prove a decent arrangement, he thought practically. Of course, he had no idea how much wealth was involved, but that hardly mattered at this point.

He was not going to do this. He should not.

But if he did, he could give up all these havey-cavey business dealings he had to manage here in Town. Damn, but he was weary of the subterfuge, the low forms of life he had to coddle or threaten for information. He could retire to the country. Be the gentleman his father would have wanted him to be. The man he had almost become before tragedy struck and forced him to use his wiles to keep solvent. For a while it had seemed challenging, adventurous, even at times great fun, but now….

No, he was not going to marry this woman. It would not do. He had managed by himself for too long to share his life with anyone.

Then he thought about the boy, thrust into such a vulnerable position by the title he had yet to grow into. Guy couldn't deny he would probably enjoy being a parent. He thought he might like children and regretted he could never father any.

Hell, he felt half-child himself, still playing at Turks and Thieves in the dark of night with deadly playmates. He thought of Smarky, scourge of Spittalfield, and Bardy the Bold with his Saracen dagger and delight in death-dealing. Excellent reasons right there to tell Lily no. He could put her in danger by mere association with him.

But she was already immersed up to her neck in trouble, now wasn't she? Who else of her acquaintances would fend off her enemies for her, if he didn't agree to do it?

There was the woman herself, the biggest temptation of all. Lily had spirit, courage and a lively imagination. He could certainly do worse for himself and never any better, by his reckoning. But did he have the right…?

The imp could arouse him with only a smile and most likely realized this power. Aside from her unique and fascinating looks, there was something slightly wild and delicious about Lily, something he could not begin to describe, that tantalized him.

Her scent, sweet and undefinable, perhaps. Or her voice, dulcet of tone and faintly raspy. Seductive when she intended, compelling attention even when she did not. Definitely more than the sum of her lovely parts, Lily Upchurch Bradshaw was an original.

Despite that, he knew that he need not worry about falling in love with her. If ever there was a man safe from that sanguine emotion, it would be himself, considering the practice he'd had avoiding it. Love, to him, meant marriage, children and a future. His father's madness precluded Guy marrying well. Until Lily.

There *was* that one almost overwhelming aspect of Lily that he hated to admit enticed him because it seemed unworthy, even salacious, to consider it. He shouldn't, but he certainly did factor it into the equation.

The plain fact was that Guy had not tupped a woman these past nine years without the onus of accidental pregnancy looming over him like a threatening storm cloud. Freedom from that fear danced here within reach, daring him to reach out and embrace it. To embrace *her.*

Another woman had come to him asking for help less than a year before. Sara Ryan had been a beautiful woman. And in dire straits, too. Yet the idea of bedding *her,* much less marrying her, had never even occurred to him. Why would he even consider such a thing with this one? Well, she had asked, for one thing. And then there was that other benefit....

"You are considering it, aren't you?" she asked, her eyes sparkling with the anticipation of victory.

As sheer flattery went, Guy could not help being affected by her enthusiasm for her plan. Even so...

"I am considering it very carefully," he told her, "since one of us must give a thought to caution."

One golden eyebrow rose. "The infamous Devil Duquesne, a cautious man?" she taunted. "Who would have thought it? Now your reputation will be thoroughly destroyed."

Guy could hardly let *that* pass unremarked. "You do tempt me," he finally said.

Lily sighed. "Enough to accept?"

Chapter Three

Lily wondered if he had been right about her clothing affecting her behavior. Whether it was freedom from the constraint of female apparel or pure desperation that prompted her aggression, Lily saw that she had shocked not only him, but also herself.

Here she had just proposed to the infamous Devil Duquesne, the man people whispered about, feared even, because he was reputed to be dangerous. He did private enquiries and settled disputes in ways that were often permanent, so they said. The government employed him to ferret out spies. Perhaps he was one himself.

Jonathan had loved gossip and had delighted her with all sorts of tidbits out of London whenever he had gone up on business. Well, she was testing this piece of his tittle-tattle, surely.

Duquesne's eyes had narrowed, assessing her yet again, as if from a different angle. He smiled, a near smirk, but it did absolutely nothing to detract from his appeal. Slowly he nodded, his smile growing, as if he couldn't contain it within that cloak of cynicism. Was he going to say yes? Would he really marry her?

Lily almost panicked, very nearly withdrew her bold idea for a solution. If she did marry Duquesne, she might create another whole set of problems.

"Doubts now, Lily?" he asked, crossing his arms and regarding her intently. He looked amused.

"No. None." She would stand firm by her decision. If he would have her, if he would commit to the cause of her protection and that of her son, she'd be willing to wed the devil himself. If that was trading her body and her fortune, so be it.

"If I say yes, you should know that I would expect something from you other than money," he told her.

She was well aware of what that would be, of course, but she had already offered that on a silver platter. "I know."

"Besides that," he said, his expression now rather serious. "If I should…in the future, fall victim to my father's malady, I should expect you to keep me…at home. *My* home, of course, not yours. That is, if you could possibly arrange it."

Lily softened inside, her heart going out to him on the instant. "Oh, most assuredly, Guy. I would never, never consign you to…" She cast about for a nice word for the terrifying place she had just escaped.

He shifted as if highly uncomfortable in speaking of this. His gaze rested on the floor between them. "I considered placing my father at Plympton. It is close to home, privately run and not as bad as one might expect, but I simply could not bring myself to do it, to uproot him from his familiar surroundings. You see, though he's not the man he once was, he has moments, even days, when he functions quite normally."

"Plympton? They mentioned that, Guy! Tonight I heard that name. They were planning to move me there. Where is it?"

He unfolded his arms and braced them on the edge of the desk as he looked up at her. "Roughly twenty miles or so from Edgefield to the north. The old mansion Lord Younger sold off some years ago."

She knew of it, but had not known it was now used as an asylum. "I see. That puts proof to the fact that Clive must be behind this scheme against me, then. It is also near Sylvana Hall, as you know. Once I was certified insane, he could keep watch and perhaps continue drugging me if I were at Plympton."

He nodded. "So, could you agree to this condition? You would, of course, hire a man who would see to my needs and ensure I would be no danger to anyone should the worst happen. You could live wherever you chose."

Unable to help herself, Lily approached him and touched his face, much as she would Beau if he were this troubled. "Oh, Guy, you speak as if this is a definite thing for you to dread."

He covered her hand with his, a light contact recognizing her gesture. "It is a possibility we must address, Lily. As yet, I've suffered no symptoms akin to my father's and I hope I never shall, but I want you aware of what might happen in future. It is wise to plan for all contingencies, don't you think?"

Lily closed her eyes and pressed her lips together, unable to imagine this man incapacitated in any way, especially with regard to his mind. She nodded. "I agree. If you will look after me and my son, I give you my word I shall move heaven and earth to follow your wishes in this." She looked up at him so that he could see she was sincere. "Guy, I will do it anyway. Whether you want me as a wife or not. I shall do it as your friend."

Never had she seen such an expression of relief. And something approaching awe. He cradled her face with both his hands and lowered his lips to her forehead. His mouth felt warm against her skin and very gentle.

Then he pulled back and searched her eyes with his. "This is a terrible risk you're taking, Lily. You don't really know me. You cannot know all I have done or am capable of doing."

She sighed and rested her palms on his chest, feeling the warmth, the beat of his heart, through the rich, worn fabric. "I know that you are compassionate with regard to your father. I know that you listen to me and truly hear what I say. And while you do have a reputation for ruthlessness—" she smiled at his surprise "—a ruthless man is precisely what I need."

His small laugh was self-deprecating as he shook his head. "What gods do you suppose have thrown us together tonight? Ours will likely be a match made in hell."

She straightened, grasping the lapels of his robe. "Then you will do it?"

He dropped a kiss on her lips, just a brief, perfunctory touch borne of camaraderie, it seemed. His voice was light and full of mischief. "Of course I will do it. I'd be a complete fool to refuse such a deal."

Lily felt unaccountably lighthearted, considering the weighty matter at hand. "Excellent!" She backed away from him, a bit self-consciously, breaking his contact with her face and hers with his chest. It was devilishly hard to think when they were touching.

He pushed forward from the desk where he'd been leaning and began to shuck off his robe. "Then we had best get to it. We'll need a special license, back-dated, of course." He spoke as if to himself now. "Justice Jelf will get that, for a hefty fee." All the while, he was donning a jacket that had hung over the back of a straight chair by the door.

Lily watched as he bent behind the desk and then sat to pull on his stockings and boots. It seemed too intimate an act to watch, so she turned away, still listening to his running commentary to himself. "Horses. Hammersley's, I think. We'll ride to Sylvana Hall after, by way of Edgefield, to change your clothing."

"I thought you were sending for Beau and Mrs. Prine," she said, interrupting him.

He looked up from his task. "Not now. I think we should make our stand on home ground. I had thought at first to hide you and your son until I could straighten out this tangle of yours with the authorities. However, if we are married and appear to have been so before Bradshaw made his move, he'll play hell explaining why he kidnapped my wife. We'll level charges against him if necessary."

"But…but we were *not* married then," Lily argued.

He grinned and stood up, stamping to settle his feet into the scuffed Hessians. "Ah, but we *will* have been. Once Tommy Roundhead does his magic on the locks at the records office. Happy first month's anniversary, darling. May we have many, many more."

Lily shook her head in wonder. "I have a distinct feeling ours is going to prove a unique wedding."

"My lady, you cannot even imagine how unusual it's going to be." He opened a drawer of his desk, retrieved a wicked-looking pistol, checked the cylinder of it and added the ammunition. Then he tucked it into the waistband of his trousers where it seemed right at home.

Lily swallowed hard and shivered, suddenly aware of just how dangerous this man might become if crossed.

She watched as he stretched out his hand, inviting her to take it. Or perhaps daring her to do so. "Are you up for a sprint across the back alleys of Mayfair and a night ride into Whitechapel?"

Lily locked her palm to his and intertwined their fingers. A promise. A binding betrothal, however brief. A daring leap into the unknown with a man who might be teetering on the edge of sanity even as they said their vows. Assuming they survived the trip into the bowels of London and lived to take any vows. "Sounds like a dashing evening, my lord. I'm game!"

His grin was pure deviltry and she returned it in kind.

Good as his word, Guy led her out the back of the house and through the tangle of vines at the back gate. The moon cast its weak glow on the path they took, one she knew was traversed by tradesmen and those who were obliged to enter the great homes from the rear entrance. And perhaps by thieves and denizens of the night with no business being here.

She was nearly breathless with exertion and apprehension when he came to a halt and looked up at the high stone wall they had been following and the imposing iron gate in front of them. "It's locked at night. We'll have to climb it." He crouched down. "Put your foot in my hands and I'll boost you. Grab the top and pull yourself up."

Lily took a deep breath and did as he said. Images of their being hauled off by the local watch and trying to explain this distracted her, but she made it. Lying along the top of the foot-thick stone wall, she watched him shin up the bars of the iron gate and join her.

"Now take my hands and I'll lower you down," he said calmly, as if he did this sort of thing every night. Perhaps he did. She complied, coming to rest on solid ground with a thump of her overlarge boots. He followed, taking a moment to brush his ungloved palms on his trousers. "There!"

"Where are we?" she demanded. "And what are we doing here?"

"Earl Hammersley's. He's a friend of mine. We're going to steal two of his horses."

"No!" She grabbed his arm as he started for what looked to be the stables. "You cannot do this! If he's a friend, why not simply ask to borrow them?"

"He's out of town this week. They're visiting Julia's family. His man would never loan his mounts without his approval. Don't worry. I will explain it to him later."

Still, Lily dragged her feet, hoping to dissuade him. "Guy! This is a hanging offense!"

"Don't be absurd, sweetheart. They don't hang nobles." She heard laughter in his voice. The man *was* crazy.

"Well, imprison us then! Guy, this is *madness!*" she rasped in a loud whisper, hating to use that word, but there was none other fitting this deed so well as that.

He kept walking, dragging her along with him. "Oh, stop quibbling, darling. This will be child's play."

Lily groaned.

They reached the stables and he walked right in as

if he owned the place. "Jemmy? Are you asleep, man?" he called.

A moment later a young fellow appeared out of what looked to be the tack room, rubbing his eyes and running a hand through his hair. He did not seem alarmed. In fact, quite the opposite. "Lord Duquesne? What are you doing here this time of night?"

"Came to borrow two nags. Lady Julia's Pepper and Lord Michael's gelding. What's his name?"

"Cinnamon, sir. But you know very well I can't loan them without his lordship's permission. He's told me—"

"I know, I know," Guy said with a sigh. "Turn around."

"Beg pardon?" Jemmy asked.

"Turn around."

The boy, obviously used to following the commands of his betters, did as he was told. Guy pushed him to his knees and slipped a small thin rope around his wrists, expertly tied it off and then secured his ankles, trussing the boy up like a Christmas goose.

"You can get loose with a little effort, but not before we're long away. Tell Lord Michael I'll return his horses in prime condition. He won't be angry with you since you couldn't prevent this."

"But, my lord, you know how he treasures his horseflesh! And I am responsible!"

"Of course you are, lad, but this gets you off the hook. Tell his lordship I've done this to save my wife."

"Your wife!" Jemmy exclaimed, his wide-eyed gaze flew to Lily.

"Lady Lillian," Guy said by way of introduction. "Tell Hammersley."

"Yessir," Jemmy agreed, now resigned and not even struggling to free himself. "Congratulations, my lord."

"Thank you, Jemmy." With that, Guy proceeded to lead the horses from their stalls and assemble the tack. Lily lent a hand, saddling the beautiful black mare herself.

Within minutes they were leading the horses out the back gate, unlocked with the keys Guy seemed to know were ensconced within a hollow in the stone wall. Lily supposed he had been here many times before to know the place so well.

"The earl *will* understand, won't he?"

"Certainly," Guy assured her as he gave her a leg up into the saddle. "Michael might value his mounts above most of his possessions, but he treasures his wife more than life itself. He'll figure I'd do the same."

What would it be like to be loved that much? Lily wondered. She supposed she would never know, but even Guy's pretense of it felt comforting. He had stolen horses for her. Wrong as that was, she experienced a thrill over it. She could never imagine the very proper Jonathan having done such a thing.

His courting of her had been romantic to a degree. They had met quite by accident when a wheel had broken on his trap along the road to Maidstone. Her father had stopped to offer assistance or a ride. She had felt that noble gaze assessing her as she sat beside the vicar, and knew she was the reason Jonathan had accepted the ride. After that, he became a constant visitor, soon a suitor, then her husband. Her father had heartily encouraged her early marriage. Even she admitted she could hardly have expected to do better than a baron, or the man himself. Theirs had been a quiet, steady bond that had strengthened with each passing year and the birth of their son. Perhaps Jonathan's heart had not been strong enough, even then, for the intense sort of love Guy spoke of his friends having. Nevertheless, she felt blessed to have had a good and faithful husband.

She adjusted her reins and prepared to ride, settling comfortably into the man's saddle. She had never ridden astride before and thought she might quite like it.

"On to Whitechapel," Guy announced, obviously eager for the adventure.

Lily nudged the mare closer to the gelding, seeking reassurance in Guy's nearness. She also hoped his sudden enthusiasm for the remainder of their escapade would somehow communicate itself to her. Her reservations were growing by the minute as the moon waned and the darkness of the alleyways swallowed them up.

Guy remained alert, his gaze continuously sweeping the narrowing streets leading them into the infamous hell that was Whitechapel.

Conditions deteriorated the farther they rode, bound for the heart of Rupert Street with its rickety tenements and stench of poverty. Rats skittered off refuse left to rot. Gutters ran with offal and worse.

He glanced at Lily who was barely visible beneath the one flickering oil lamp that remained unbroken past the turn onto Rupert Street. Weapon at the ready, he swiveled quickly at the sound of scuffling feet.

"Stand away," he ordered the figures who appeared out of the cavern between the buildings.

"Aha, 'tis himself!" one of the footpads said with a snarking laugh. "Who'd ye be after then, Duquesne?"

"Tommy Roundhead," Guy growled.

"Cost ye, guv," the fool declared, still sniggering.

"Cost *you* if you don't fetch him," Guy replied, cocking the pistol. It was the expected ritual.

Not two moments later Roundhead stepped out of the alley, immediately recognizable by his overlarge pate. "Duquesne? It's only Thursday."

"Not here for the scuttle tonight, Tom. I've need of you," Guy told him. Without waiting for an answer, he shifted the pistol to his left hand and reached down with his right.

Tommy grasped it and swung up behind Guy on the gelding. "Watch Nell," Tom snapped at the underlings who protected his lair. Nell Gentry, a former street girl, was Tommy's common-law wife and was prone to wander unless he kept a constant eye on her.

"Turn slowly," Guy muttered to Lily. "Ride ahead of me at a walk, the same way we came in."

She nodded and did precisely that. Guy could see around her, but just barely since the streets were so narrow here. He held his breath, weapon cocked and ready lest they be attacked. Tommy would be a deterrent to that since this block was his territory, but he might not be recognized soon enough for his power to be that effective.

They rode out without incident, Lily keeping her mare to a walk when Guy knew she must itch to gallop hell-bent for safety. Tommy hung on to the back of the saddle, unused to riding, nervous as a cat without whiskers. Once on the ground, he would be fearless again. And invaluable.

Once they crossed the Thames, Guy took High Street, turned off on Pramble Close and drew up in front of the house of Justice Jelf.

"Gor, Duquesne!" Tommy exclaimed. "What truck have ye got wi' Jelf? I'd as soon not come in wif ye, if it's all th' same."

Guy agreed. "Stay with the mounts. Anything happens to these horses, Tommy, I'll rip the ears right off your head. Understood?"

"Righto, guv. Lend me that gun then."

"Not on a dare," Guy replied, helping Lily dismount. "You're well armed. Never known you not to be."

Tommy laughed softly, took the reins of both mounts and wrapped them around his left hand. "You be long?"

"Long enough to wed. Ten minutes at most."

"Ha! Ripe lie if I ever heered one."

Guy ignored the aside, took Lily's arm, ushered her to the door and rapped smartly on the panel.

It was midnight by now, but Jelf would be awake, most likely with a card game in progress. Still it took a good five minutes and sore knuckles to get him to the door.

"Eh?" the man snapped as he opened the door a crack. Sure enough, he was dressed, though his shirt hung open to mid-chest and his dark hair was rumpled as if he'd run his hands through it half the night.

Justice Lord Jelf looked much as he had on his worst of nights during their last year at Eton. How he'd managed to secure his current position, Guy could only guess, but it certainly came in handy at times.

"What do you want at this hour, Duquesne? A game?" He cast a lazy glance at Lily.

Guy pushed the door wider and moved past the justice. "I want to get married. You sober, Galen?"

"Sober as a judge," Jelf cracked, laughing at his own poor joke. "Married, you say? When and to whom, if I might inquire?"

"This very minute, to her." He inclined his head toward Lily. "Get your book and the paperwork. We're in something of a rush."

"Where's your license?"

"In your desk, I expect. Go and get it." If there was a form in London Galen Jelf didn't have copies of, it had not yet been printed up in quantity. A profitable sideline, as it were.

Jelf raked Lily with a sly look of interest. "Sure you've got the bride here, Guy, and not the best man? Though it's pretty enough, whatever you've chosen."

"We can do without the comments, Jelf. We married last month, understand? I want no question of that should anyone inquire or check the records."

Jelf smiled, a knowing expression. No doubt thinking Lily was in an interesting condition and Guy was doing the right thing.

"You owe me, Jelf," Guy reminded him.

"And now you shall owe me, my friend. Fifty pounds is the price. Are you solvent?"

"As salt in water. I'm good for it. She's rich," Guy said.

Lily nodded and stuck out her hand to shake. "Lily Bradshaw. Nice to meet you, Justice Jelf."

"Aha, it speaks! Felicitations then," Jelf said smoothly. "Come with me, children. It's a nasty deed you commit, but I'll stand for it. Do we want fictional witnesses or do you have someone in mind? How about Kendale and Hammersley? Will they vouch?"

"Absolutely. Good thinking. I'll post them my thanks tomorrow."

They repaired to Jelf's study where he lit a lamp and produced a handful of papers from a drawer. Pushing the pen and inkstand toward Guy, he watched as the blanks were filled in. He signed, too, with a flourish and then opened his book to commence the civil ceremony.

"You understand this will not be recognized by the Church? I'm not ordained and this is no House of God."

Guy nodded. "So long as it's legal."

"It serves for Jews and Catholics," Galen muttered, and turned the page to begin.

Guy regretted the need for this, knowing any woman on earth would prefer her wedding to be otherwise. Hell, any man would, too, come to think of it.

Jelf's curt statements and questions bore none of the sentimentality or religious overtones of the Church of England service. Cut-and-dried, it was over in a trice. A done thing.

"By the power vested in me by the Crown, I pronounce you man and wife. She's yours to kiss, Duquesne. Have at it."

He immediately headed for the doorway. "Douse the lamp and close the doors behind you, if you won't mind. I'm holding three eights and they're just foxed enough to count me out if I'm away more than five minutes." He threw up a hand in farewell. "Luck to you both. Barring that, may you have an interesting life." His voice trailed off down the hallway toward the back of the house.

Reluctant to face her before, Guy now shot Lily a look of apology. Then he quickly bent and pressed his lips against hers, hardly taking time to feel the softness of her lips. Later, he promised himself.

"I'm…amazed," she said.

"Then my kissing's improved by leaps," he replied.

She leaned over to extinguish the lamp. "Let's ride," she ordered.

Guy snatched up their copies of the marriage license and certificate on the way out. By first light, the duplicates of the papers would be snug in the files, awaiting anyone who might question the marriage of Viscount Duquesne and Lady Lillian Upchurch Bradshaw. Roundhead would see to that.

In the meantime, there were thirty miles of hard road between here and Sylvana Hall. Not much of a night, as wedding nights went. And God only knew what they would face in the morning.

Guy handed Roundhead the papers and told him specifically where to put them. "Tommy, it's essential you get these in place before daybreak. Then go to Smarky. Tell him to go and have Bodkins pack for me. He's then to deliver my things to Edgefield along with whatever information he can gather about a bloke called Brinks. Suggest that he begin that enquiry at St. Mary's of Bethlem."

"Bedlam?" Roundhead queried with a laugh. "Aye, guv. Whatever you say." His grimy hand shot out and Guy filled it with a small wad of bills.

"Also, I'd like an accounting of a Mr. Clive Bradshaw. Have Smarky collect that or farm out the task as he sees fit, but I need it soon."

"Aye, I'll tell 'im. Safe journey, guv," the man muttered, and vanished into the darkness between the justice's home and the house adjacent to it.

Guy lifted Lily to the mare's saddle and mounted the gelding to ride beside her. They crossed the Thames once again by way of Westminster Bridge, wound down York Row, silent in the early morning hours save for the clop of hooves.

The horses advanced at a brisk walk along Lower

Minette Street, a narrow byway hardly worthy of a name, in order to reach the main road more quickly. They were still not in what Guy considered a safe area of the city, but at least he could breathe a bit more easily than he had done with Lily accompanying him through the crime-fouled streets of Hades.

From the corner of her eye Lily watched two shadows detach themselves from doorways she and Guy had just passed. They were being followed.

"Easy," Guy whispered. "Ride just ahead of me. Don't look back." She had hardly heard his words. Her pulse thundered in her ears. Her muscles had tensed, alerting the mare who began to dance sidewise, her head jerking the reins to the left.

Suddenly as that, two men dashed out of the darkness. One grabbed her mare's bit with one hand, attempting to drag Lily from the saddle by her leg with the other. She screamed and the mare reared, breaking the brigand's hold. Lily grasped the mare's mane and held on.

The fellow struggled up from the cobblestones where he'd fallen, cursing foully as he flew at her. A huge shadow enveloped him from behind and Lily heard a distinct snap.

With a cry of terror, she dug her heels into the mare's flanks, but with reins tangled, only succeeded in guiding her into a tight circle.

"Hold fast!" Guy ordered. "And ride!"

She loosened her grip and let the frightened mare have her way.

Lily glanced over her shoulder. Like a circus trick rider, Guy bounced once and swung onto the gelding that was already nearing a gallop. Behind them, two dark heaps lay unmoving on the cobbles, barely discernible in the blue-gray glow of the moon.

"Face ahead and turn right," Guy shouted as he caught up to her.

They cut sharply down another side street that led into a small park with overhanging trees. There Guy drew up and she did the same.

"Are you hurt?" he asked politely.

"Who were those men?" she gasped, trying hard to steady her jerky breathing as she ran one hand through hair dampened with the sweat of fear.

"Old acquaintances out to settle a score, I expect. Not to worry."

"Not to *worry?*" she snapped, piercing him with a look of anger. "They meant to…accost us!"

"And so they did," he replied, reaching forward with one large hand to gentle the gelding with a pat, his voice as matter-of-fact as if he commented upon the fair weather. "But that's the end of that."

"You…you *killed* them?"

He sighed audibly and sat straighter, looking back the way they had come. "Yes, well, it's time we rode on if you are not too shaken."

Shaken? Two men lay dead in the street! She knew without asking he had broken her attacker's neck with his bare hands. Had likely done that to the other man, as well. He had not even drawn that pistol he wore in his belt or warned them off.

Lily shivered, unable to speak of it. Instead she meekly followed as Guy took the lead and guided them to what appeared to be a main thoroughfare.

"This is Lambeth Street," he informed her idly, as if

they were merely out seeing the sights of London. He set a calm pace, seeming in no rush to get where they were going or to avoid anyone coming after them as a result of the dead robbers.

Whom had she married? Lily wondered.

She had to admit she might not have lived to wonder about it at all if he had not reacted to the attack so forcefully. Even now those two might be following, still bent upon mayhem if he had let them go with a warning. Another violent shiver racked her.

"Cold?" he asked, obviously having noticed.

Lily shook her head.

"Everything will sort itself out," he told her gently. "You'll see."

Everything might have a bit too much help in the sorting, Lily thought with a mirthless laugh that sounded like a groan. For now, all she could do was hope she never need see this frightening side of the Devil Duquesne again.

Only now did she realize that his reputation was based in reality. The rumors were true.

For all his wit and good humor, the man apparently could kill without compunction, without any remorse whatsoever. Had he already gone as mad as his father, the earl?

And to think her marriage to Duquesne was a fact now, only to be undone by the death of one of the parties involved. Chills ran up her spine as she glanced at him.

The devil wore a smile.

Chapter Four

Lambeth Street forked onto St. George, which, in turn, connected to Kent Road. Once they reached it, Lily recognized landmarks. Meadowlands stretched to their left beyond the humble dwellings and mean business establishments strung along the roadway. They kept a steady pace.

"We'll pause for a rest when we reach the crossing at the Darent and then again at Wrotham," Guy told her.

He was dividing the journey into thirds, Lily noted. Ten miles at a stretch would not exhaust the horses if they paced them properly. Lily knew she would be more than ready to dismount for a while when the time came, unused as she was to riding astride and without the cushion of her petticoats.

Her worries about her new husband's sanity had dimmed somewhat on further introspection. She supposed she should be glad he had the experience to deal with such threats instead of bemoaning the fact that he was capable.

Hadn't she deliberately hit Brinks on his head more

than once to save herself? Would she not have killed him—given the means and strength—if he had rallied too soon and threatened her? In the heat of the moment, in fear of her life, she might have done so, Lily admitted. Who was she to pass judgment on Duquesne?

If she were wise, Lily knew she should put all thought of the incident behind her and not dwell on it. There were too many problems ahead.

"You have a good seat," he commented.

"So have you," she replied, then broached a topic they had not yet discussed fully. "Should anyone ask, when did we meet? And where did we marry?"

"Tell the truth. We met on the green of Edgefield town when you were a lass in short skirts. And recently we became reacquainted."

"I warn you, Beau tends to be rather outspoken, even with his elders. He could give everything away."

"Ah, I cannot imagine a child of yours being forward, Lily. Who taught him such things? I wonder."

She heard the laughter in his voice and it should have reassured her. He is not mad, she told herself firmly. Here he was, teasing her about her son, behaving in a perfectly normal way.

"I suspect it runs in Beau's blood. You knew my father."

"Not well, save for attending an occasional service of his when I was young, and of course that day when he pressed me to haul you both to Dr. Ephriam's. But those references do make your point sufficiently. You must miss him terribly."

She smiled to herself. "Oh, yes, I do. I only wish he could have known my son. Beau is very like him."

"Ah, secure in his opinions and not averse to sharing them?" He chuckled. "Better a bit headstrong than a milksop who cowers in corners, eh? Will he resent your bringing home a husband?"

Lily sighed. "We shall see. There is no anticipating how Beau will react. You'll have to win him over." She realized how demanding that had sounded. "If you wish to bother with it."

"Why wouldn't I bother? He's your son, Lily. It's important that we get on well. I look forward to the challenge."

If nothing else, he must realize that Beau was her heart, the one person left in this world she would die for if need be. The wise thing for her to do would be to foster Guy's affection for herself and her son so that he would stand a bulwark between them and any threat to their well-being. God only knew she wanted them both on his good side.

They rode on, the moon casting shadows across the deserted roadway and finally illuminating the stone bridge that would allow them to cross the river near Derwent.

Lily reined to the right and trailed Guy to a small clearing beside the river. He slid from his saddle and held up his hands to her. "Come, I'll help you dismount."

When her feet touched the ground, Lily swayed, catching his forearms to remain upright.

"Steady there, my girl. Is something wrong?" He guided her over to a spot away from the mounts and helped her to sit on the soft grass. How gentle he was now. It was as if no one had ever disturbed his serenity.

She pressed her hands to her face and rubbed briskly. "I felt a bit faint for a moment."

He released a sigh and shook his head. "When did you last eat?"

"Luncheon yesterday, I believe."

He struck his forehead with the heel of his hand. "Damn me, how could I ignore something so basic as food? Rest here. Let me tether the mounts and I'll find something for you immediately."

Lily scoffed at the urgency in his voice. "Wherever would you find food this time of night? Every dwelling we have passed is dark as pitch. People are asleep."

"Then I'll wake someone. You cannot ride another twenty miles in this condition. I'd look over my shoulder and find you lying in the road."

She tensed at the reminder of those men sprawled motionless in the street. "Please, no. Water the horses and forget foraging. I'll survive."

He ignored that. Lily lay back on the grass, supported by her elbows and watched him. Not more than five minutes later he had the saddles off, the horses bound to saplings that grew by the shallows and had returned to her.

"Here. Keep this at the ready. If you need it, pull back the hammer, point and pull the trigger." He handed her his heavy pistol, then struck out for a cottage just visible in the distance.

His long strides ate up the ground, as if his mission were crucial.

Lily looked down at the weapon. She had never held one or even looked at one closely. Minding what Guy had told her, she pulled back the hammer until it clicked so that it would be ready should anyone approach. Not that she would shoot it *at* them if they did. But she could fire above their heads and frighten them off.

Satisfied she was prepared for anything, Lily sighed and lay down upon the sweet, scented grass. She was so tired, so sleepy. Why was Duquesne determined to go to so much trouble for her? She was mildly amused that he seemed so worried for so little reason. Her stomach rumbled beneath the gun that rested upon it and she wondered idly what he would find for them to eat.

Above her the moon beamed down and stars twinkled through the few sparse clouds passing overhead. Such welcome silence after leaving the sounds of the city. Such peace after their brush with danger. Her eyes closed as she drank in the stillness of the night.

Guy juggled the cloth-wrapped bundle of sausages and bread he had purchased from the disgruntled farmer he had awakened. Simple fare but hearty, the victuals should suffice until they reached her home.

He smiled to himself as he approached and saw that she had fallen asleep. But was she only sleeping? She looked so deathly still. Had she fainted? Damn, she was already weak from hunger. And she had imbibed the brandy at his house on an empty stomach. With all that in mind, he hurried his steps and crouched beside her, laid their meal on the ground and firmly shook her shoulder.

"Lily? Wake—"

The boom deafened him and a hot streak of fire grazed the side of his thigh. Before he could recover, her hands were at his face, pounding, clawing, pushing.

Guy grabbed her wrists, suffered a sharp knee thrust that barely missed his essentials before he pinned her to the ground. "Lily! It's me! Leave off!"

Suddenly she went limp beneath him. He felt her chest heaving from her efforts and from fright.

"Easy now," he huffed, his own breath uneven. She was a fighter, his Lily. Slowly he released her arms and moved off of her. "Are you all right?"

She pushed to a sitting position, shaking her head and placing her hands over her ears, rubbing them as if that would restore her hearing. His own were still ringing from the loud report of the gun.

Then he remembered the sting on his leg and ran his palm down the side of his breeches. A long tear in the fabric felt a bit wet and sticky. "My God, you've shot me," he said with a short bark of a laugh.

She issued a sound somewhere between a scream and a groan as she scrambled to her knees and began running her hands over his shoulders. "Where?" she demanded. "Where are you hurt?"

"Settle down, Lily. It's only a scratch and hardly even bleeding." But he enjoyed her moans of sympathy and those agile hands exploring his body. If they had the time, he might play the invalid and enjoy it, but they would need to get back on the road if they were to make Sylvana Hall by daybreak.

He recovered the pistol and carefully tucked it away. Lesson learned.

"Sit back now and calm yourself," he ordered, glancing around them in all directions. "We should leave here shortly. Someone might have heard the shot and come looking for poachers."

"Not until I see the wound!" she argued.

He pulled a handkerchief from his pocket and handed it to her. "Go and wet this at the bank while I saddle the horses."

"You cannot ride!" she announced as she discovered the patch of blood on his trousers. "We must find a doctor!"

"Do as I say!" Guy thundered. It was time he took firm charge of her before she went into hysterics.

She jumped up immediately.

He stood, swept up the bundle of food and strode off to where he had left the saddles. His thigh stung like blazes, but he dismissed the discomfort. There would be time enough to see to it once they reached their destination.

Lily was scurrying to the riverbank, his handkerchief waving like a flag as she ran. "Lily, mind the slippery—"

Splash!

Guy closed his eyes and clicked his tongue. Now she would be soaked to the skin. Lily was just too…too *active* for a damsel in distress. He liked self-sufficiency in a woman, but this was ridiculous.

She sputtered an epithet and splashed, making her way back up the bank.

"Need help?" he called, choking back his laughter.

"No! I'm fine!" He could hear the shiver in her voice. Though the night was fairly warm, she must be chilled after the dunking.

"Come here and let's see the damage," he ordered, dropping his saddle on the ground.

"I'm only wet to the waist," she muttered as he reached her and began running his hands over her shoulders.

She turned her face up to his and the moonlight illuminated her features a ghostly blue. Her gaze fastened on his. Her slightly parted lips beckoned. Without a thought to resist, Guy leaned toward her and brushed his mouth across hers. The sigh she issued drew him deeper into the kiss, tasting her fully for the first time ever.

Sweet urgency, an innocence hardly touched, honeyed depths waiting…just for him. Guy surrounded her with his arms and held her fast, melding her body to his, his palms cupping and caressing her hips…her curvaceous, very *wet* hips.

His good sense intruded and he released her. "Best save this for a more propitious time," he whispered.

She gulped and nodded, crossing her arms over her chest.

Guy turned away abruptly, shook his head to clear it and picked up one of the small padded blankets used for cushioning the saddle. Then he returned and began to mop the excess water off of her.

She jumped back, her boots squishing. "Stop! I'll smell like horse sweat," she protested.

He laughed and tossed her the blanket. "Better that than to drip all the way home. I'd offer to exchange but I'm afraid Brinks's breeches won't fit me." Especially now that he had nearly burst out of his own. Damn, he could use a quick dunk in the river himself. "Will you be all right?"

"Yes, will you?" she countered, handing him the wet handkerchief.

He pushed aside the thought brought on by the wet curves of her beneath his hands and the mind-rending effect of that kiss.

Later he would pursue it, he told himself again, just as he had after the strange ceremony that united them legally. Now was still not the time, unfortunately.

Stripping her of those wet garments and making love on the grassy bank of the Derwent was not an option he could consider. "Come, we need to ride out before the sound of that shot brings half the populace down on us. We haven't the time for explanations."

She hurried over to the mare and began the chore of saddling up while he finished his own task with the gelding.

In short order they crossed the Derwent and were once more on the road to Maidstone. Guy reached into his makeshift sack, withdrew a link of sausage and handed it to her. "Here, eat this before you starve to death. No use being wet *and* hungry."

"What about your wound? We really should see to it. Is it bleeding still?"

"Not anymore. As I said, it barely broke the skin." He sighed. "We make pair in our deshabille, eh? But you're no complainer, are you, Lily?"

"Depends," she said, the word barely discernable through a mouthful of sausage. "Any bread?"

Guy handed her a portion torn off the loaf and then joined her. How strange it was to feel so easy in the company of a woman, he thought as he chewed. Despite the way she had aroused him with her response and the fact that he had left both of them wanting, Guy somehow knew Lily expected no apology for it.

She was a strong lady, his wife, and canny, too. Guy still could hardly believe how well she had weathered that attack in the street and the way she'd calmly accepted his need to eliminate those two. Smarky had warned him last week that they were dogging his heels and determined to make an end to him. Lily had accepted what had to be done without question. A truly welcome measure of trust.

With her there seemed no need for entertaining banter or observing false niceties. He was good at both when he put his mind to it, but this camaraderie with her was infinitely more comfortable. "I think I'll like being married," he commented, apropos of nothing.

She issued a small hum, a wordless expression signifying her doubt. "Well, so far it has been rather…interesting," she added with a rather broad hint of sarcasm.

But Guy suspected that despite her disgruntled remark, her current discomfort and the dire event that brought them to this pass, Lily was enjoying her adventure. There was something to be said for a woman with a mettlesome spirit.

He smiled to himself as he looked down the road at their future. "I can promise you it will get better."

"I'll definitely hold you to that," she said as she popped the last bite of sausage into her mouth and daintily licked her fingers as he watched.

By the time they neared Wrotham, Guy was on fire for her. He had replayed that scorching kiss and the feel of her body in his memory so many times during the silence of their ride, it proved a painful seduction of the senses.

In his mind he touched her, tasted her, heard that enticing little moan of hers repeatedly. He could hardly close his eyes to blink without seeing her lips parted, waiting, inviting, inciting… But he knew he must wait.

Damn, he would be a randy wreck by the time he did get the proper opportunity to seduce her.

How could a woman appear so erotic in those clothes? Her hair curled every which way, the style of it nearly the equal of a poorly built bird's nest, a golden halo made silver by the light of the moon. He thanked God when the moon waned, though that left them wandering the road in the dark. At least then he couldn't glance sidewise at her and concoct visions of Lady Godiva with formerly concealing locks trimmed to just below her ears.

He chuckled to himself as he reined up near a small brook just off the roadway.

"What is it?" she asked, her voice betraying her weariness.

"Wrotham's just ahead," he told her, regretting the necessity of halting yet again. Ten more miles, perhaps less, and they would reach their destination. Neither the horses nor Lily were likely to get that far without wearing themselves out completely.

He led the way off the road before they reached any dwellings. Lily could not afford to be seen by any locals who happened to be awake. Not in her present array. Someone this close to her home might recognize her and she did look rather scandalous.

In the darkness just before dawn, Guy could barely make out the shapes of Lily and the mare, but the lack of rustling leather told him she was not busy unsaddling. Poor dear must be completely done in. He'd let her ride with him on his gelding so she could rest. "We will be going to Edgefield first. It is closer. There, you can change. Some of my mother's things are stored in the attics. They're out of style, but at least you'll have skirts."

She sighed loud and long. "Yes, I suppose that would be best. But only long enough to change. I must get to Beau as soon as possible."

"Let's not unsaddle then. Just walk about for a few minutes to stretch out the kinks and then we'll go on."

"All right," she said, but Guy could tell from the direction of her voice that she had sunk to the ground beside the mare.

He led the horses down to the brook. While they drank, he brushed his hand over the gelding's flank and felt only a light film of sweat. "Good old fellow," he muttered. "I hope you are up to hauling the two of us."

In the distance he could hear the sound of a coach, hoofbeats and the jingle of traces. Perhaps the mail, he thought, for it ran at all hours. But as he listened, he heard it continue on through the small village just ahead without stopping.

A chill skittered up his spine. Was it Bradshaw? Had he come from London in search of Lily? By this time she might have been discovered missing from the hospital.

"Lily? We should go," he said, rather more sharply than he intended. "If we cut cross-country, we can make Edgefield in less than an hour and be at Sylvana Hall before sunrise. A coach just passed that might be headed there."

"Clive?" she asked, scrambling to her feet.

"If it is, the winding road will delay his carriage at least an hour. Also, he'll probably stop at the Goings Cross station to water up and rest the horses."

"Let's go," she ordered.

He lifted her to the gelding's back and swung up behind her, holding the mare's reins to lead her along. They would follow the line of the hedgerows to Edgefield property and the trespass would go unnoticed at this time of night.

With a bit of luck they could make themselves presentable there and still reach Sylvana Hall before that coach did if that was where it was headed.

His every instinct warned him it was necessary to make haste.

Chapter Five

Lily nestled against Guy even as she cursed her weakness. Though she had endured more in the past two days than ever before in her life, she wished she could have borne up better and finished their trip with a bit more dignity. Instead here she was being coddled like a child, seeking the warmth and comfort of a protector.

She sighed and tightened her arms around his waist. At least he would be well compensated for his trouble. And she had to admit, it felt good to rest in the shelter of his arms.

How warm his chest felt next to her face as she burrowed closer. His scent surrounded her, filling her head with all sorts of imaginings she should not be having. Bare skin, the taste of it on her lips, the heady heat of his mouth on hers.

She could hear his heart beat right next to her ear, which lay pressed to his shirt. Like a brand, his palm and strong fingers burned into her rib cage as he held her fast.

Now and then she sensed his mouth rest lightly

against the top of her head. Not for the life of her could she sleep in this position, though her eyes could not seem to remain open.

He halted and she forced herself to push away from him and sit up. Enough of this. She must be strong, assert herself again and show Duquesne that he would not be required to do everything for her. If only she had begun to think for herself long ago instead of relying on those around her, she might have been better prepared for what had happened to her. She had no one to blame but herself for her complacency, if one didn't count Society's expectations of women.

Dawn was just peeking over the horizon, its light filtered by clouds that threatened rain.

"We are here," he said softly.

They had obviously arrived at Edgefield. Before them stood the rear entrance of a huge, sprawling manor. The house was built of the same local stone as Sylvana Hall. Though much larger than her home, this building looked centuries older. Ivy covered much of the lower half. The adjacent gardens were overgrown and unkempt. The dooryard lay unswept and the horses stamped fretfully on the uneven ground.

Guy released her and dismounted, helping her down without any great ceremony, as if he did so every day. "Come, let's raid the kitchen. You must be famished. Then we'll go up and find you something to wear. Can you stand?"

She realized he still held her upright, his hands upon her waist. Impatiently she pulled away. "Of course I can stand. I could have ridden alone if you had allowed me."

"O-oh, snappish, are we? Well, I don't wonder. A bit

of food is what you need to set you right." He took her hand and pulled her along the flagstones that served as a walkway to the door.

They entered a room that seemed straight out of the Middle Ages with its enormous fireplace and hanging pots. Thankfully, she saw that someone had built a fire there. Lily headed straight for it, chafing her hands and holding them out to feel the warmth. She still felt chilled from her half dunking at the river's edge.

She looked around as Guy greeted a heavyset woman who seemed vaguely familiar to her.

"Good heavens, is that blood?" the woman demanded, pointing at Guy's leg.

"It's nothing," Guy told her. "A scrape that hardly broke the skin. Won't even need stitches, though some of your special salve wouldn't go amiss."

"Let me see to it!" the woman insisted.

"No, no, I'll tend it directly when I change clothes. First, I'd like you to meet someone." He turned to Lily. "Mrs. Sparks, this is my wife, Lady Lillian. You'll remember her father, Vicar Upchurch? Could you scare us up a bite to eat? We've had a long night's ride."

The older woman gaped at her. Lily almost laughed thinking what a sight she must make with her men's clothing and wild, cropped curls. "Good morning, Mrs. Sparks. I am delighted to see you again."

She recognized the woman now as one of her father's old parishioners. It had been years since Lily had attended the village church at Edgefield. After her marriage, she and Jonathan had gone to services in Maidstone.

"My husband speaks very fondly of the capable staff here at Edgefield," she said to the woman. Guy had never mentioned a soul who resided here other than his father and had said precious little about the earl except to tell her he was insane. Lily hadn't a clue how the place was staffed or what quality service was afforded—certainly not a like number of the twenty-six hard workers employed at Sylvana Hall—but it never hurt to begin a new acquaintance on a positive note.

Ah, she saw she was right. Mrs. Sparks snapped her mouth shut and managed a quizzical smile. "Thank you…my lady. If you and Guy, uh, his lordship…would have a seat in the dining room, I'll—"

"Could you do up a tray for us, Mrs. Sparks?" Guy interrupted. "We will breakfast in my chambers. Cold meats and bread, a bit of cheese and some strong coffee would be perfect. I'll be down to fetch it when I've shown my lady to her room."

The woman's eyes rounded even more as her head bobbled in an uncertain nod. "Of course. But I could cook you a—"

"No time for a full meal. We have business at Sylvana Hall and should be off there as soon as possible."

Mrs. Sparks darted him a look that said she needed to speak with him alone. Lily looked back to the fire, affording them a modicum of privacy, though she fully intended to listen.

The woman's whisper was quite clear. "Sir, he's not awake, but perhaps you should—"

"I will be back later today or first thing tomorrow to see him. This other matter is of some urgency. I must ask that you tell no one of our arrival here this morning. Should anyone inquire, you had word of my marriage several weeks ago and were ordered to keep the news to yourself. Agreed?"

"You know I won't talk out of turn. I never do. But I would like to be kept informed so I know what's going on with you."

"You're the dearest of the dear, Sparks." Lily heard the smack of his kiss and the resulting grunt of disapproval from the recipient.

"Off with you then," Mrs. Sparks grumbled in a near whisper. "And see to your lady wife. His Nibs will be that upset you didn't bring her in to meet him if he finds out you were here."

"I doubt he'd know her from the bedpost, but I'll introduce them soon. Meanwhile, keep up the good fight."

Then he raised his voice and called to Lily, "Come with me, sweetheart."

Sweetheart? Lily grinned in spite of her exhaustion and went to join her husband. How strange it seemed, like a dream where nothing made any sense at all, following a man she hardly knew through a rambling old house up to his private chambers. Even more unusual that she felt no dread, not even a jot of fear, only a light-headed sort of curiosity.

She obviously needed sleep, but that was unlikely at this juncture. When he offered it, she took his hand and went up the stairs with him like a child joining another in exploring a maze.

"Your home away from home," he said without apology as they entered an enormous sitting room fitted with furniture left over from the previous century. "Charming, don't you think?" he quipped. "Make yourself comfortable while I fetch the clothes. Riding habit?"

"Yes, that would be perfect," Lily said, still looking around her, noting the lighter rectangles of wallpaper where paintings had been removed. There was a notice-able lack of finery here, as if everything with any great value at all had been sold off.

She had expected as much, having heard rumors of his financial hardships. Still in all, the place appeared quite comfortable, if unassuming. She sank into a heav-ily upholstered chair and closed her eyes, not worrying for a moment about fouling the fabric with her still-damp breeches or her muddy boots. A warm fuzzy blan-ket drifted over her and she felt him tuck it around her neck.

"Back in a moment," he said.

She heard a door close, snuggled more deeply under the blanket and drifted off to sleep.

When a sound jarred her awake, she looked up to see him standing in front of her.

"Sorry to wake you so soon, but I thought you might want to wash up a bit and change before we eat."

Lily nodded, brushed aside her covering and reluc-tantly pushed out of the enveloping chair. Still groggy, she slid out of her coat and began to unbutton her waist-coat while Guy laid a dark blue velvet riding habit across the nearby couch.

Though wrinkled, the garments were of classic cut. The shirtwaist of white had a simple ruffle at the neck. The hat that he perched on the arm of the couch was in the style of a gentleman's top hat, made feminine by a band of tulle tied at the back and left to hang loose. Peeking from beneath the rest was a filmy ruffle of white. Probably a chemise, she thought.

He tossed a pair of matching gloves of dyed leather onto one of the cushions. "There you are. Sorry, I could find no riding boots."

"These will suffice until we reach Sylvana, thank you." Lily halted in unfastening her shirt, aware for the first time that he was observing her rather hungrily as she undressed.

He smiled wickedly and shrugged. "I suppose I must wait in the other room?"

Lily rolled her eyes and laughed. "I suppose you must."

"I'll just go and change myself then."

He headed for a door that was closed, not the one they had entered on arrival. "Here's the dressing room that connects to my bedchamber. I've brought a ewer of water in there. In the interest of haste, I thought you'd want to wait until you reach Sylvana Hall to have a proper bath."

"Thank you," she replied, sounding too formal for the occasion, she knew. "That was most kind. I'll only be a moment."

He bowed and left, exiting the way they had come in.

Lily removed the small vials she had taken from Brinks and put them safely away. Then she peeled off the remainder of Brinks's clothes and hurried into the riding habit. She then went into the small dressing room, found the ewer and basin and dashed water on her face. It refreshed her somewhat, though she still felt as if she had cobwebs in her head.

He had put out brush and comb, so she made use of them, bemoaning for the first time the unflattering riot of curls left by her clumsy hacking with Brinks's knife. The former length and weight of her hair had served to help control its unruly mass. Now that it was short, it spiraled every which way.

"You look like a poorly shorn lamb," she muttered to the mirror and stuck out her tongue at her image.

A knock on the door opposite the one she had entered interrupted her grim appraisal. "Yes?"

"Breakfast!" he announced.

Lily scurried to join him, gazing quickly around the other chamber of his suite, the bedroom. Beside the window sat a small table set with two plates laden with slices of ham, bread and a pot of jam. Steaming cups of coffee beckoned with a delicious aroma.

She noted that he now wore fresh linen, buff breeches and a coat of dark green gabardine that complemented a finely embroidered waistcoat. His scuffed boots needed a shine, but otherwise, he appeared quite presentable. Handsomer than ever, if she were perfectly honest with herself.

Lily studiously ignored the large four-poster bed that stood close by. Not that she was all that eager for her conjugal duties, she insisted to herself, but she would dearly have loved to crawl onto that deep feather mattress and sink into oblivion for about twelve uninterrupted hours.

But she must get to Beau, she remembered. He would be worried about her sudden absence. And worse, Clive might already be there.

Guy held out her chair. "You look lovely in blue," he told her.

Lily laughed self-consciously at the flattery. "Said like a wary husband with an eye to the future. No need for pretty lies with me, sir. I just looked at your mirror in there."

"Then you have a grave need for spectacles if you don't agree with me," he quipped as he joined her at table and they began to eat. In spite of his reassurance, he kept looking at her hair throughout the meal.

As she sipped the last of her coffee, Lily tugged at one curl that kept dangling below the rest. "I made quite a mess of it. I fear a knife is not the perfect instrument with which to effect the latest coiffure."

He held up one finger as he rose and strode over to his bureau. When he returned with a pair of scissors, Lily held up her hands and began to protest. "We have no time for this."

"Won't take a moment," he ordered. "Just let me fetch the brush and comb." He did so and stood behind her, one hand at her nape as he pulled the brush through her hair. "A nimbus of gold," he said softly. "That was my first thought when I saw it gilded by the lamplight."

Lily remained silent as he brushed, feeling the boar bristles gently massage her scalp, the touch of his fingers on her neck sending tingles through her. Then he stopped, took the comb and separated a section. She heard a snip, then another. Oh, Lord, he was cutting off more! But instead of jerking away to prevent it, Lily let him have his way. It could hardly look worse than it did.

"There you are. You'll be all the rage. Your friends will faint with envy and men will fall at your feet in admiration. Have a look." He handed her the small mirror that matched his brushes and comb.

Lily laughed with delight. "What have you done?" She combed her fingers through the feathered strands and fluffed it at the crown. "I quite like it!" She grinned up at him. "You have missed your calling, sir! If you could speak French, I daresay you'd make a fortune at this."

"Mais oui, madame. Merci beaucoup." He tweaked

a curl beside her ear. "It seems a shame to cover that masterpiece, but it is time to don your hat and be off again. Are you up to riding five more miles this morning?"

Lily jumped up and rushed through the dressing room to gather the hat and gloves. "Right you are. Beau will be that worried about me, I'm certain."

Rejuvenated by her breakfast, Lily could hardly wait to get home. In the back of her mind she worried about how her son would take the news of her marriage, but was nevertheless eager to reach Sylvana Hall.

Surprisingly, Guy seemed even more anxious to reach there than she. "Do you think he's in danger even now?" she asked.

"I believe we should take no chances by leaving him to face company alone," he replied. "If the coach that passed us belonged to your brother-in-law, he should be arriving at the Hall very shortly. It was traveling slowly, but even with the delays, it will be there soon if that's where it was headed."

"It should be interesting to see Clive's reaction to my presence at Sylvana Hall if he believes he left me locked away in London," Lily said with a bitter smile.

"*Interesting,* at the very least."

They went out through the kitchens where a grubby lad held the reins of their borrowed mounts. She noted the mare was now outfitted with a sidesaddle. Guy lifted her up, saw her settled and then swiftly mounted the gelding.

Without another word, they rode hard across the meadow and through the woods that lay between Edgefield and Sylvana Hall. Even the dreary misting rain did nothing to dampen Lily's eagerness for this last, most urgent leg of their journey.

* * *

They topped a hill that backed Sylvana Hall. Almost the entire estate could be viewed from that high vantage point. Guy motioned toward the road that wound onto the property from the opposite direction. A coach was visible in the distance, perhaps half a mile away. "We need to be there before he arrives," he told Lily. "You should find your son and keep him close until we've had a chance to speak with him about the marriage. Can you have him avoid his uncle until then?"

"No great chore in that," she replied. "He's not overly fond of Clive and the feeling is mutual."

"I'll deal with Clive Bradshaw. Shall I send him packing?"

She frowned as if uncertain. "I have always heard you should keep your enemies close."

"Good point," he replied, sending her a smile of approval. The girl had a head on her shoulders.

"You won't…kill him, will you?"

He frowned, still looking at the slowly approaching vehicle on the road. "Not immediately."

She cast him a doubtful look, then seemed to come to some inner decision. "Do I have your promise?"

Guy nodded.

"Then let's ride," she ordered, and took off at a gallop.

By God, he liked a woman with nerve and Lily had more than her share of that. When he thought of all she had endured, he decided it was enough to fell most men he knew.

He regretted she had been witness to his darker dealings, but he'd had no choice at the time but to dispense with those ruffians.

When they reached the back entrance to the Hall, she

dismounted without waiting for his help. Once inside, she guided him through to the foyer. "You might wait here or in the parlor," she said. "I'll be down directly as soon as I've seen my son."

"Take your time. I expect the little fellow will be wanting an accounting of your absence. What will you tell him?"

"Not the whole truth, surely," Lily said as she removed her hat and brushed her curls off her brow with the back of her wrist. "I shall think of something not quite so frightening."

She shot Guy a warning look. "You have a care. I doubt Clive will be thrilled with our news." She hesitated, then added, "But promise me you'll be…prudent? At least until we know what's afoot?"

"Madam?"

They both turned. The butler, Guy guessed. He was fifty or so, nearly bald, dressed all in black and looking as if he had been sucking lemons. Very proper indeed. He regarded Guy with a raised brow.

"Lockland, this is my husband, Viscount Duquesne. Mr. Bradshaw is due at any moment. As soon as you greet him, show him into the parlor where his lordship will receive him."

The butler appeared almost as dumbstruck as Mrs. Sparks had at Edgefield. Guy wondered what reaction Clive Bradshaw would show when informed of Lily's elopement.

What Guy most desired was a confrontation that would give him an excuse to wipe the beautifully tiled floors with the scoundrel.

He winked at Lily, then strolled into the parlor and left the door standing open.

While he waited, he helped himself to a dollop of brandy from the cut-glass decanter on the long table against the far wall. The appointments in this room alone were probably worth the entire houseful left at Edgefield.

The rug was Aubusson, of course, and there was a Wren-designed mantelpiece with—if he wasn't mistaken—vases dating back to the Ming dynasty. Directly above those rested a portrait of some long-dead baroness with her fuzzy little dog. Looked as if it were done by Reynolds. Guy peered closer and nodded, recognizing the signature. The Barons Bradshaw had obviously lived well for some time.

"My lord, Baroness Bradshaw and Mr. Bradshaw," the butler announced.

Guy looked over his shoulder before turning around slowly. So Clive had brought his mother with him. The dowager baroness certainly looked well able to defend her whelp if need be. Blond hair, obviously dyed, lay slicked from a center part and mostly confined beneath a fashionable black bonnet. That added a formidable austerity to her square face and haughty features. Her full lips looked carved from stone. Her eyes, the gray of granite, were granitelike. Unfortunate for her, Guy thought. Without the hardness, she'd be a handsome, if not pretty, woman.

Though she was tall and sturdy instead of porcine, the corset beneath her traveling costume looked fit to burst from sheer indignation. He smiled at her and turned to the son, regarding him with the same innocuous expression.

Clive bore a startling resemblance to his dam, though he had not yet attained her height or breadth. In a wrestling match, Guy would have put his money on the mama.

Bradshaw's hair was thinning, a blond more faded than his mother's. Pomaded flat to his head, it gave way to curls around his ears and nape. When he ungloved his hands, Guy noted how soft and uncalloused they were.

Here was a man who would hire out his villainy, at least the physical aspects of it. Had he? In the interest of holding rage at bay, Guy thought it best not to dwell too deeply on that at the moment.

"Welcome to you both on behalf of Lady Lillian. Won't you be seated?" Guy turned to the butler. "Lockland, that will be all, thank you." He was not about to order up refreshments for these two.

"And who might *you* be?" the woman demanded, her tone imperious, her face as pruned as the snobbish butler's. Guy wondered whether they might secretly be related.

"I am Duquesne, madam. Lady Lillian's husband," he said with no little satisfaction at the abrupt change of expressions on their faces.

Bradshaw glared. "What do you mean, her *husband!*"

Guy shrugged, took another sip of brandy and exhaled with pleasure at the pleasant burn. "I assume that question is rhetorical. We were married last month in London."

The old baroness sank into the nearest chair and looked a bit out of breath. But it took her precious little time to recover. She frowned fiercely at him. "Not *the* Duquesne who…"

Guy smiled and raised his snifter in a mock toast to

himself. "One and the same, madam." He watched as she shot a frantic frown at her son.

Clive said nothing, merely glared at Guy through narrowed eyes. The fellow looked perfectly evil when he did that. Probably practiced in a mirror to obtain just the right effect. Guy figured he could match it easily, but chose not to at this point. Instead he sipped his brandy and maintained his pleasant attitude. He had promised Lily prudence.

"I cannot stay here," the dowager baroness groaned.

Guy almost retorted that no one had asked her to, but held his tongue, mainly to see what Clive would do next.

"Nonsense, Mother. Lily will want us here. If for nothing else, to help celebrate her *marriage.*" He bit off the last word as if it had a bitter taste.

The rapid clatter on the tiles outside the parlor prevented Guy's pithy reply.

A small sandy-haired boy, definitely Lily's son, dashed past the guests and halted directly in front of Guy.

Huge blue eyes, their gaze assessing, traveled over Guy's face, down to his boots and back up again. Small lips quivered for a second, then firmed. Little fists clenched, unclenched and clenched again. No doubt, the lad wondered just what his mother had foisted on him in the way of a stepfather.

In Guy's experience, one began as one meant to go. Respect should extend both ways. The boy was a peer and looked rather deserving of it at the moment.

Guy held out his hand. "Lord Bradshaw."

After but a second's delay, Lily's son clasped hands and shook as firmly as any man might. "Lord Duquesne."

Nothing else. No indication by word or deed that they had never met before. Had Lily warned him to hold his questions? They were certainly there in his eyes. She had obviously told the boy something, for it was clear he knew of the marriage.

It was also evident that he was in no hurry to greet their guests.

Guy smiled kindly at the boy, hoping to communicate that they had a common purpose, which was to make Lily happy and to keep her safe. He wondered how she had explained her absence.

The smile must have sufficed, for Beau turned abruptly and made a short bow to the dowager. "Grandmother. Uncle. Have you come to visit for a while?" The tone of his voice was much too formal and did not offer any great encouragement to them to stay, Guy noted.

"Why, yes, we have," Clive answered for the both of them. "And how are you faring today, Beauly?"

The small shoulders stiffened. "I do not prefer that byname, sir."

Guy interrupted. "Oh, I'm certain *Clivey's* only just shed his own. He probably doesn't understand how quickly one with your sudden responsibilities matures. Permit me to suggest that we all address you correctly as befits your station. Henceforth, you shall be Bradshaw, if that pleases you."

Beau nodded once. "It does, sir." He glanced at Lily with a slightly apologetic nibble of his lip. "Except for my mother, who may call me as she likes."

"Of course," Guy agreed with a smile for his wife. "Mothers must retain that privilege." He leaned down a bit and said in a stage whisper, "Wives, too. She calls me Guy."

"This is an absurd conversation and most inappropriate," the dowager announced. "You, boy, are impudent. Children should be seen, not heard. I am retiring to my room now." She snorted as she rose and flapped a hand at Lily. "Send me up a tray. I shall not be down until noon."

"She has a room?" Guy muttered, more or less to himself.

"Without delay, ma'am. Rest well." Lily then looked at Clive as if she expected him to follow suit.

"Lily, I would speak with you alone. Immediately," he demanded.

"Indulge a new bridegroom, if you would," Guy said by way of preventing any such tête-à-tête, "but I would consider that highly improper." He raised one eyebrow and added, "I am plagued with the fault of jealousy, you see. A failing, I know, but there it is." He finished his brandy and firmly set the glass on the mantelpiece next to the Ming vase.

Clive rolled his eyes and shifted impatiently. "Well, at least send the boy upstairs!"

"A lord, ousted from his own parlor by order of a guest, sir?" Guy shook his head. "If you would have private speech with *me* concerning your, uh, concerns over the marriage, then we might take the matter into another room." He lowered his chin and stared at Clive from beneath his lashes, as evil a look as he could summon. He had practiced his, too. "Or perhaps…*outside,* if you prefer?"

He saw that his meaning had been taken. Both Lily and the boy were swinging gazes to and fro as if watching a match of tennis. She appeared worried, but Guy ignored that. Her son looked fascinated. Guy understood that. Boys liked a good scrap.

In fact, he awaited Clive's answer with an eagerness he had not felt since he'd fought Billy Whitsun over the favors of a barmaid when he was fifteen. His blood was up and his fists itched for action. If they must suffer a viper in their midst, Guy wanted it to be a frightened viper.

"Forget it," Clive snapped. "We shall discuss this later."

"At your pleasure," Guy remarked dryly, carefully disguising his disappointment as Clive turned on his heel and stalked out of the parlor.

Little Beau had covered his mouth and his shoulders were shaking with glee.

Lily frowned. "Behave yourselves, the both of you! This is no matter for levity!" She pointed to the couch and issued an expectant look. That was a mother's expression of admonishment if Guy had ever seen one. And he certainly had in his younger days.

He made a wry face at Beau that Lily was not privy to as they marched in unison to the appointed place and took seats side by side. He was in league with a seven-year-old, about to take a scolding for what amounted to a schoolyard challenge.

Beau kicked sideways, gently nudging Guy's leg in what seemed a gesture of support. The little fellow had obviously suffered this before and knew what to expect.

Lily shook her finger at them in turn. "Now then, I want no more of this tweaking Uncle Clive's anger, Beau. He is our guest and must be afforded civility at all costs. You are not to lord it over your grandmother or your uncle. That is not considered good form at all." Her gaze leveled on Guy. "And you, sir, are not to issue any threats or ultimatums."

Beau leaned closer and whispered, "What is that? *Ultimatums?*"

"If-you-do-this, I-will-do-that sorts of things," Guy explained. "Ultimatums."

"Oo-oh," Beau said, dragging out the word. *"If you insist on being a boor, I shall pound you?"*

"Precisely. You have an incredibly quick mind, Bradshaw!"

Beau grinned. "Thank you, Duquesne."

"Hush! Both of you stop this! Beau, go back to the nursery and take up your nines. Twenty repetitions and no slacking, do you hear? Guy, I shall like further words with *you!*"

"You're at the nines already?" Guy asked Beau, truly astounded. The boy was young for the task of multiplication.

"I get stuck on times-seven," Beau confessed with a sigh.

"Sixty-three. That is a hard one to remember."

"Go!" Lily snapped, pointing to the door. Guy could see she was barely containing a laugh. He strongly suspected the canny Beau could see it, as well.

When the boy had clattered up the stairs, she plopped down beside Guy. "Well, that was easier than I thought it would be."

"Clive's retreat? The man's a yellow-livered coward."

Lily laughed, leaning her head back against the damask as if exhausted. "I was speaking of you and Beau. Nothing like a common threat to draw two blokes together, eh?"

"Aha, a devious plan! And I never even suspected."

"Worked rather well, wouldn't you say?"

Guy met her gaze and loved the laughter in hers. "Beau's a fine boy, Lily. He has your wit."

"And Jonathan's wicked sense of humor and lack of respect for authority. That, you will have to help me mind. He'll be incorrigible before he's ten if we allow it free reign."

"Incorrigible has its advantages," Guy argued, laying his arm along the back of the couch. "Your lad is a marvel. Did you see how he wanted to fire away at me when he stormed in here? But he held back."

"I must tell you, he was not that taken with the idea of a stepfather, but I told him he must trust my judgment and wait until we were private with you to voice any questions. He did promise, and Beau's as good as his word."

"I'll speak with him as soon as he finishes his lessons." Guy shook his head in wonder. "My God, he has a handle on that temper, doesn't he? I am impressed to hell and gone. I like him, Lily."

"We shall see how long that lasts when your wills clash. Now would you mind terribly if we repair to our rooms? If I do not sleep soon, I cannot vouch for my own temper."

"Good idea. I expect we'll need our wits about us once our guests have fully digested what our marriage means to the grand scheme Clive might have cooked up for you."

"Yes. If indeed he is the cook," Lily said with a protracted sigh. "Did you think he was at all surprised that I was here instead of in London?"

"Hard to judge since the news of our marriage gave him such a turn." Guy had to admit he entertained a few doubts in Clive's direction now that he'd met the man.

But who else could have instituted such a daring bid to have Lily locked away in a madhouse? Who else would profit by that?

He stood and offered his hand. "Come. Show me where to lay my head. This business of being a husband is damned tiring thus far."

She pulled herself to her feet and shot him a coy glance that was pure Lily. "But I trust you're not yet bored with it."

He drew her to him for a hug, encouraged when she did not pull away. "Not in the least. I haven't had this much excitement in days."

"And this day's only just begun," she said, moving easily out of his arms and leading him out of the parlor. "Wait until you see where you have to sleep."

"Knowing young Bradshaw, I'd guess that won't be in the master's chamber."

Lily laughed merrily and led him up the stairs.

Chapter Six

Lily showed Guy to her own room since he had rightly guessed that Beau had appropriated the master chamber. She had allowed that after Jonathan died, mostly because of the convenience to her. She did not want to sleep there, and it was adjacent to hers with an adjoining door. If Beau wakened with nightmares, she would hear him. The nursery was located on the floor above and used as his schoolroom.

Guy strolled through her bedroom smiling, hands clasped behind him as he looked around. "Very ladylike. Of course, you realize I shall require a frilly nightgown to fit in here."

Lily laughed. "Close your eyes and you won't mind the ruffles. The bed is more comfortable than those in the guest rooms."

He raised an eyebrow. "Lumps in them to discourage long visits? Fortunate in view of the current guest list, I expect."

"It has not discouraged them before this. They've lived here almost constantly since Jonathan died, and not by my invitation."

"You should have tossed them out," Guy said.

"Hindsight proves that's so, but as I said, now I suppose we should keep Clive here rather than have him elsewhere concocting further schemes to get rid of me. Here at least we might observe his actions, perhaps note the correspondence that goes out so we might learn what he's up to next."

"We shall see," he muttered noncommittally.

She reached to smooth out a wrinkle in the coverlet at the foot of the bed. "Why don't you lie down for a few hours? I must see to Beau's lessons and go over the menus for the day with Cook. Then—"

"Lily…" His look was admonishing and rather impatient.

Words caught in her throat as he approached and reached for her hand. She had guessed this would happen. That he would insist on his husbandly rights the moment the opportunity of privacy presented itself. Well, it was to be expected, she supposed.

She sighed, wishing she were more rested. Well, this would probably only take a few moments. Still, something told Lily she could be wrong about that. This man might not be quite as perfunctory as Jonathan had been.

There was something deliciously wicked about the way he smiled at her when they had discussed this duty. She prepared to surrender and have done with it.

But instead of setting about it with the heated kisses she was expecting, he merely held her hands in his and chided her with a look.

"What is it?"

"You must be the one to rest," he said. "Those circles beneath your eyes look like bruises. Do you want to leave the room because you think I have it in mind to press my rights?"

"Oh. No…that wasn't the reason. It's simply that there is so much that needs doing this morning." She might have known the moment she resigned herself to his consummating their marriage immediately, he would veer off in another direction entirely. The man was definitely an unpredictable sort.

In fact, even as tired as she was, Guy himself looked almost as tempting as the soft mattress. She needed distraction, but other matters were certainly more imperative at the moment. "I should see to Beau. You stay and sleep."

He tugged her around to the side of the bed. "Beau will survive your absence for a few hours and I'm certain anything your cook prepares will prevent us starving. Go to bed."

"Remember, Clive is on the premises. What of Beau's protection?"

"I'll take care of that. Since Beau rose for the day just before we came riding in, we can hardly require the little fellow to go back to bed while we catch up on our rest. You are the most tired. I'll see to him, then wake you in the afternoon."

Lily shook her head and pulled her hand from his. "No, he doesn't know you. He will be—"

"He will be *fine*," Guy insisted. "This will give me a chance to become better acquainted with him."

"But what of his questions? He knows virtually nothing yet of why we married. In company he was polite, but who knows what…"

Guy smiled and brushed a hand over her hair. "Not to worry. Beau and I will get on fine."

"But suppose Clive or his mother—"

"You are not to fret about them. Lock these doors and you will be safe. I promise you on my life that your son will be looked after. You have my word, I won't let him out of my sight for a moment."

"Well…" Lily eyed the plump pillows longingly. How long had it been since she'd made use of those? Her eyelids drooped and her muscles felt leaden. She frowned up at Guy. "Are you certain?"

He leaned down and brushed his lips against hers, then rested his mouth for a moment against her brow. "Sleep well, Lily. I have it all in hand."

She welcomed the small intimacy, loving the warmth of his gesture, his gentleness and consideration. He made it so easy to forget what he was capable of when he was crossed.

Then he released her and strode to the hall door where he turned and shook a finger. "Mind you lock up. I'll knock when it's time for you to wake."

When he had gone, Lily turned the keys in the locks and quickly slipped out of the riding habit. Still clad in the chemise that had belonged to his mother, she crawled beneath the coverlet, snuggled into the feather-stuffed pillows and sighed with relief.

She trusted Duquesne. He had exhibited no signs of madness on the way from London. Even when the pistol had discharged and grazed him accidentally, he had taken it all in stride. He had not attacked Clive when the man had practically asked for it. Every move and every suggestion Guy had made was logical and showed good sense. Indeed, he seemed in perfect control of his actions and his emotions.

His killing those cutthroats on the streets of London

troubled her, but in retrospect, he'd been left with no choice. It was the way he had done it, with seemingly no effort at all and without showing a jot of remorse afterward that bothered her.

Jonathan would never have been able to do such a thing, even if it had meant both of them dying there on the street. He had been all that was proper, conservative and above reproach. Lily quickly decided she appreciated Guy's abilities more than she worried about his methods.

Guy had seemed Jonathan's antithesis at first meeting. He could be decidedly improper and in no way a traditionalist. In fact, he was notorious. But honor, duty and strength of purpose seemed to mean everything to him. Jonathan had espoused those virtues. Guy lived them with a roughness that shocked her. She recognized the key differences between her husbands even this early on—their respective attitudes toward the regard of their peers and their inherently opposite personalities. Guy had a passion for life that Lily had only recently discovered she shared. Perhaps that should frighten her, but instead it buoyed her courage.

His word, she reminded herself. Guy had given his word Beau would be safe. And she had to trust someone. At least her new husband possessed the wherewithal to act in defense if need be. And he had no cause whatsoever to harm her son.

At the moment she could not summon any reason not to take Guy at his word. He could be so kind when the occasion called for it. The memory of his lips on her brow melded with a much earlier one of his soothing her as an injured child. That warmed her clear down to her bones and reassured her that she had chosen well.

She recalled how calming he could be when her world seemed upside down, and how he had held her so comfortably when she was unable to ride another mile. And who else had ever caused her to laugh when there was so little occasion for mirth?

Lily drifted into dreams, smiling at his silly jest about wearing frills, wondering just what kind of nightgown he really would wear. Or if he would wear one at all.

"Age quod agis...Age quod agis...Age quod agis."

Guy heard the high clear voice of Lily's son repeating the Latin phrase, each time emphasizing a different syllable. Then the strong young voice dropped to a mutter. "Ballocks."

Time to interrupt lessons. The boy might not have bitten off more than he could chew, but Latin obviously put a bitter taste—and also inappropriate English words—in his mouth.

"Good morning again," Guy said as he entered the nursery where lessons were going on. Or were they? "Where is your nurse?" he asked the boy, surprised that a boy left to his own devices would still be attending to studies. Any lad worth his salt would be seriously slacking off.

"Grandmother ordered her to assist with upacking. And she's not a nurse! She's a governer-ess." Beau's lips, so like Lily's, pushed out in a pout. He was a handsome little rascal, even when piqued.

"She assigns you your studies?" Guy asked.

The boy squirmed for only a second before answering. "Mother does that. Mrs. Prine sits with me to do them." He frowned even harder. "Unless Grandmother takes her away."

"Your grandmother was up here just now?"

The boy nodded. "I am to master two phrases before I am allowed to leave the room." He thumped the book with his knuckles and sighed. "Grandmother might test me."

"Age quod agis," Guy said, nodding. *"Attend to what you are about.* That's a good 'un. What is the other you need to learn?"

The little shoulders slumped. "I am allowed to choose. Why should you care what I learn? You're not my father."

"I know. *In vino veritas,"* Guy said solemnly.

Beau cocked his head and parroted the phrase. "What does it mean?"

"One forgets to lie when one is foxed."

The boy cocked his head, a sly look in his eyes. "Grandmother would cane me if I were impertinent."

"Over my dead body," Guy assured him with a grin. "What is nine times seven?"

"Sixty-three," Beau answered without hesitation, his posture had improved. "I know the nines. And the tens are easy."

Guy stood then and slapped his hands against his thighs. "Excellent. So, what now that you have finished your work for the day?"

"I wish to ride," Beau ventured, obviously prepared for a negative reply.

"I suppose you have a decent mount?" Guy asked, noting the boy already wore riding boots.

"I do, sir. My mother says I have an excellent seat, too. I will go alone."

At *seven?* Guy could not believe Lily would allow that. Even Guy himself had not had free rein at that age.

He did recall how eager he'd been for it, how ready, or so he'd thought at the time.

Not that Lily treated Beau as though he were still a baby. Guy had noticed how she limited her displays of affection for her son to a light touch on the shoulder or a brief smile of reassurance. He remembered how his own mother had done the same when he'd begun to assert his independence. None of that tousling of hair or outright hugs or kiss on the cheek unless they were alone.

Seeing the two of them together had brought memories flooding back, good times long forgotten in the bitterness of the intervening years. He had thought more about his early relationship with his father than he had for some time.

Whether that was beneficial or not, Guy wasn't certain. He did know that it made him too aware of all he had lost and dearly wish that somehow he could have it again; family, caring, someone to talk with when things went awry. How long had it been since he had needed that? He didn't *need* it now, he told himself, but it would be nice to have.

Well, he had family now, for good or ill. He might as well try to fulfill his role in it.

He cleared his throat and looked out the window. "I'll ride along, if you don't mind, Bradshaw. There are a few matters we should discuss and the fresh air will do us both some good, I believe."

Beau grabbed his hat and quirt from the table by the door. "I will ask Mother to come, too."

"She is asleep."

"Is she sick?" Beau asked as he halted, his entire body tense, his voice reduced to a worried whisper.

"Not at all, merely exhausted from all the excitement of the ride and then the arrival of your visitors."

"Then I shouldn't leave her," Beau said, his wish to ride obviously warring with his need to protect. How much did the boy know about what might be going on?

"She is safe in her chamber with the door locked so no one will disturb her," Guy promised. "Besides, we won't need to go far."

The boy exhaled slowly and gave a nod. "Very well." He marched out of the nursery, slapping the riding crop against his leg.

Guy followed, not terribly excited about riding out after having ridden most of the night, but he needed to establish how he and the boy were to get on. Doing that while engaged in an activity Beau loved seemed a perfect opportunity.

After Beau's pony and one of the mares in the stables had been saddled, they galloped out across a field. Lily was right. The lad rode as if born to it.

Only when the mounts tired did they rein in and dismount beside a small brook. "This is a beautiful place," Guy commented.

"It is mine. All of it," Beau declared. A warning?

"Lucky fellow. It looks prosperous."

"You aren't to have the estate even if you *are* married to my mother."

Ah, so it *was* a warning. "I already have one, thank you. It borders yours," Guy told the boy and pointed. "Just there, beyond those trees."

"Then why did you marry her?"

Guy smiled and fiddled with a long blade of grass as he spoke. "She's a lovely woman and I admire her very much. I have sworn to protect her and care for her."

"I am her son. *I* will protect her!" Beau argued.

Guy shrugged. "You're good with your fists then? And weapons, if it comes to that? I don't mean to overstep, Bradshaw. I only thought to give you a bit of help until you are taller."

"Taller?" The boy scoffed. "Stronger and older, is what you mean."

Guy nodded, stripping the grass into shreds as he looked off into the distance. "Yes, that, too. And as you grow, I will teach you all I know, if you'd like."

Beau looked pensive. "What do you know?"

Guy tossed the grass aside and wiped his hands on his breeches. "How to hold what is mine against all takers. Things a man needs to defend himself, his property, his people and his good name. Are you interested?"

To his credit, the lad took his time considering the offer. Then he met Guy's gaze directly as any adult. "Yes, but you must promise not to make me call you Father."

Guy's widened his eyes as if shocked. "Why would I do that? You had a perfectly good father from what your mother tells me. I had thought instead we might be mates. I've never had a friend your age, even when I *was* your age."

"Neither have I," Beau admitted. "Then you have no plans to send me away to school? I am seven now."

"Send you away?" Guy gasped, and pressed a palm to his chest as if horrified by the idea. In fact, he was. "I should say not, even if you insist!"

"Grandmother said you would. She said so this morning when she came to the nursery. She warned me you'd ship me off straightaway."

So the old biddy already had begun a campaign to

turn Beau against him. "My word on it, there is *no* chance of that happening. You are needed here. So shall we shake on it, Bradshaw?"

"If you like, Duquesne." They shook hands solemnly. "Now you must teach me to shoot."

.Guy winced. "You mother won't like that idea if I know her at all. Allow me a while to persuade her if you don't mind."

Beau thought about that, tongue in cheek. "A little while then. Are you sure you can persuade her, Duquesne?"

Guy answered in kind. "Given time I believe I might." Another seven years or so, he figured. "Until then, I see no reason why we may not begin instruction in self-defense, do you?"

Beau wriggled excitedly and a smile bloomed on his young features. "No reason at all!"

"Then on your feet, man! This is as good a place as any to begin."

Lily woke to the sound of her son's happy laughter. She smiled to herself, so delighted to hear it. What had him so tickled? Quickly she rose and donned her blue velvet robe over the chemise just as she heard the knock on her door.

When she opened it, shock held her silent. Both Guy and Beau stood there covered in grass stains. Beau's coat sleeve bore a wide slash of mud and his boots were even more scuffed than Guy's.

"We apologize for our appearance, madam, and are on our way to shed our dirt," Guy explained with a wink. "But Bradshaw here wants to announce to you that he is newly proficient in the art of tumbling. Show her, old man."

Beau backed up and kicked out his right foot. Guy grabbed it and thrust upward, helping the boy to complete a perfect backward flip and land on his feet.

Lily gasped.

"Attacking!" Guy shouted, backing down the hall, then running at Beau with arms outstretched as if to scoop him up.

At the last minute Beau threw himself forward and dropped to his knees, tripping Guy, who went sprawling over his head to land in a heap at the feet of her mother-in-law.

"What is the meaning of this!" the woman screeched, leaping back to avoid Guy's body.

Lily watched her husband spring to his feet and run a hand through his hair. Then he sketched a rough bow. "Your pardon."

"I should think you would beg it, you ruffian! What have you done to my grandson?" She narrowed her eyes at Beau. "Young man, you go to your room this instant!"

"Remain where you are, Beau," Lily said quietly. "I will see to my son, madam. You will excuse us, please."

The dowager huffed, then turned with an imperious glare and marched off down the corridor. The three of them silently watched her go.

Then Lily pointed emphatically to her own open door, addressing both Beau and Guy with a pointed stare.

They exchanged a guilty wince and complied.

As soon as she shut the door, boy and man collapsed in a fit of laughter, rolling like puppies on her carpet.

"Cease this instant and explain yourselves," she ordered. "What have you been doing?"

Guy sobered immediately. "I regret if we upset you, love. I promise from here on out, Bradshaw and I will restrict our roughhousing to the out of doors."

"That is *not* the point," Lily exclaimed.

Beau ran to her and clasped her around the waist. "Mama, please don't be angry. We've had such a rousing good time and you're spoiling it." He looked up at her with that liquid blue gaze of pleading and gave her his sweetest smile. "I have not played for ever so long."

Lily glanced heavenward and shook her head, throwing her arms up in defeat. "Go, then. Have a bath, the both of you."

Beau skipped off down the hall, whistling. Lily shook a finger at Guy. "You see that he doesn't hurt himself. That appears to be an excellent way to break one's neck."

Guy smiled at her. "Says a girl who insisted on climbing trees?"

"And has the scar to remind her of the foolishness," she retorted.

Guy nodded, then shrugged. "Our lad gave a good account of himself, though. You have to admit it."

"And you, sir," she replied, "give me headaches. I did not think to have two children to rear!"

"If I am a boy for him now, he will become a man for me," Guy explained.

"You are supposed to be a father to him," she argued, keeping her voice low.

"In all but name, I will be. But he needs a friend more at the moment and I like to think I am becoming that."

Lily sighed and placed a hand on his chest, giving him a slight push. "I cannot pretend to understand you, Duquesne."

He shrugged and smiled sweetly. "No one does, but I've never minded."

She closed the door and leaned against it, almost as exhausted as she'd been when she'd lay down to sleep a while.

What was she to do with this husband of hers? What an enigma he was. How many sides were there to this Viscount Duquesne and who was the real man inside?

When the family gathered in the morning room for the noon meal, Lily was unsure what to expect, but she feared it would not be conducive to the digestion.

Mrs. Carroll, the housekeeper, had placed a lovely arrangement of yellow roses on the sideboard and another on the table. The silver appeared newly polished and the linens pristine. Though much less formal than the dining room, Lily preferred the more intimate space when not entertaining. Her former mother-in-law obviously did not approve the choice. But when had she ever agreed with anything Lily did?

Though still quite attractive, Bernadette's frown aged her unnecessarily, Lily thought. In contrast, Clive's oily smile did nothing whatsoever to enhance his appeal.

Guy sat at the head of the table at her insistence after seating her at the opposite end, as was proper. Bernadette and Clive sat to either side.

"Where is the boy?" Bernadette snapped.

"He is having a tray in the nursery," Lily explained.

Bernadette grimaced. "How you indulge that child!"

Lily looked down as she spread her napkin over her lap. "Beau is mine to indulge." The last time Beau had attended a meal where Bernadette was present, the woman had criticized his every move at table and thoroughly spoiled his appetite.

Clive lifted his glass. "I suppose we should toast the bride and groom, Mother," he drawled, his eyelids at half-mast. "Here's to the future." He sipped. "And to luck, whatever sort might befall you."

Bernadette harrumped. "A cursed union, to be sure."

"Cursed?" Guy asked pleasantly, leaning forward as if quite interested in her answer. "Cursed by whom?"

"Mother…" Clive warned.

At that moment the maid entered with the soup tureen and began to serve.

Thankfully Bernadette refrained from answering. Lily supposed it was due to the rule of never discussing private affairs in the presence of the servants. Not that they didn't know everything that went on.

The remainder of the meal passed in silence except for the clink of the cutlery against porcelain. Guy shot her an occasional smile and wink. If he minded the tension in the room, he concealed it well.

When they had finished, Bernadette excused herself and left, the silk skirts of her morning gown rustling like a rasp.

Lily left, too, urging the men to remain and have their coffee. After that debacle of a luncheon, she hoped Guy would take charge and find some means to persuade Clive to leave Sylvana Hall and take his mother with him. If Guy did not, she felt she must.

It was not as if they had nowhere else to go. There was the house in London, not the most prestigious address, but a decent one. There was also the dowager house that stood a mile away, again not what Bernadette had been used to when she was the baroness, or even after the old baron had died.

The woman had always lived here at the Hall except for the years that Lily and Jonathan had been married. During that time, Clive and his mother had traveled the Continent, availing themselves of the hospitality of friends and distant relatives.

Only now did Lily suspect that Jonathan had not wished them to reside here and most probably had forbidden it. Why would that be? she wondered. Had he suspected Clive was dangerous? No, surely she was imagining things, reading more into them than was there.

Perhaps she would be wiser to allow Clive and his mother to remain at Sylvana Hall so she could keep him under close observation, as she'd first thought to do, but Lily was not certain she or Guy could tolerate the two.

And for another thing, Beau did not need to endure the constant harping of his grandmother or be at risk from the possible machinations of his uncle. Guy could not be with him every minute.

Had Clive truly been the one who wanted her declared insane? If so, he must be an excellent actor because he had shown no surprise to see her returned. Wouldn't he have done so if he thought her securely tucked away in Bedlam?

However the fact that he had traveled all the way from London the very same night that she and Guy had, and that he and his mother came here immediately, seemed to verify his guilt. That was hardly proof, but it was enough to convince her she would be better off with Clive living somewhere else.

Chapter Seven

Guy leaned back in his chair and sipped his coffee, his gaze fastened on the man they suspected had betrayed Lily. The silence had the intended effect.

"Lily's quite mad, you know," Clive said.

"Is she now? I confess I hadn't noticed. Is that why you had her spirited away to St. Mary's?"

Clive frowned. "Where?"

"Bedlam. Someone kidnapped her and had her forcibly confined at St. Mary of Bethlem hospital."

Clive laughed, his eyes wide as he set down his cup with a clatter. "That's absurd! She has fed you the lies of a highly disturbed mind, Duquesne."

Guy pursed his lips and regarded the man carefully. He did appear surprised. Or had missed his calling as an actor. "So you had nothing to do with that."

"With what? She imagined the entire thing. I'm sorry, but she is a lunatic. How can you be wed to the woman and not have witnessed this?" He sighed. "In your defense, I suppose she might not yet have had one of her spells when you were with her."

"We haven't been together much since the ceremony," Guy said. "Why don't you explain further to me what set her off?"

Clive shook his head and donned a sad expression. "It's not too late for an annulment, you know. I'm certain she never told you of her affliction and that is certainly grounds for an immediate dissolution."

Guy nodded slowly, his hands clasped in front of him. "So you would have me set aside the marriage." He shook his forefinger. "Now you must admit, Clive, that does sound suspiciously like a suggestion you would make to further your own aims."

"My aims?" Clive's eyebrows shot up and he pressed a hand to his chest. "I have no aims, Duquesne. What do you mean?" His voice had risen a full octave.

"It means that I know what you're up to and if I could prove it, you'd be under arrest." Guy pushed away from the table and stood.

He reached just forward of his plate and picked up a piece of silver, rotating it between his thumb and forefinger. Then he peered down his nose at the man he had despised at first sight.

"It also means that if anyone…anyone at all… touches my wife again for any reason whatsoever, I will carve out his eyes with this butter knife." He placed the dull utensil just to the right of Clive's plate, paused for effect, then added, "And then I shall kill him. Very slowly."

With an evil smile of promise, Guy left him there with his mouth hanging open and a look of horror on his face.

Guy needed to speak with Lily. The hell with keeping the two close to see what they were up to. He knew already. These people were abominable. He had sooner spend a week with the worst bully-boys in the stews than another hour in the house with Clive and his mother.

He found Lily in the kitchen discussing dinner with a heavyset woman he had not yet met.

"Duquesne!" Lily said, greeting him with a sunny smile. "I'd like you to meet Mrs. Kale, our cook. Mrs. Kale, my husband, Viscount Duquesne."

He smiled at the new face, doughy as an apple dumpling, creased with laugh lines and dotted with raisin-dark eyes. She smelled of cinnamon and nutmeg. He liked her immediately.

"The meal was excellent, Mrs. Kale. I am most happy you are here."

"Thank you, milord," she said with a giggle, dipping in a brief curtsy. "If you've a sweet tooth, I keep biscuits in the larder for any lads what fancy 'em. The young sir can vouch they're grand for taking the edge off hunger."

Guy closed his eyes and took in a deep breath. "Ah. You are a jewel beyond price. I can smell them from here."

Lily laughed. "Because there's a fresh batch just baked there on the table. Now cease cozzening Cook and come stroll the garden, Duquesne."

"One biscuit first, and then I am all yours, my lady."

Mrs. Kale reached for a tin on the worktable and held out a warm crisp cake to him. "Have a nice walkabout," she said.

"Another conquest," Lily commented when they were out of Cook's earshot. "Beau's already eating out of your hand. You simply ooze charm, don't you, Duquesne?"

"Your in-laws are not so taken with me," he argued, licking a crumb off his finger. "These are sinful concoctions."

"Wait until you taste her almond delights. I forbade her to make them more than once a week or I should weigh twice what you do."

She reached to break off a pink rosebud, but Guy got to it first. He snapped the stem, then straightened. "The petals are shamed by the softness of your cheek, my love." He drew the flower down the curve of her face.

"Oh, please!" she said, laughing merrily. But she took the rose, her hand brushing slowly over his as she relieved him of the bloom.

"Bathed in sunlight as you are, I lose my very breath to look at you," Guy said seriously. Perhaps he was doing it up a bit brown, but it was near the truth. She was lovely, especially so when she smiled and her eyes sparkled with humor.

"Come now," she admonished, her shoulders shaking with mirth. "You needn't play the part when we're alone, though I confess I shouldn't mind a whit when our guests are listening."

Guy sighed theatrically. "You wound me. How am I to court a wife? I've some success at everything else in skirts, but I swear I am at a loss here as to how I should go about it."

"First of all," she said with a pretty moue and a tap on his chest with the rose. "Do not tell her of your other victories. It puts one off to think of her husband rollicking about with dollymops and shop girls."

He nodded. "Properly noted. And?"

"And second, do not desist from pretty words when she instructs you to do so. It is merely modesty rearing its ugly head that makes her protest." She grinned. "And third, you might diplomatically hint to our company that we should like to be alone."

He rolled his eyes. "May I put that first? That's actually why I sought you out in the kitchen."

"You wouldn't mind asking them to go?" she said, frowning.

"Is that a joke? I have the urge to abandon you here and run full-speed to find them." He noticed the worry lines crease the creamy smoothness of her forehead. "I promise to be tactful. I understand that she is Beau's grandmother."

"You are so generous. But please don't go just yet," she said, lacing her hand through his. Her voice had grown soft, its faint rasp caressing his ears like plush velvet. "This is so pleasant, the first time I have felt safe and calm in a while now."

She felt safe with him. Guy felt his chest puff out and his mouth tug into a satisfied smile. He knew she was playing him like a fiddle, but he didn't care. She was right about one thing. This walk was the most pleasant thing he had done in ages, next to kissing her.

Anticipating a repeat of that in the very near future—like tonight if he could arrange it—made the sun shine that much brighter. It warmed his insides like fine brandy.

Lily was his wife, he thought, admiring her upturned smile. She seemed to like him and he liked her. By her own admission, she had truly loved her first husband, so there was little danger of putting her emotions at risk. He and Jonathan Bradshaw were as different as roses and ragweed and Lily could never fall in love with the likes of him. That was fine since he had no intention of loving her back.

There was no reason at all why they should not enjoy one another.

Perhaps he had done her an injustice by agreeing to this marriage, but he could not see how at the moment. He would make her and her son happy for as long as he possibly could and then release them immediately if he felt his faculties dimming.

Certainly a man would realize when that began to happen.

Following Guy's order for them to leave, Clive and Bernadette had departed in high dudgeon at four in the afternoon for the dowager house, a mile down the lane. They were not returning to London as Lily had hoped, but at least they were out from underfoot for the moment and she felt much more at ease.

Guy had solved the problem and all was right with her world, Lily thought happily as she came down to dinner. They were to dine early, at eight, so that Beau could join them.

"Ah, here she is, loveliest woman in Kent," Guy exclaimed, standing to greet her as she entered the dining room.

"No, in the world!" Beau argued, scrambling to his feet, as well, giving her a little bow of the head immediately after he saw Guy do it.

"Thank you, gentlemen. I am flattered." She allowed Guy to seat her, then looked to her son. "Good evening, Beau. What has occupied you this afternoon?"

He grinned. "I played war with the small soldiers Duquesne fetched from his home. He has more, he says." The boy sent Guy an adoring look as he wriggled back into his chair.

Guy had ridden over to Edgefield soon after Clive and his mother departed. "How did you find your father?" she asked him.

"Having a good day, actually. We walked about the grounds for half an hour until he tired. He seemed much better than I have seen him in a long while."

"Is your father ill?" Beau asked, tiny worry lines creasing the space between his deep blue eyes. "He isn't going to die, is he?"

"No, I don't think so, not anytime soon." Guy placed his napkin just so as the maid began serving. "He is ill, but I believe he's improving."

"That's marvelous!" Lily said. "We should all go over to visit. He must get lonely."

Guy did not answer, instead casting her a frown.

Beau began to chatter away about his pony and how well he got on with the mounts she and Guy had appropriated from his friend Hammersley's stables.

Lily could have hugged her son for carrying the conversation right through the dinner of roast duck and steamed vegetables, even if he did plague Guy mercilessly with questions. That established the fact that her husband possessed infinite patience with children and also eliminated the need for her to come up with proper topics of discussion that must include a seven-year-old.

She had begun to feel nervous about retiring for the night. He would join her in her bed. Neither of them had suggested they do anything else about the sleeping arrangements. Both knew that consummating the marriage was necessary.

The day she had married Jonathan, she had felt these same qualms. Fortunately her first husband had proved extremely gentle and the soul of brevity when it came to the marital duty.

After a while, she had quite enjoyed sleeping next to Jonathan after he accomplished the necessary deed to produce a child. Even the deed itself was merely awkward, not really onerous. She had so missed being held.

Duquesne was no Jonathan, however. He seemed a man of much greater passion. Thinking of his kisses nearly caused her to swoon. Even now she could feel herself blushing over her dessert.

She glanced up from her custard dish and found him regarding her with a quizzical look.

Beau, who was carrying on some discourse about the proper training of horses, suddenly asked, "How do you break horses to ride? Have you ever done that, sir?"

Guy held her gaze. "First of all, you never break one. That destroys the spirit and it shall be nothing more than a slave. What pleasure is that? You establish trust. Once your new friend realizes that you intend no harm and expect the same consideration, then you begin to create a bond that will serve the both of you well. It is not a question of taking what you want, but an exchange of favors. You provide what is needed and so, receive what you would like."

Beau laughed. "That is too easy, I think. Have you ever done it yourself or did you learn that from a book?"

Guy smiled. "Personal experience soon affirmed what I learned by reading. The concept works well for me, even when dealing with non-equine friends." He raised an eyebrow and held her gaze as he took the last bite of his blancmange.

"Hmm. I shall try it one day and see if you are right," Beau announced, stifling a yawn with one hand.

Lily watched Guy turn his attention to her son. "I daresay you will, Bradshaw, and I wish you luck. For now, I think a good night's sleep would do you good. You are about to fall forward into your pudding."

Beau laughed and pushed out of his chair. "May I be excused?"

"Of course you may, sir," Lily said fondly with a nod of approval for his manners. She held out her arms as he approached her for a good-night kiss. "I shall be up to hear your prayers in a little while."

After Beau released her, he marched to Guy's place and held out his hand. "Good night, Duquesne."

Guy shook it. "Good night, Bradshaw. See you in the stables at nine?"

Beau shot her a questioning look. He knew he had lessons first. She remained silent.

With a small shrug, he turned back to Guy. "Perhaps we ought to make it ten, sir. I should be finished with business by then."

"Business before pleasure, I always say. Good man." He cuffed Beau lightly on the arm. "Ten it is."

Beau beamed as he took his leave of them. She had seldom seen him as animated as he had been since Guy had come home with her. Even when Jonathan was alive, the boy had seemed more reserved and too old for his years. She only hoped Guy would know how to handle Beau when their wills clashed, as they surely would.

Everything seemed to be going entirely too well. That alone made her wary. Judging by her past, that was always the time when disaster struck.

Somehow, though, she felt better able to deal with whatever came about. Perhaps knowing that Guy would protect them caused her to feel that way, but she liked to think she was more capable of managing for herself than she had once been.

Reflecting on her actions the previous night gave her hope she wasn't as incompetent as some women might have been in that sort of circumstance.

Tonight might tell the tale. She would need courage.

Guy went to the library and poured himself a brandy as he waited for Lily to settle her son for the night. He wondered whether he would have been welcome to hear those prayers she insisted on. Would the boy include him? Probably. The little scamp had taken to him right off. Guy hadn't expected to like a child that much, at least not right away.

Perhaps he had paternal instincts, after all.

He sipped the liquor, feeling its warmth flow through him as he gently rocked the snifter, enjoying the feel of the fine crystal in his hand.

He looked around at the fine selection of leather-bound volumes that graced the dark oak shelves from floor to ceiling. Bradshaw had possessed excellent taste and had made fortunate choices in his life.

Guy felt almost unworthy to fall instant heir to the collection. He raised the glass in a silent toast. *I will hold it intact for your son. And your wife.*

"*My* wife," he corrected, saying the words out loud. He drank again, more deeply, feeling the burn. Tonight he would make their marriage real, here in this house where she had lived with the man she loved.

A sudden spurt of jealousy made Guy want to dash the glass into the fireplace, but he resisted the urge. Jonathan had been good to Lily. He had fathered a fine son. And from all observations, had managed his estate extremely well. Guy could not help but respect the man for all that. But the envy was there, not for the possessions, but for the love of a woman and child.

"Pour me one of those?" Lily asked quietly.

Guy did so, handing it to her after she took a seat on one of the leather armchairs that flanked the smoldering fire in the hearth. She had changed from her evening dress of blue faille to a brown velvet dressing gown edged with off-white lace. Her golden curls curved about her face like errant commas.

"My, don't you look charming," he said, polishing off the brandy and taking a seat in the opposite chair. He crossed an ankle over his knee and brushed nonexistent lint off his boot. "Prayers all said?"

She sighed, feathering the long, slender fingers of one hand through her hair. "He almost fell asleep on his knees."

"Did you speak with him about why you were gone?"

A dark look shadowed her eyes. "No, only that I had to leave unexpectedly and had no time to say goodbye. If I told him the truth, it would frighten him too much."

"He needs to know there is possibly danger afoot, Lily. Children worry more about what they imagine is happening than what actually is. If they are informed, they feel better prepared to deal with it."

She assessed him with those wide blue eyes. "So speaks a child who was not kept informed?"

He nodded. "But you are his mother and you know him best. I don't like to presume."

To Guy's dismay, she began to cry. Not loudly or inelegantly, but a simple shedding of tears that streamed down her face and beaded on the velvet of her gown. "I...trust you with him," she whispered, her voice quavering.

Guy found himself kneeling at her feet, brushing her tears away with his fingertips. "Ah, Lily, please don't cry." He leaned in to kiss her cheek.

She cradled his face in her hands and placed her lips to his, a tender gesture unlike anything ever bestowed upon him. He could taste the trust in her soft, vulnerable mouth. Her sweet, mellow scent that enveloped him was one of welcome. But it was the sigh that did it. Drew him nearer so that he embraced her fully and drank from the well of closeness that she offered.

Want took on new meaning for him then. He desired her far more than any woman he had ever held, but the feeling encompassed much more than that. Guy truly wanted all of her, mind, body and heart. And he had no right. No right at all to have her love him. It would only mean heartbreak for her later if she did. Losing a beloved husband to death was bad enough. Losing a man she loved in the same manner he had lost his father would be devastating to a kind heart such as Lily's.

He almost pulled away. But suppose he refused to make love to her? She might believe it was because he thought Clive was right about her, after all. She might even think he had only married her for the money. God, what should he do?

But Lily answered the question. "We should go up to bed."

Guy stood, wordless in the face of her suggestion and helpless to deny her what she obviously wanted from him. What he wanted, too. She had been quite frank about missing being married. He took her hands and lifted her from the chair.

Silently they left the library and walked slowly up the staircase to her room. When they entered, she went directly to the bed. The covers had already been turned back. With her back to him, she shrugged out of her robe and stepped out of her slippers.

The sight of her white slender foot on the bed steps alerted him to something. This was not just a woman. Lily was a lady. Guy had precious little experience with the type. None whatsoever, in fact. There had been those who bore the title without the sensibilities, of course, but none so innocent as this. Her voluminous nightrail covered her from neck to ankle and she looked as if she meant to keep it on.

What did she expect from him? And why was he simply standing in the middle of the room like a novitiate?

"There is a robe you may have in the dressing room," she told him.

Be damned if he'd don something Bradshaw used to wear. He wanted no reminders of husband number one.

He propped his hands on his hips, cocked his head and observed her for a few seconds. "No, thank you. I think we should begin as we mean to go."

She lay propped against the pillows like a sacrificial lamb, fingers laced across her breasts. Now she stared at him. "What do you mean?"

He shrugged. "I will undress in here and I don't believe I need a robe. Do you mind that?"

Her mouth opened as if to speak, but no words emerged. She simply shook her head.

"Fine."

He walked over to the chair beside the bed and began loosening his cravat. That discarded, he sat down and removed his boots, tossing them to one side. Again he stood in full view of her and continued to undress.

Amazing how arousing it was to do such a thing when he'd never paid it much mind before. Damn, he didn't want to terrify her with the sight of his nudity, but it wasn't as if she hadn't seen a man in the altogether before. She had been married for a number of years.

He was down to his smallclothes and shed them quickly, his member springing forth with a will of its own. He glanced at Lily to see her reaction and saw that she had her eyes tightly closed.

This was not good.

He strode over to the bed, climbed in beside her and pulled the covers up to his waist. He propped his elbow on the pillow next to her and rested his head in his hand, just looking at her. "Open your eyes."

She peeked up at him. "You forgot the lamp."

"I didn't forget," he informed her.

"But...but you should turn it out, don't you think?"

"Before we sleep I will. Can't have a fire hazard."

She swallowed hard and her eyes were wide open now. No tears there, he noted. Just a bit of panic. "Why?"

He didn't even pretend to misunderstand her question. "I want to see you. Don't you want to see me?"

"But we always..."

"New rules, Lily. We get to make our own. Are you afraid of me? Is that it?"

She frowned. "Afraid?"

"Yes, afraid. Take off that gown, I dare you," he told her with a wicked grin. "Bet you a crown you won't do it."

For a long minute she seemed to consider it. Guy held his breath, nearly wild with anticipation.

Then she sat up abruptly, wriggled the hem up around her waist and whipped the nightgown over her head, tossing it to the floor. "So there. I am not afraid!" But she had pulled up the sheet to cover breasts that he had only glimpsed. An enticing glimpse it was, too.

Guy grinned, thinking this could be fun if she let it. "What do you think? Should we toss caution to the winds and be wild?"

"Certainly not," she said with a huff. "You are behaving like a…like a…"

"A licentious libertine?" he supplied.

"Precisely!"

"But you knew I was that when you proposed to me."

He teased the top of the sheet with a provocative finger and peered up at her from beneath his lashes, still grinning. "You can be one, too. I'll never tell."

She gripped the sheet tighter, locking her arms beneath her breasts to hold the fabric firmly in place. "You'd like to reduce me to that, wouldn't you!"

"I would *love* to reduce you to that. And you would love it, too, I promise."

Again she huffed, but he could see she was beginning to breathe very fast. The pulse in her neck raced, plainly visible. Aroused or frightened?

"Relax, Lily, we have all night. I'm not planning to rush you."

"Rush me?" she demanded. "You have me unclothed as I have never before been in the presence of a man and you are lying there naked as the day you were born and just as shameless as you were then, I'll wager."

"It's true. I have no shame," he admitted with a heart-felt sigh. "You should have none, either. From the little I've seen, Venus herself would envy what you have and she displays it all for crowds to see. Not that I'd advise you to do that sort of thing, but—"

"This is a totally inappropriate conversation," she admonished.

"Anything is permissible between husband and wife," Guy informed her. "And never shared with anyone else. Pillow talk is not to be bandied about, ever. One of my rules."

She rolled her eyes. "You have rules?"

"Certainly. One of them is never to do it in the dark."

"Why? Forget the one you happen to be with?" she snapped.

"Ah, jealous already. See? You're smitten with me. I knew it."

"Damn you, Duquesne. Why are you deliberately trying to make me angry? I had talked myself into this, but I didn't realize you would be so—"

"Irreverent," he finished for her. "I know, and I sympathize with your feelings, I really do, but you see, I am the man I am and I doubt I'll ever change. If we're to get on together, you'll simply have to loosen up those stays a little. Are you really angry with me?"

She puffed out her cheeks and blew out a harsh breath. "No, only a bit shocked. And uncomfortable."

Guy had to give in. This was too new to her and she wasn't ready. He tossed back the covers and got up, knowing her eyes would clamp shut the minute he did so.

He trudged over to the lamp, twisted the key to extinguish it and then returned to the bed. "There. You'll soon have broken another of my rules."

"You actually have more than two?" she asked, sounding a little braver and much relieved. "Pray tell, what is the other?"

"I never go to bed with an unwilling woman. And here I am. No matter what you *say* you've decided, you aren't quite willing, are you?"

She remained quiet until he stopped rustling around to get comfortable. Then she said in a small voice, "Strangely enough, I find that I am. Still. That is truly odd, don't you think? I must be more dissolute than I knew."

Guy breathed a prayer of thanks for her honesty, her forthrightness and the fact that he wouldn't have to delay much longer.

"There is nothing dissolute about you, Lily. Or this." He leaned close and kissed her as gently as he knew how.

Maybe he understood her fear just a little. He found he was afraid, too, but his fear had nothing to do with coupling in the dark. He could fall in love with this woman too easily.

Loving someone terrified Guy and that feeling began to invade him now like the curling tendrils of a hardy vine. How much stronger hold would it have after they had shared the ultimate intimacy?

Chapter Eight

Lily moved her hand and touched him tentatively. His chest felt hot, his heartbeat pumping furiously against her palm. The fire in the kiss almost burned away all thought, but she clung to awareness, not wanting to miss a single facet of the excitement he was arousing in all her senses.

Never before had her fingers caressed steel-firm muscles such as this. His subdued strength sent fiery sparks darting through her, coalescing at places where sensation had lain dormant far too long.

"Your hair," he whispered. "Like silk. Soft… sweet…scented…golden…silk." His tongue teased her ear as his palm caressed her neck and shoulder.

She breathed in his scent, unable to get enough of the subtle, enticing spice he exuded. Intriguing, somehow foreign and dangerous, it beckoned irresistibly.

The rumbling groan deep in his chest excited her so, she must have made some sound in reply, for he deepened the kiss, devouring her mouth as if he could not live without it. Realizing her effect on him sent a surge of power through her.

He slid his arm beneath her waist and pulled her closer while his other hand stroked down her arm and smoothed over the curve of her hip. Lily tensed, suddenly uncertain about allowing this man liberties no one had ever taken.

Jonathan had never... No! She would not think of him now.

"It's all right," Guy whispered, again touching his lips to her ear as he spoke. "We'll go more slowly."

"No," she snapped, impatient with herself for hesitating. And for her wicked anticipation. "Have done with it. Finish it now."

He pulled back a little, still holding her. She could barely see the outline of his head in the darkness. "Perhaps we should wait. Are you afraid, Lily? Is that it?"

She shook her head vehemently. "Not at all afraid, I swear. And it must be done."

He sighed loud and long. "We don't *have* to. No one is keeping watch, you know."

"I *want* to," she told him firmly. "And I want to *now*." With that made clear, she clasped one hand behind his neck, fitting her mouth to his.

This time it was she who heightened the passion, kissing him deliberately and feverishly while she pushed away the sheet between them and pressed her bare body to his.

He responded swiftly, rolling her to her back and covering her full length, one leg insinuating itself between hers. She felt his member hard against her thigh and prayed he was not too large. He was a much bigger man than...

"Lily," he breathed her name, a harsh rasp next to her ear, then entered her slowly.

The feel of him pushing inside her, filling her completely, stole her breath away. It was as if every nerve she had stood on end and quivered. Though she wanted to be done with this, neither did she want it to end.

His hips moved against her, then he withdrew to thrust forward again. She bit back a moan, certain that to voice any pleasure would be unseemly. Women were not supposed to like this necessary evil. *Necessary,* she thought, unable to quell a shuddering sigh of ecstasy.

Again he whispered her name, a nearly painful sound as he began to move more quickly. She lifted her body to receive him, increasing the indescribable feelings to fever pitch. Suddenly he thrust almost violently and she felt the heat of him suffuse her.

When he stopped, a wave of disappointment washed through her. She felt she had almost reached some pinnacle of pleasure. Did women do that? Was there ever enough of this to satisfy? Did she dare ask him to prolong it next time? Would there even *be* a next time?

He rested his weight on his forearms, his hands tangled in her hair, his face above hers. Slowly his mouth descended and tasted her swollen lips, tugging lightly at the lower one that felt so sensitized. "Still prefer brevity?" He moved his hips again, a pleasant weight against her, but he no longer filled her as he had before.

"That…that will do," she muttered.

He moved off of her, disengaging their bodies, but instead of letting her go, he cradled her close.

Lily welcomed that, though she still felt frustrated, almost bereft. Yet this closeness was the part of marriage she missed, Lily told herself. Men were the ones who craved coupling, who took such great pleasure from it. Women permitted it, so she had been taught, to keep their husbands happy and to procreate.

She had never missed it all that much. But something about that bothered her now. Perhaps she really *had* missed being bedded, as in never having had it properly done.

She suspected that Guy knew far more about this than Jonathan had.

Just thinking about such a thing seemed so disloyal to Jonathan. It made her feel small-minded and altogether too wicked. He had been a wonderful husband, giving her their precious Beau and nearly everything else she had ever wanted.

To desire doing this simply for gratification must be terribly immoral for a woman. "I was a good and modest wife," she murmured against Guy's shoulder.

He kissed the top of her head. "I'm sure you were the best ever. But modesty is somewhat overrated at times."

Lily was now inclined to agree with him, but she said nothing else. She had done her duty. Their marriage was consummated, their business deal confirmed.

Wanting more seemed greedy and she did not want Guy to see that baser side of her nature. The side that wanted him besotted with her, wanted him to lust after her, to make her love him and to fall hopelessly in love with her. What foolishness.

That was wishing far too much for a woman of her practicality. Romantic thoughts, and especially lecherous ones, had no place in this scheme and were very likely triggered by the act of consummation itself.

She should be perfectly satisfied to have Duquesne as a good friend, one who would lend his protection to her and Beau. Her son was everything to her and it should remain that way.

If only she had the excuse of trying to conceive, she would not need to conceal her hunger for him.

"I wish I could have another child," she said. The thought slipped out of her mouth quite accidentally.

"Ah, Lily…" He sounded so sad.

"I know you would not want to and also why you would not, and there is no possibility anyway. I should never have said it. But you are so wonderful with Beau." That was entirely true. It delighted her that he took such interest in her son. She patted his chest where her hand rested, enjoying the texture of his skin and the leashed power of the muscles beneath it. She made her voice light, whimsical. "You are such good father material. It seems a shame to waste you."

"Thank you," he said after a few seconds of silence. "No one has ever paid me such a compliment."

When his hand began to wander and his lips touched her temple, she pulled up the covers and released a loud sigh. "Well, good night, then. Sleep well."

He might be ready to begin again, but she needed to acquire more control over herself than she had right now. The temptation was simply too great to tell him how she was really feeling and what she truly wanted him to do.

Guy suffered in silence. She'd obviously had enough of him, though he had purposely left her wanting. His mistake, assuming she would then see the benefit of prolonging their love play the next time. He should never have thought of it as love play in the first place. It had been precisely what she had named it, the obligatory consummation. And now it was done.

So much for enthralling her with his expertise in bed. With a disgruntled sigh that he carefully expelled so she wouldn't hear it, Guy rolled away from her and attempted to sleep.

Tomorrow held tasks he would sooner put off, the business aspects of their agreement. He had to examine account ledgers, both his and hers, make arrangements for repairs to his estate and contact a solicitor about naming young Beau heir to the Duquesne properties.

Perhaps he would take the little fellow with him when he rode into Maidstone to see to the deed. Guy rather enjoyed the lad's company and Lily needed to catch up on her rest after her ordeal in London, their harrowing trip here and dealing with her in-laws. He would arrange for guards among the footmen to watch over her. Though he felt sure Bradshaw was no longer a threat, Guy wouldn't bet on it.

While mentally listing her trials of late, Guy wondered whether he had rushed fences with the bedding. Yes, he should have insisted on delaying this until she had fully recovered. Surely exhaustion and tension, combined with her natural reserve, had been the reasons for her abruptness.

Perhaps his own lack of sleep had impaired his judgment in dealing with her tonight. Yes, that was surely the case. He ought to have waited until they were both well rested.

He vowed that from here on out, he would keep her delicate constitution in mind. But then memories of her escaping Bedlam on her own, proposing to a man she knew to be a raconteur and then riding hell-bent cross-country like the excellent horsewoman she was, made him think again. Lily, delicate? No. Not in body and certainly not in spirit. He almost laughed at the thought.

She was no wilting violet, but a passionate, resolute and resourceful woman. Why then did she seem so confounded by the act of love? Why had she rushed him through it?

She had admitted at the outset that she missed being married. Had he misunderstood what she'd meant by that? The only thing he could figure was that she still loved her husband and saw Guy's attentions as a duty only to be endured and hurried along. Well, hadn't she called it *necessary?*

Her refusal to allow him to satisfy her confused him. He had dealt with rejection before, but never in this circumstance. Never in bed.

Damned if he would deal with it again, even for the incredible pleasure of possessing her for the space of a few minutes. He had his pride. If she wanted him again, she could bloody well ask.

Anger at and jealousy of a dead man kept him awake and uncomfortable most of the night.

The next morning Lily awakened alone. She was glad of that. It would have proved most awkward waking up naked next to Guy after last night's event. Perhaps he had thought so, too.

She stretched her arms wide and smiled at his consideration of her modesty, even though he didn't think much of the virtue.

She wasn't entirely certain how she felt about what had happened. A thoroughly wicked shiver ran through her just thinking of all she had allowed him to do. She could still feel his touch on her skin and was loath to wash it away.

When she performed her ablutions in the dressing room, her mind wandered somewhat salaciously as she drew the wet washcloth over her body. Perhaps tonight he would want her again. She met her own gaze in the mirror and smiled. This time she might be able to ignore prudence altogether.

"Nonsense, Lily!" she muttered. "You are not some silly goose with romantic flights of fancy. Behave yourself!" She actually giggled, glad at the moment she had no personal maid about to look askance at her private antics.

From the first, when she had wed Jonathan, she had elected to bathe and dress herself as she had always done. It infuriated her mother-in-law and even caused Jonathan to raise a brow. But this was the one concession to her modest upbringing Lily had insisted upon, the absence of a maidservant to attend her personal needs.

Admittedly, that insistence had as much to do with retaining marital privacy as it had with her former habits. Maids were notoriously nosy.

For instance, if she had one now, the girl would be well aware of what had gone on in Lily's bed the night before. And this morning, every servant in the house would be privy to it.

She abandoned her ridiculous musings, dressed quickly and went downstairs to begin her day.

Mrs. Prine informed her that Guy and Beau were in the nursery doing lessons, and that a guest had been waiting in the parlor for her this last quarter hour. It was Mrs. Oliver, the wife of the vicar who had succeeded her father at Edgefield Church, the housekeeper informed her.

Lily hurried to greet the guest, embarrassed at staying so late abed this morning. It was nearly ten, early for visitors by city standards, but not so for country folk. "Mrs. Oliver, how nice of you to come."

The woman beamed. "So you've married our lord Guy. The news was most welcome, my lady."

"Thank you." Lily accepted the envelope Mrs. Oliver handed her.

"It's a formal invite, my lady. We'd be most obliged if you would come. There's those that'll be there who recall when you was but a child tagging behind the reverend as he visited the infirm. They watched you grow up and missed you when you married Lord Bradshaw and moved up here."

Lily regretted the social distance her first marriage had demanded. Her father had died soon after she and Jonathan wed and her main tie with Edgefield Village had been severed.

Though she had never met the wife of the current vicar before this visit, the woman seemed sincerely eager for Lily to attend the tea planned in her honor by the women of her father's old congregation.

No doubt Guy's housekeeper had made the rounds in the community and spread the news of his marriage immediately after she and Guy had stopped at Edgefield Manor on the way here. "I would love to come, Mrs. Oliver. How dear of you to plan this for me."

The vicar's wife nodded with satisfaction. "Then we'll expect you the day after tomorrow at two in the afternoon."

"This is ladies only, I presume?"

"Oh, yes, ma'am. It is the regular time for our weekly Ladies Circle meeting. I do hope you won't mind a bit of discussion about our plans for good works."

Aha, so there was an underlying motive in addition to honoring the former vicar's daughter and their local lord, Duquesne. Lily took Mrs. Oliver's hand and pressed it between her own. "Only if you allow me to contribute to your efforts."

"Oh, ma'am, that would be ever so grand of you! Perhaps you would also consider attending services at Edgefield now and again. What with your father the former vicar and the earl and Lord Duquesne furnishing the living there…"

"Of course." She had missed the lovely old church and its congregation. It was much less imposing and certainly nearer by than the one she and Jonathan had attended in Maidstone. "We would be delighted. I shall speak to my husband about it."

She had no idea whether Guy would agree to attend church services with her or even if he was religious at all, but Lily resolved to go the very next Sunday and take Beau. Her memories of the church there were very happy and she was certain he would love it, too.

After she had seen Mrs. Oliver to the door, Lily went up to consider what she would wear to the function. Nothing too fussy, she thought as she entered her bedroom. Something sedate. Perhaps the blue merino with the lace collar. She had so enjoyed the blue riding habit that had belonged to Guy's mother, the countess.

Almost everything else hanging in her wardrobe would be considered half-mourning and it was time she came out of that. It had been two years. The first twelve months she had passed wearing unrelieved black, as was proper. The second, she had changed her dress only in so far as adding a bit of trim here and there or donning the occasional dark purple of late.

The colorful dresses she had worn before becoming a widow would seem like new to her. She rummaged in the trunk that had remained closed for so long.

"Lily?" Guy greeted her as he passed her open door.

She saw he was in riding attire. Though she knew she blushed, Lily managed to keep her composure. This was a morning like any other, she kept telling herself, but avoided meeting his gaze. She must pretend nothing had happened between them and hope that he did not insist on discussing it. Surely he was gentleman enough not to do that.

With a deep breath, she introduced a topic to distract him just in case. "You missed our guest. You were with Beau?"

He shrugged and ducked his head, looking a bit guilty. "We were out early riding and I thought to give him a hand catching up with his lessons. He's diligent, that one. Smart as a whip."

She concealed a grin. "Is he now? Well, not if he was trotting about the fields when he should have been at his studies. What is he about at the moment?"

"Totaling the accounts for grain. I gave him the figures from your books." He came closer then, touching the dress she was holding up for inspection.

"But those books are too difficult for a boy of seven, Guy," she said gently, pressing a hand on his arm, unable not to touch him when he stood so close. "We must not give him too great a challenge with his limited knowledge of mathematics."

Guy scoffed. "It took me only five minutes to show him how it's done. The boy amazes me, Lily," he said, shaking his head. "I think he's a thirty-year-old in the wrong body."

Her laugh burst out unexpectedly. In some respects, Guy seemed more a boy than Beau. She found it endearing that Guy's hardships had not left him bitter and that he could still take joy in something so simple as a little boy's achievements.

Guy was like no other man she had known. Not gruff and strict as her father had been, nor concerned with propriety and etiquette like Jonathan. And Guy was as different from Clive as two men could possibly be. Jeremy Longchamps, Jonathan's friend and Lily's one suitor, didn't even enter the realm of comparison. She decided Guy was perfectly unique.

Lily realized then just how few men she had known well in her life. She had no frame of reference for dealing with one such as Guy. Considering that, perhaps she had not done so badly after all.

What a relief that he seemed so at ease with her despite last night, not at all sly and suggestive as she had feared he might be. Her feelings of awkwardness fell away.

"Come in, sit with me for a while and I'll give you a bit of gossip."

"Gossip?" he asked with a grin. "That sounds delicious. What are you doing there?" he asked as she laid the gown she was holding across her bed.

"Deciding on the appropriate thing to wear day after tomorrow," she told him, gesturing at the dress. "That's to do with the gossip, by the way." She lowered her voice as if to tell him a secret. "Did you know that Lord Duquesne's staff has spread the word in the village that he's wed that scamp who used to scratch her name on the back of the pews in Edgefield chapel?"

"No! Has he really dared such a thing? Do you suppose the rascal abducted her or was it the other way 'round?"

Lily laughed merrily as she lifted the blue gown and held it against her front. "Will this do for a tea, do you think?"

"At Edgefield?" he guessed, frowning at the dress.

She looked down at it. "What's wrong? Is the lace too much? The color too bright? I've worn mourning for so long now, I thought—"

"No, no, the frock's lovely," he answered, coming closer and putting his hand on her shoulder. "I think you shouldn't go unless I accompany you and I daresay that's out of the question."

"I'm afraid so. Ladies only."

He nodded, somewhat absently. "I thought as much."

"For heaven's sake, Guy. They are neighbors and my father's former flock. They're doing this especially for me, for *us,* really. I must go."

His smile appeared again. "I'd prefer you take someone with you. How about Mrs. Prine and Mrs. Kale? Will that do?"

"If you insist." In fact, she was flattered by his continued concern. She felt more secure than she had since Jonathan had died. No one, especially Clive, would dare touch her now that she was married to Guy.

Guy, a true gentleman despite his reputation, one who seemed perfectly willing to bow to her wish for modesty and to do precisely as he had promised with regard to her protection and Beau's. Surely her troubles were over and her new life begun.

Guy decided Lily would be safe enough traveling the five miles to the church at Edgefield if the other women went along. Clive was well aware now that Guy was on to his scheme. That in itself should prevent anything further happening, at least not right away. But he would keep a careful watch to be sure.

For now, Guy intended to concentrate on building a better marriage. To that end, he had come to Lily's room to speak with her about last night. That had proved impossible when greeted with that blush of hers. He couldn't make himself embarrass her more than he obviously had done.

For his own good, he needed to gain a bit of perspective on his and Lily's new relationship. She was a lady to the core and he had known that from the beginning. Still he had hoped for a bit more of her adventurous spirit to surface in the bedroom.

It was as if she had become a different person once they reached Sylvana Hall. Not shy and retiring exactly, but entirely too conscious of the starch in her petticoats. Danger had quickly dispensed with all that in London, but now she had reclaimed her training. He wondered whether he would ever see that devil-may-care, caution-to-the-wind side of her again. God, he hoped so.

He had been profligate for too long, used to a much different sort of attachment. His experience with women of Lily's station was admittedly lacking. The single ones had avoided him because he had no wealth to offer, and also because of his reputation. The others he had avoided. He had no wish to cuckold their husbands for the sake of momentary thrills.

He had left her this morning while she'd still slept. After a brief glance, he'd refrained from looking at her. Damn, but he had wanted her again. He still did, right now, but it was the middle of the morning and she was hardly likely to desert her daily duties just to accommodate his lust.

The idea made him smile, but it was a grim expression that mirrored how he felt. He and Lily had things to work out, but they were things best left to the night.

When he strode into the stables, Beau stood there waiting, the little leather quirk slapping rhythmically against the top of his small, scuffed boots. The boy grinned. "Where shall we ride now, sir?"

"I thought I left you working."

"All finished," the boy said with a grin.

"I need to visit my father," Guy told him, "and then I'm on to Maidstone to handle a bit of business."

"Excellent. I should like to meet him," Beau said, climbing upon the mounting block and propelling himself onto the saddle, working his little boots into proper position in the stirrups.

"Your mother will be worried if you simply disappear."

"I told Mrs. Prine I was riding out with you."

Resigned, Guy nodded and headed out in the direction of his father's estate. Beau caught up, jouncing along happily. "Is he truly mad?"

Guy almost reined in to send him home. "Who said he was mad?"

Beau shrugged. "I hear the servants talking. They were not mean about it. One, and I shan't say who even if you whip me, declared it was a shame his old lordship left you to do all of the work of an earl without your having the grand title to go with it." He clicked to his pony to go a bit faster, then said over his shoulder, "I think a viscount shouldn't mind a bit of work. That title is grander than baron, and I don't mind working."

Guy nodded. "Point taken."

"So is he mad, then?"

Again, Guy nodded and answered the boy's question as frankly as he had asked it. "He is. You'll want to wait downstairs while I see to him."

"I'd rather not. I've never seen a madman before. Of course, I saw my mother, but I expect a woman's is a different sort of madness, don't you think?"

Guy almost gaped, but managed to absorb the shock of the boy's words before it was noticed. "Hold up a moment. What do you mean? What's this about your mother?"

"At the picnic," Beau replied, slowing his pony to a walk. "She had a fit. Uncle had to restrain her. I was upset until he explained. Oddly enough, he was very kind that day." The boy shook his head as if in wonder at the event. "Very unlike his usual self."

Lily had experienced a former episode that she'd neglected to mention? A shiver of unease crawled up Guy's spine. "When did this happen?"

"Last month. We brought her home and put her to bed. When she awoke, she seemed as well as ever."

Guy remained quiet as he mulled over the unwelcome news. After a while he asked the boy, "Were there any other incidents such as that?"

The boy shrugged. "I don't know. I feared it was the madness that made her leave without saying goodbye to me. But now I suppose it was only that she wanted to go and meet you."

Was that a note of jealousy he heard? Guy wondered. He smiled at the boy, hoping to relieve any worries. "I know for a fact that she was delayed. Your mother never intended to be away long enough for you to know she was gone. She was most anxious to return and see you."

Beau brightened at that, his expression hopeful.

"Thank you ever so much for bringing her home. She seems quite herself now, wouldn't you say?"

Guy forced a nod. "I pray that's true." He needed to find out whether she had drunk or eaten something at that picnic. Surely she had.

He rode in silence until they reached his father's house. They left the horses tied to the post near the entrance to the kitchens. "It would be best if you stayed downstairs with my housekeeper," he told the boy.

The earnest blue gaze, so like Lily's, met his, then drifted away, his face a study in disappointment. "Very well."

Guy introduced Beau to Mrs. Sparks, saw him settled in with cakes and milk and then went up the stairs to make a short visit with the earl.

When he entered the master suite, he found his father thrashing about, babbling nonsense and grinning at things that weren't there. Suddenly his grin turned to grimace and he cried out, an unearthly sound between groan and scream. His wrists were secured to the bedpost with linen strips. He strained against them, threatening to break bones or tear fabric.

Guy wondered if he was looking at himself thirty years from now. His father had looked remarkably like him before his illness. Now the earl's hair had turned almost white, his face gaunt and his large, muscular body to skin and bones.

Marcus Mimms, his father's old valet, sat in a chair beside the bed, sadly observing the earl. "He sees her, he says. The countess. Always at first. Then it goes bad. Almost always goes bad."

Guy wondered how many times the old fellow had been obliged to witness this sort of behavior over the years. Laying a hand on the broad shoulders of his father's trusted servant, Guy asked, "How long has he been this way?"

"Since early morning. He's somewhat quieter than he was." The former batman slicked down his own sparse hair with a shaky palm. "I expect he'll be sleeping soon. A good long sleep, that's what he needs." He glanced over at the bottle on the table. "If you'd hold him, sir, I'll give him the medicine. Easier when I don't have to do it by myself."

An opiate. Guy knew laudanum was the only thing that truly calmed his father after one of his spells, but he wished there were an alternative to it. He had seen the wasted humanity in the opium dens in London and the mere thought of it sickened him.

"I'll be hiring some help for you as soon as I can find someone suitable," he told the valet, thinking of his one attempt to do that and how it had brought him Lily instead. Thank God he had not employed that Brinks fellow who turned out to be such a rotter.

With a sigh, he held his father's head steady while holding his nose so he would open his mouth. Guy thought of Lily doing the same to Brinks in order to gain time to escape. How brave she had been. And resourceful, too.

Marcus emptied in the required dosage. Moments later, the thrashing stopped and his father drifted into sleep.

"I was wrong. It is the *same*," said a small, terrified voice from the doorway. "Just the same."

Guy turned, aghast that the boy had been privy to the scene. "What are you doing here? You were to stay with—" He stopped midsentence when he noted Beau's distress.

As quickly as possible, Guy ushered him downstairs and out to where the horses were tethered.

"I want my mama," Beau whispered, turning a pale, imploring face up to Guy. His wide blue eyes brimmed with tears.

"So do I. We'll go home now and leave Maidstone for another day," he said gently, lifting the boy into his own saddle. "We'll ride double, if you don't mind."

Such a small weight physically, such a heavy one otherwise. Guy hardly knew what to do with a little one who was upset, but the boy was in no condition to manage his pony. One of the stable lads could return it later.

Beau always acted so much the little gent, a body could almost forget he was but seven years old.

Lily would be furious about this and he could hardly blame her if she was. What had he been thinking, bringing a child along on such an errand? Any fool should have guessed his curiosity would never allow him to remain downstairs where he was put.

Guy mounted behind the saddle and held Beau firmly with one arm, feeling the boy's heartbeat fluttering rapidly against his palm. A protective feeling swept over him. This was Lily's son, a defenseless child. In her mind, Guy's gravest responsibility. "Your mama's fine, Beau. You'll see."

The small head nodded, but he heard a sniffle.

With a silent curse, Guy urged the mare to a gallop.

As it happened, Lily had no chance to castigate him when they returned. Beau clung to her like a shadow for the rest of the day. Guy had given her a very abbreviated version of what had gone on.

Lily looked worried, but she kept up a good front before her son, lightening the mood with chatter about ordinary, inconsequential things. After an early supper, she excused herself to put the lad to bed.

When she had not come downstairs after an hour, Guy went up to see about them both.

Lily was just exiting the boy's chamber. She grabbed his arm and urged him down the corridor and into the room just past hers. "Now tell me what really happened," she demanded when the door was shut.

Guy sighed, pressing his fingers against his eyelids and wincing. "He witnessed Father in a full-blown fit. It reminded him of the time—" Did he dare mention the picnic Beau had told him about?

"What time?" she insisted, glaring at him like the outraged mother she had every right to be.

Guy opened his eyes and watched her closely as he answered. "Apparently he saw some parallels in my father's behavior and yours the day of your picnic with the Bradshaws."

She frowned, obviously puzzled. "Picnic? Oh, the day I fainted?"

Ah, this would be trickier than he'd thought. "I fear Beau's description was a bit more vivid than yours."

Her eyes widened and she looked stunned. She swallowed hard. "Tell me. What did he say? What did he see?"

With all his heart, Guy wanted to take her in his arms and tell her to forget it, to banish from her mind anything he had said about it. But that would neither help her nor her son. This needed clearing up.

"You had a spell of hysterics that day, Lily. Beau said that Clive had to restrain you. They brought you home and put you to bed. Don't you remember any of it?"

She was already shaking her head. "No. No, all I recall is falling to the grass. When I awoke, I was in bed
at home. A simple faint. That's what I thought it was."

She began to pace, her hands twisting the handkerchief she held. Guy worried that she might experience
another episode if he allowed her to upset herself any
further.

He stopped her and pulled her to him, enfolding her
in his arms as he'd wanted to do the minute he'd seen
her after returning home. "We will sort this out, Lily.
That's what I'm here for."

She pushed away and frowned up at him, her beautiful face a study in anger mixed with worry. "I am not
a lunatic. I *know* I'm not!"

"Of course you aren't," he answered calmly, forcing
a smile as he gently tucked a golden curl behind her ear.
She batted his hand away and turned her back to him.

His heart seemed to shrivel inside his chest. After all
these years of watching his father decline, must he now
watch a wife suffer the same fate?

Not if he could help her, he declared inwardly. There
had to be something he could do.

"I shall sleep in Beau's room tonight," she said.
"That way I can reassure him if he awakens." She
looked over her shoulder at him, her brow creased with
the announcement, as if she expected him to object.

"Excellent idea," Guy agreed. What else could he do
without sounding like a demanding beast? As badly as
he wanted to hold her through the night, she would not
believe that was his sole intent. Maybe it wasn't. "Shall
I move him to the trundle so you may have his bed?"

"No, thank you," she whispered, looking vastly relieved. In a hasty, almost guilty, gesture of thanks, she

approached him and squeezed his forearm. Quickly she rose on tiptoe and kissed him on the cheek. "Good night." Then she hurried out of the room before he could respond.

Guy raked a hand through his hair and gripped the back of his neck, feeling the muscles there drawn tight as a drum head. God, he wanted a drink. He knew better than to drown his sorrows, but this occasion seemed to call for a thorough soaking.

However, he knew he could not afford that escape tonight. Not when Lily might call out to him. Or worse yet, when Beau might wake and cry out that something was wrong with his mother and he needed Guy's help.

After he went to bed, Guy lay awake for hours, both doors of the dressing room that separated the bedrooms standing wide open so that he could listen for sounds of trouble.

That morning he had wanted time to think. Now he had entirely too much of it.

Chapter Nine

Lily spent most of the night trying to recall exactly what had happened at that picnic. She did remember how Beau had hovered around her that evening after she'd recovered from what she had thought was a fainting spell from too much sun.

Flashes of memory did surface, but they were indistinct, as in a strange dream. She must have consigned the entire episode to being that very thing and thought no more of it.

Now she worried, about herself and also about Beau and that day's effect on him.

This morning as her son awoke to find her sitting in the chair beside his bed, enjoying a second cup of coffee, he looked vastly relieved.

"Good morning," she said cheerfully, offering him her brightest smile.

"Are you well today?" he asked in a small voice.

"Of course, darling, never better. But I can see that you're still worried. Shall we talk about your visit to Edgefield?" she asked conversationally, sipping her coffee and smiling. "I believe that's what upset you?"

He wriggled off the bed and stood beside her chair. His fingers toyed with the lace on the sleeve of her dressing gown. "Duquesne's father frightened me," he admitted.

"I should think so," she replied evenly. "Whenever someone exhibits behavior we don't understand, it does give us a turn." She paused, brushing the golden curls off his brow. How she wanted to take him onto her lap and hold him close as she had when he was younger, but he would surely resist. He was growing up so quickly. "Did I frighten you the way the earl did, Beau? Tell me what happened that day at the picnic."

A sound at the doorway caught her attention and she turned. Guy stood there, leaning against the opening.

Beau glanced from one to the other.

"Go ahead, dear," she said to Beau. "It's all right."

"We had only just gotten there," he began hesitantly. "You were sitting on the blanket and then you lay down. I thought the sun must be making you sleepy."

Guy entered the room and quietly sat on the edge of the bed, folding his arms over his chest. "What were your uncle and grandmother doing?" He looked expectantly at Beau.

Beau's trust in her husband was evident as he continued. "Grandmother was telling Sandy to put out the food and dishes and make ready to eat. I don't believe she noticed you at all. Uncle had walked down to the water, to watch some swans, I think."

"So none of you had yet eaten or had anything to drink?" Guy asked.

Beau shook his head.

"Where were you?" Lily asked.

"Sitting near you, fixing the sail on my boat." His eyes grew wide. "You made a cry and began to thrash about, and everyone came running, the ones who were not already close by. You leaped to your feet, making that very strange noise in your throat." He cast a nervous look at Guy. "Much as his lordship did yesterday. Then you ran to the pond, swinging your arms about as if being chased, though you weren't. Uncle grabbed you quick to save you splashing into it."

Lily was too appalled to speak. She looked to Guy for help, for some explanation.

His attention seemed fixed on Beau. "Then what happened?" he asked.

Beau swallowed hard, his gaze on her, and bravely went on. "You struggled with him, but he lifted you anyway and carried you to the buggy. Grandmother and I dashed after you both. You had fallen asleep when I climbed in. Then we all came home. I was sent here, to my room, and ordered to stay. They put you to bed and locked the dressing room door between us so I would not go in and bother you."

Guy unfolded his arms, smiled gently and laid a hand on Beau's shoulder. "But I'd wager no lock could keep you out of here, eh?"

Beau beamed up at him. "No, sir. I have Father's key. The moment I heard them leave, I went in and stayed until Mama woke up." His little chin jutted out. "I wasn't scared then."

"Got over it when it counted," Guy said with an appreciative nod. "Very enterprising of you with that key, and quite the thing to do, looking after your mother. It's exactly what I would have done in your place." He was obviously highly pleased with Beau's disobedience.

Lily was simply glad they were in league to protect her at all cost. If that meant Beau disobeying his grandmother, so be it.

Guy stood and scooped up the clothes Beau had discarded the night before. "Allow me to be valet this morning, Bradshaw. It's gone on nine o'clock and you're still in your nightshirt." He held Beau's breeches so he could step into them. In a trice, her son was dressed and busy pulling on his boots.

Guy placed his hands on his hips and leaned forward slightly. "Now what say we have some breakfast? I daresay your mother would like to complete her toilette without her gentlemen observing. Do you suppose we could cozzen a bit of porridge from Cook?"

"Porridge?" Beau made a face and a rude noise, his preoccupation with her condition obviously forgotten for the moment.

"Perhaps black pudding then?" Guy suggested, herding Beau toward the hall door. He winked at her over his shoulder.

Beau pretended to gag, then giggled as he and Guy went down to breakfast together.

Lily shook her head in wonder at how easily Guy had distracted Beau from his worries. She blessed him for that.

If only that would work for her, as well. But it seemed something was dreadfully wrong with her, after all, and her fright nearly equaled Beau's.

Lily could not recall drinking anything immediately before the seizure or whatever she had experienced that day. So how could she have been drugged? It made no sense.

Could she have been wrong about Clive's motive for taking her to Bethlem Hospital? Perhaps her actions at the picnic and then later at the soiree really had convinced him that she needed to be committed. Perhaps those bottles Brinks had for her really had contained medicine meant to calm her hysterics.

Were the insane ever aware that they were?

She must ask Guy. He would know if anyone did.

Guy's heart ached for Lily, for Beau and for himself. For too long, he had avoided involvement in anyone else's problems because it had been all he could do to manage his own. Even now he wondered whether he would have taken on this responsibility if he had been aware it would become more than a matter of mere physical protection.

The small hand holding his gave it a tug. He looked down into the lad's wide, trusting eyes.

"Thank you for coming here," Beau said.

Guy's doubt disappeared. He forced a smile. "Certainly, Bradshaw. Where else would I be?" Knocking about London, up to no good, doing whatever was necessary to gain a few groats and maintain the status quo, that was what. No way to live.

At least he could do some good here now that he had put his mind to it. And his heart into it, too, he thought wryly. The old pumper seemed quite full at the moment even if it did ache like a sore tooth.

After breakfast, when he had Beau settled with his lessons, Guy went down to the library to compose two letters. The time had come to call in favors.

He needed Smarky here right away, even if he hadn't completed his investigation in London. For a fair price, the man would stay and be more vigilant than anyone Guy could hire locally. And though it would doubtless take a fortnight to get Thomas Snively down from Edinburgh, Guy would explain the problem in brief and send for him, too.

If Snively could not leave his post at University to come himself, he would surely send someone with more expertise than old Dr. Ephriam.

Guy knew that his father was a lost cause, but Lily was not. He would not let her be. Perhaps if someone had intervened in the earl's treatment early on, he could have been saved.

At thirteen, Guy had been too young to know what to do, but a few years later he had employed an eminent London doctor. By that time, he had been assured, there was nothing to be done but to keep the patient comfortable, protect him from himself and dose him with laudanum to calm him after one of his spells.

Guy decided he needed to go further afield in this case and locate the best physician to be had to evaluate Lily's true condition and exhaust every possibility of finding a cure for it before she grew worse.

"Good morning again," Lily said as she swept into the room, lighting up the place like a sunbeam. Guy stood immediately and returned her greeting with a smile of frank admiration.

The butter-colored morning gown that molded her figure rustled as she took the chair that faced the desk and arranged her skirts. A small confection of white lace and ribbon adorned her carefully styled curls, disguising the fact that her hair was hardly longer than his finger.

He ached to touch the wayward ringlets that had escaped their confines, to trace a path over the bloom of her cheek with a finger and caress those rosy lips, kiss them as he had done the night before last. Strange how she could arouse him to fever pitch without even trying.

"I came to thank you for distracting Beau earlier and for looking after him."

Guy shrugged off her gratitude. "He balked at the assignment I gave him after breakfast, but began it nonetheless."

"I peeked in. He was so engrossed, he never noticed me. Latin phrases, perhaps?" she teased.

He laughed with her. "Letters. His penmanship leaves much to be desired." He glanced down at the desk and made a face. "A fault we share, so it seems."

"Ah, but practice makes perfect. Someone should have held a rod over you, though I cannot imagine that happening."

Guy could not for the life of him equate this vibrant young woman with the one who could supposedly lose her reason and wits on the instant. But then, he could still recall how strong and imposing his father had been at one time.

She glanced at the desk and the pages lying beneath his pen. "Am I interrupting your correspondence?"

"Not at all. I've finished," he assured her. He decided to be totally honest about what he was doing. That, in itself, was out of the ordinary for him, used as he was to concealing his intent to others. But Lily was his wife and this concerned her, more than anyone.

"I've written to a physician in Edinburgh in hopes he will travel here and give us his opinion."

"Someone you know well?" she asked, resignation in her eyes.

"Very well. We worked together for months when I was investigating a case in Scotland and became quite good friends."

"What sort of case?" she asked politely.

"Murders. Several done by the same man. Thomas Snively had treated him as a patient and helped me to locate him."

"A madman," Lily guessed, looking away as if she couldn't face him.

Guy sighed. "Yes. Thomas is very accomplished in matters of the mind. He has made that his specialty and even teaches it at University. He's widely read and well traveled, always with the goal of learning more in his field."

"Then we shall welcome him when he comes. Perhaps he can help," Lily said without enthusiasm.

Guy wanted so much to take her in his arms and tell her he would solve everything. Somehow, he felt she would not be all that receptive after being told what was commonly called a *mad doctor* was coming to treat her for lunacy.

"Also, I plan to have a friend of mine come down from London as added protection for Beau," he said, hoping to shift the subject. "His name is Smarky O'Rourke."

A frown creased the smoothness of her brow. "Smarky? What an unusual name."

"He's an unusual fellow." Guy sat down, folded both missives and addressed them.

"George will post those for you," Lily said, her voice and her expression subdued. "Shall I ring for him?"

"I'll ride to the posting station and do it myself," he declared as he sealed the letters. That would give him a chance go by the dowager cottage to see if Lily's in-laws were still there. He hoped to discover they had changed their minds after what had happened and gone on to London. If not, he meant to put the fear of God into the both of them if they were to stay on the estate.

An hour later, after having a word with the butler and footman to keep an eye out for trouble while he was gone, Guy cantered down the lane to the cottage, if one could call it such. It was a square, two-story stone structure, roughly one-third the size of Sylvana Hall, a charming place that some former baron had built with his sainted mother in mind. Saintly certainly didn't fit Bernadette, he thought with a grimace.

He dismounted and walked up the front steps. Before he could lift the knocker, a young man opened the door. When he saw Guy, he stepped back. "Sir?"

Guy smiled. "Viscount Duquesne to see the Bradshaws."

"I'm sorry. They…they are not here, my lord."

"Where are they?" Guy asked.

"Gone to Maidstone for the day, I believe."

"Ah. Then I'll not wait. Who are you, by the way?"

"They call me Evan, sir. Evan Reese."

"Do you work for the estate or are you privately employed by the Bradshaws?" The handsome fellow was nattily dressed and very well-spoken for a servant.

"Lady Bradshaw has hired me on as a man-of-all work, sir."

Ah. Guy wondered what sort of work she had in mind. The lad looked sturdy enough to handle just about anything. "Are you the only one about?"

Light eyes shifted to the right, avoiding Guy's. "Yes, sir."

"Well, Evan, tell them I came 'round if you will." Guy wanted them to know he was keeping a close watch.

He walked back to his mount and turned to look at the house. A curtain at a window of the top floor stirred. Evan Reese had gone back inside, but had not had time to reach that window. So at least one of them was home and they were not receiving guests today. At least not this guest. Guy smiled and resisted the urge to wave at the one watching him.

He knew he had Clive scared, if not *running* scared. Perhaps his visit would make an end to the plot against Lily if there were one.

Of course there was one. Guy mentally shook off the doubt that persisted in rearing its head at the odd moment. Why else would she have been taken all the way to London for committal? To add validity to the act that might not have passed inspection locally, that's why. And why would the guard have been planning to give her medication to convince the authorities she was mad when they came to evaluate her? Because she was not really insane.

Guy damned himself for not having absolute trust in her faculties. She certainly had absolute trust in his, otherwise she'd not have put her life and that of her son into his hands. But he could not help thinking her just a little mad to do that. After all, his own faculties were certainly more at risk than hers.

He galloped on to the post station, hurriedly mailed his letters and returned to Sylvana Hall, still uneasy about leaving her for very long.

"Has he gone?" Bernadette asked Ephriam. "Did Evan convince him that I'm not here?"

"Yes, he's ridden off." He straightened the curtain. "Shouldn't you have spoken to Duquesne to see what he plans?"

"He has cast me out of my own home. That *was* his plan."

"Darling, please don't be distressed." Ephriam went to her then and knelt at her feet, as willing a slave as he had been for years.

Bernadette leaned her head against his. "But how can I help it, Augustus. This marriage of Lily's is disastrous. Now what am I to do? Clive is so upset. He has hardly spoken since."

"There, there. He's a grown man, sweetheart, not a child you need to protect." When she would have argued that Clive would always be her son and her reason for living, he shushed her. "I will speak with him if you like. Calm him and assure him that everything will come right eventually."

"Will it, Augie?" she allowed artful tears to course down her cheeks. "Will there be justice for all this?"

"Absolutely, my sweet. You'll see." He reached for the bell cord. "Let me summon that new footman of yours to fetch you some tea. Doctor's orders!"

"He's a man-of-all-work, dear. That's the proper term." Bernadette cradled his face in her hands and gazed soulfully into his eyes. The lines around them, the faded blue of the irises and the pinkish cast of the whites reminded her that he was no longer young. Thank goodness she had hired Evan.

Lily spent the remainder of the day arranging her wardrobe. Guy's things would be arriving soon and he would need a place to put them. She packed away the drab mourning attire she had grown so accustomed to wearing and replaced it with her brighter gowns and accessories.

Performing the mundane task soothed her, made her feel as though everything was quite normal. Perhaps it would prove to be. She had a new husband who seemed to like her very well. Her son accepted him. The daily routine of those at Sylvana Hall would scarcely change except for the better. Not having Clive and his mother about would lighten the load, and probably the disposition, of the servants. How relieved she was to have them out from underfoot.

She tried not to think of her own added duties as a wife, but that was difficult. Not that those duties were unpleasant, by any account, but she could hardly go about sighing and blushing or someone might suspect.

A small smile escaped even now as she allowed a moment's anticipation of the adventures that might lie ahead, after dark.

"So here's where you've been hiding!"

Lily jumped and dropped the frilled petticoat she was folding. "Good heavens, Guy! Announce yourself next time."

He laughed and sauntered into the bedroom, his hands on his hips. "Look at you, all housewifely. I would think you'd have a maid to sort your laundry, at the very least."

"We do. I was merely making room for your clothing and storing my widow's weeds."

"Ah, yes, you're only just back into colors." He plopped down on the bed and lifted the ruffled petticoat with its pale blue crocheted-lace edging. He fingered the handiwork. "You do this?"

"Goodness, no. I haven't the patience for any sort of needlework." And no mother to have taught her, she thought sadly. "But I do paint a bit, so I'm not totally unaccomplished. And I do play tolerably well."

He grinned that naughty grin that always stirred something in her midsection. "You certainly do."

Embarrassed by what might possibly be ribald teasing, she returned to her folding. "I'm sure I don't know what you mean. You've never heard me play."

He caressed the soft garment he held. "Let me guess. The violin?"

"Hardly." She held up a camisole. Realizing how intimate she was being with a man in the room, she quickly rolled it up and tucked it in a drawer.

He hummed appreciatively and rubbed the ruffles against his lips. "The oboe?"

Lily laughed. "You know very well it's the pianoforte. It is the only instrument in the house. And I would be willing to wager you've searched the place thoroughly."

He looked artificially wounded. "You believe I would be so bold as to pry?"

She inclined her head and looked at him. "It is what I would do if I were you."

With a sigh, he collapsed back on the bed, his arms spread wide, a fetching sight. "Lord bless us, I've a wife who understands me." He cut his gaze to meet hers. "We do rub on rather well so far, don't you think?"

Lily smiled at him, pleased at this small, precious slice of domesticity. Tempted to lie down beside him, yet knowing that wouldn't do in the middle of the afternoon, she turned away. "Yes, it seems we do, at that. Thank goodness."

He curled up off the bed and straightened his jacket. "So, I shall leave you to your chores and go and do mine." He closed the distance between them, grasped her face in both hands and kissed her soundly before she knew what was happening.

He released her just as quickly, before she could respond, and left her standing there with her mouth open.

And wanting.

Damn the man. She touched her lips with fingers that trembled. Did he never do the expected?

The rest of the afternoon, Guy looked for things to do so that he could avoid Lily. He had a purpose, of course. He had very nearly eaten her up earlier. And she would have been willing to let him, he was sure. Then she would have lain there as she had before and would have allowed him anything. For Guy, that was not enough. He could hardly bear this passivity that seemed to engulf her here in this place.

Maybe it was the ever-present memory of Bradshaw that caused her to be so. In London and on the way here, she had let loose her inhibitions. Wearing men's clothing, even though Guy had joked about it, might be what had prompted her to act differently then. If so, he was all for getting her a pair of breeches right away.

But Lily's softness and gentility had an appeal all its own. If only she would give her passion free rein, Guy knew she would be happier. And he certainly would. If it killed him, this waiting, he meant to show Lily eventually the absolute joy they could bring one another.

He believed the longer he teased her and put off their next coupling, the more ready she would be for it and the less likely to let her shyness intrude.

To tell the truth, he wanted her to give him everything that she was and also to accept him, faults and all. Maybe that was selfish.

Of course it was. Expecting her to change when he wasn't able to do so himself? Worse than selfish, it was unrealistic. But Guy knew he could never be the strait-laced gent she seemed to expect in bed.

He could never be another Jonathan Bradshaw, not for her or anyone else.

Perhaps she could not be what he wanted, either, but Guy knew he had glimpsed a glorious wild streak in Lily that was too natural to be feigned. It was there somewhere, and somehow he meant to bring it to the fore again.

If he had to change a little, maybe lean toward the gentler side of his own nature, maybe they would both benefit. It wouldn't hurt to try.

His father had advised him long ago to begin as he meant to go. Guy had taken that to heart. It was good advice and had served him well.

His beginning in bed with Lily did not do him credit.

Chapter Ten

At their informal supper, Guy launched his plan to draw Lily out of the prim role she had assumed. Firing double entendre comments that went over Beau's head and provoking her with suggestive looks proved difficult while, at the same time, attempting to play the noble husband and circumspect stepfather.

The lecherous looks weren't a pretense. She'd worn a deep red gown to dinner that set him afire. Though her breasts weren't overly large, she certainly knew how to show them to best advantage. Her waist appeared wasp-thin while her shoulders shone with a pearl-like luminescence. The hooped skirt she wore swayed enticingly. He had never cared much for the fashion, but tonight it was all he could do not to pant.

She was on to him, casting him the occasional come-hither glance from beneath her lashes as they ate the fancy turtle soup she had ordered Cook to prepare. The expense was a complete waste, since he could taste nothing but the memory of his lips on her the night before last.

She had swept her golden curls back and caught them at her crown with a simple crimson ribbon and small silk flower.

"Dressing for dinner certainly has its advantages," he commented, his voice a grumble of frustration. He'd have liked to eat her up with his soup spoon.

His own dinner clothes were outdated, some older things he had stored at Edgefield when he'd returned from school. At least he was dressed decently for the part of a country gentleman dining *en famille.*

Her dimpled smile distracted him from his thoughts. So did her voice. "More soup?"

He laughed wryly. "I think perhaps I'm ready for dessert."

"No dessert until you finish everything else," Beau announced with the last slurp of his soup. "It's Mother's rule."

Guy laughed and shook his head. "By all means, we must follow Mother's rules."

Lily continued to smile at him, one eyebrow cocked, ever the lady. And yet he enjoyed some success. Instead of going all cool and icy on him because of his teasing, she found some humor in it. He felt ridiculous.

When they had at last finished the strawberry trifle, Lily excused herself. "If you two will excuse me, I shall leave you to enjoy your after-dinner drink."

She was instilling proper protocol and procedures in her son, Guy realized. Tradition. More rules. The ladies left the gents to their cigars and brandy once the formal meal was finished. He wondered whether she thought it was necessary to work on his manners, as well. He toyed with the idea of offering Beau a cigar. That would teach her a thing or two.

One of the footmen arrived as if by magic to serve them.

Beau was having goat's milk, something Guy could never tolerate. He opted for the more traditional brandy.

When they were alone again, Beau spoke, sounding very grown up. "I wanted to speak with you, sir."

So this was not all to do with tradition. Guy sipped the liquor and nodded encouragement.

The small face frowned, laughably serious with its mustache of milk. "It is about school."

Guy shrugged. "We had that discussion. I promised not to send you away. Are you still worried that I will?"

Beau's brow furrowed even more. "Perhaps I should go. Mother is afraid she will frighten me again. I promised her I would be brave next time, but she worries. I don't like to worry her. Is school so very bad?"

Guy sighed. "No, it can be fun. I enjoyed it very much. This is your choice, of course, but as for me, I'd rather see you go at ten, or perhaps twelve."

Hope lit Beau's face like a lamp. "Truly? Why?"

There was no point in lying to the boy, Guy thought. He only wished someone had advised him before he had gone. "Often the younger boys have problems fitting into an established group of older mates."

Beau nodded thoughtfully and drank another swallow of the milk. "They get beaten?"

Guy smiled. "Sometimes." Almost *always,* he wanted to add. It was the nature of the little beasts to ride roughshod over the weaker ones. "Of course, at ten or twelve you will have grown considerably. And I'd be happy to lend you what knowledge I have of the sports they play so you'll have something to offer the team."

Beau finished his milk, set down the glass and rose to leave. "You're a brick of a fellow, sir." He grinned and licked his upper lip. When he passed Guy's chair, he thumped his fist lightly on Guy's shoulder. "Good night, Duquesne."

Guy toasted the boy with the remainder of his brandy. A smile and nod were the best he could manage. He felt so moved, speech failed him, a truly unusual circumstance.

Guy had the urge to share with Lily what had happened, but it would probably seem insignificant to anyone else in the retelling. She might even see it as interference this early on. So he was left with hugging to himself the knowledge that he was becoming a father, after all. It was something he had never realized he'd wanted so badly, or even wanted at all.

Lily tucked Beau into his bed, heard his prayers and kissed him good-night. He seemed calmer, as if a great weight had been lifted off his small shoulders. Sharing their troubles with Guy had that effect. She had no idea what she would have done if he had not accepted her proposal, if he were not here, taking charge of things.

She returned to her room and changed out of her evening clothes. Tonight she would not go down to join Guy in the library. He would come to her.

With that in mind, she took out a simple nightgown and wrapper of ivory silk that she had never worn before. The restructuring of her wardrobe had produced things she had forgotten she had.

The dressmaker in Maidstone had made several sets of revealing nightclothes when Lily had ordered her trousseau before her wedding with Jonathan. Lily had never felt the garments quite proper enough to wear even in the privacy of her bedroom and had packed them away. The scent of lavender in this one was still a bit overpowering. She shook out the folds and fanned it in the air before slipping it over her head.

The slide of the fabric against her skin made her feel daring, sensuous. For a moment she imagined Guy's hands slipping around her waist, over her hips, gathering the liquid feel of the gown between his long, strong fingers. A sigh escaped her.

Tonight would be different. Tonight she would not require a dare. Tonight she would be the woman who had boldly asked Guy to marry her and confessed that she had missed being a wife.

How had she ever done that? What had come over her to make her so blatantly aggressive?

She looked into her mirror and produced her sultriest smile. Then she grimaced at herself. He really would think she had lost her mind. With a huff of self-disgust, she tore at the tie of the wrapper and started to change again.

"Ah, what's this then?" Guy asked, his voice a low growl of appreciation.

"Guy!" He had been standing behind her to one side so that she had not seen him reflected. She jerked the robe together and tied it, laughing nervously. "You frightened me."

His lazy smile was knowing as he approached and handed her a snifter. "Thought you might like a bit of brandy." His lips pursed as his gaze traveled down her body and back again to meet hers. "How…intoxicating *you* are. I could have done without the liquor."

Again she laughed and skirted around him, holding the brandy close to her chest in an attempt to cover the low décolletage and the protrusion of her nipples beneath the soft silk. His very voice did that to her, excited her unbearably. And his eyes, dark and heavy-lashed, penetrated her very soul, not to mention her clothing.

With her back to him, she hurriedly sipped the brandy, gulped it really, and began to cough when it burned her throat.

"Easy there," he crooned, taking the glass from her and rubbing her briskly between her shoulder blades. "Why do I frighten you, Lily?"

She shook her head vehemently, appalled at her cowardice. "You don't!"

He was her husband, after all. They had already made love. It wasn't as though he would hurt her in any way. It was herself she feared, what she might become if she let herself respond fully. "I told you I'm not afraid of you."

His chuckle was wry. "Well, darling, you scare the hell out of me."

Surprised, her train of thought lost, she turned to face him. "I do?"

He nodded, one side of his mouth kicking up in a half smile. "Indeed. You are so different from any woman I have ever known." He trailed one finger up her arm to her shoulder and played with the edge of her wrapper. "So very different."

Lily closed her eyes and sighed. She could guess what he meant by that. He was well used to courtesans and others with vast knowledge of pleasurable pursuits. She was but a village girl at heart, a simple vicar's daughter with very limited experience in a man's bed. "I don't know what you want," she confessed, feeling breathless and deliciously undone.

He took her by her shoulders and kissed her forehead.

His lips were hot against her skin. "Yes, you do. I want all of you, Lily. Everything within you. Everything you are."

Even as he spoke, he kept pressing kisses to her face while his hands caressed her arms, her shoulders, her neck. She could hardly think. Her head swam and her knees felt weak as water.

"I surrender," she whispered.

Suddenly he backed away from her and when she opened her eyes to look up at him, he frowned. His huge hands cupped her shoulders, his grip harder. He gave her a gentle shake. "No."

"No?" she repeated, her brain refusing to function properly, still mired as it was in the wonder of his touch, the heat of his lips.

"No! I'm not some conquering force come to master you this way. Or any way at all! You *surrender?* This is not a war, damn it."

"But you have won," she argued softly. "What more can I do but give you what you would have?"

His shoulders slumped a little and he began to shake his head. "Ah, Lily." His sad gaze traveled over her body again, stoking the fire that was already raging.

Then he released her, turned and left the room. For a long time Lily stood there quivering, wondering what she had done wrong. He no longer wanted her. She had somehow failed.

Guy slept little in the guest room that night. Again, he had handled things badly. Subtlety was not his forte, that was for sure. He had been too direct with Lily. He had pushed too hard, demanded too much of her too soon. Why could he not get it right with her?

When morning came, he wished he could ride out

alone and work off some of the frustration and clear his mind. True, they had years in which to come to terms as man and wife, but he found his impatience to do so outstripped his good sense.

Damn it, he wanted her. He could have had her, of course, right then and there. He still could. All he had to do was to go back to her bedroom, kiss her senseless and undress her. But what would that say to her? That he had power over her? He did, obviously, but she also had it over him if she would only recognize it. He wanted Lily to desire him as much as he did her. That was the problem.

He wanted her to love him.

When he went down for breakfast, she was in the morning room finishing her meal alone. She didn't appear to have slept any better than he had. There were slight circles beneath her eyes, marring the flawlessness of her complexion.

She bade him good morning, her greeting tentative, as if she expected him to accuse her of something. He hated the vulnerable look in her eyes that he knew he had caused.

"I owe you an apology," he said, taking the chair across from her, deciding he might as well be direct about it. "This marriage business is new to me, Lily. I behaved badly last night. Will you forgive me?"

She gave him a tight little smile. "Of course."

Guy cleared his throat and started to elaborate. But Lily was already rising to leave. A lady would consider it highly improper to discuss things of this nature at the breakfast table. Even he ought to have realized that. This evening would be a much better time. It's what he had meant to do and should have done last night, discussed things between them instead of blundering immediately into a seduction. The sight of her in that silk confection while surrounded by the heady scent of lavender, had thrown him off course.

He stood immediately. "Lily, don't go. Not another word about that until tonight, I promise."

She managed a more sincere smile. "It's not that. I have things to do this morning. What are your plans for today?" A very proper question for a dutiful wife, he supposed.

"I need to ride into Maidstone to see the solicitors about the will."

"Will you take Beau with you? It is Mrs. Prine's off day."

"Yes, I promised him. You come, too," he suggested.

"I would, but I'm off to Edgefield for that tea the vicar's wife has planned. I must go alone after all, by the way."

An uneasy feeling crept up Guy's spine. "No, I'll drive you there, complete the business in town and collect you on the way home."

He thought she would protest, but she merely hesitated, then nodded, giving in gracefully. She still looked worried.

"About the other, Lily… We'll work things out," he told her, wishing he could do more to convince her of it. But if he did, nothing else would get done for a while. Besides, he wasn't certain she was ready yet.

"I hope so," she replied, almost in a whisper. "I sincerely do." The woeful way she shook her head told him she hadn't much hope at all.

There was a table between them. And much more than that. If he planned to extend the measure of comfort he wanted to provide as a husband, Guy knew he needed to clear the air.

If last night had left him upset, he could only imagine what she must be feeling. She might even believe that it was somehow her fault. How stupid he had been that first time to try pleasing her when what she really had needed was solace. And then leaving her so abruptly after she had offered herself up like a sacrifice. What had he been thinking? Not of her, but of himself.

"We should leave at two o'clock," she told him and hastened to leave again.

"Lily?" he called as she reached the open door. She stopped and turned, a question in her eyes. He cleared his throat. "About last night…"

"Please." She held up one hand, effectively halting him midsentence. She blushed bright pink. "You promised to wait until tonight…if you wouldn't mind?"

"Yes, tonight," he muttered, watching her scurry from the room.

He sighed and sat back down. The friendship they had established in their short but eventful time together had become a stilted, overly polite acquaintance and it was his doing.

Tonight would be different. If she was unwilling to discuss it in the bright light of day, at least she had not forbidden him to speak of it at all. They would work things out together and then he would make it up to her in the best way he knew how. If ever there was a pleasured wife on this planet, come morning it would be his Lily.

The afternoon brought a light rain, dampening everyone's spirits except for Beau's. Lily had to insist on his wearing a cap and redingote. He fidgeted frightfully in the seat between her and Guy, complaining constantly about having to take the closed carriage instead of the open buggy.

Normally she would have spoken sharply to him to curtail his bad behavior, but she suspected that his worry for her had instigated it.

Guy leaned one arm against the wall of the carriage and propped his head on his hand, observing Beau's wriggling. "You surely wouldn't have your mother soaked through to the skin when she arrives at the vicar's. Can you feature what those women would say of us, Bradshaw?" He scoffed. "They'd say we prized our sport over the welfare of a lady, that's what. I don't know about you, but I'd as soon not be the talk of the county in that respect."

Beau stilled. He looked up at her. "I never thought of that."

"Well, now you have," Lily said, smoothing the skirts of her blue gown and tugging her pelisse closer at the neck.

How did Guy know precisely what to say in order to insure Beau's compliance without seeming to chastise him? It must be an inborn gift that had been denied her.

Though she seldom raised her voice to her son, she often found it necessary to be quite firm. He was headstrong and stubborn, a failing inherited from her, she knew.

Guy grinned at her over Beau's head. "Imagine me at seven," he said.

Lily suppressed a laugh. He must have been a terror. Much of the boy survived in Guy.

When they reached the vicar's house, Guy alighted first and helped her down while the driver held an umbrella over her to keep her free of the mist. "I believe we are early," he commented, noting as she did that there was only one conveyance parked near the old stone cottage. "Shall we return for you at five?"

"Perfect," she said to Guy. She startled a little when he leaned to brush her forehead with his lips.

To cover her surprise at such an intimate gesture in public, she quickly moved away from him and touched Beau's hand when he extended his arm out the window to her. "Be a gentleman," she warned her son with a pointed look. He smiled back and promised he would.

Lily trusted Guy implicitly where Beau was concerned. The two got on famously and she thanked God for that. She wished she knew how to reclaim that camaraderie between Guy and herself. He wanted that, as well, so she was certain they would somehow work things out eventually.

For now, all she had to worry about this afternoon was charming the ladies of Edgefield who were going to so much trouble to welcome her as wife to the future earl.

The carriage rattled down the lane as she hurried to the entry of the cottage where the vicar's wife awaited her in the open doorway. Handing off her umbrella and pelisse as she greeted the woman, Lily noted that two other guests were already seated in the parlor. To her dismay, she saw that one of them was her former mother-in-law.

Lily knew she should have foreseen that the woman would be invited. She was, after all, the only female relative Lily had left, even if they were only related by marriage. The vicar's wife would have no way of knowing they were not congenial.

She entered the parlor and dropped a curtsy. "Mother

Bradshaw," she said by way of greeting, determined to be pleasant and not spoil the event for everyone.

"Lillian," the dowager baroness replied with a tight expression. "You are too early. One would think such a *grand* lady would effect a grand entrance after everyone was here."

The vicar's wife shot Lily a concerned look, obviously realizing her mistake in including the former baroness. "The others will arrive soon. Won't you have a chair, my lady? Perhaps a dish of coffee to warm you? There's such a chill in the air today."

There certainly was, especially in this room. "Of course," Lily replied, heading across the parlor to sit beside the one unfamiliar guest. The dark-haired woman had immediately risen when Lily entered and now curtsied to her.

"Lady Lillian, this is our niece, Miss Sara Ryan. She is visiting from London and is thinking of residing here permanently," said the vicar's wife.

"Miss Ryan, so nice to meet you." They were of the same age, Lily thought. It would be nice to make a new friend.

"And you," Miss Ryan replied. "I know Lord Duquesne quite well, as it happens. We are old friends." The woman's expression was that of a cat with feathers 'round its mouth.

"Ah, I see," Lily said, recognizing a challenge in the woman's implication.

A maid brought in a tray with two cups of coffee and proceeded to serve Bernadette first. Then she crossed to where Lily sat with Miss Ryan.

Lily accepted the remaining cup and busied herself stirring in several lumps of sugar. As she drank it, she wondered just how well Miss Ryan *did* know Guy. "You will surely wish to renew your acquaintance when he comes to collect me," she told the woman.

"It will be delightful to see him again," Miss Ryan replied, her smile widening to display a row of even white teeth.

Lily drank the hot liquid, wishing Miss Ryan would go away. She noted that Bernadette Bradshaw had left the parlor in the meantime. It was too much to hope she had gone home. Thus far, this afternoon was an unmitigated disaster.

"I hear Lord Duquesne's father is still indisposed," Miss Ryan said. "That must have put a damper on your wedding day. Not much of a celebration, I'll wager."

"We had a quiet civil ceremony with several friends in attendance. That was what we both desired," Lily replied.

The vicar's wife dithered, interrupting the uncomfortable discourse with a clearing of the throat and wringing of hands. Lily wished she could alleviate the woman's obvious distress. Two social faux pas on the same occasion must be the devil to face.

"You have done absolute wonders with this room, Mrs. Oliver," Lily said in a determined effort to change the topic. "It appears much warmer than when Father and I resided here. I see that you crochet." Lily glanced about at the numerous antimacassars, furniture throws and an enormous fringed piece draped over the top of the upright piano.

The entire parlor seemed webbed in white thread. Lily felt much like the fly caught up in it while spiders loomed.

"Oh, yes, and thank you, my lady. Would you care to revisit the other rooms?"

Lily thought not. "Oh, but surely other guests will be arriving soon and you—" She set down her cup as she protested. Bernadette Bradshaw had come back in, wandering around the room now, examining the pictures on the wall, pointedly ignoring Lily.

"Come, come, I will show you the other rooms, Lady Lillian," offered Sara Ryan. Before Lily could object further, the woman took her arm, urged her to get up and guided her toward the hall.

"Really, I prefer to remain in the parlor," Lily stated, barely resisting the urge to snatch her arm away.

"Seeing how you used to live before you became a baroness should remind you how fortunate you are. And now you're the viscountess," she purred. "It almost makes the institution of marriage seem acceptable, doesn't it. Especially when one marries up." She actually laughed.

"Sara, really!" the vicar's wife exclaimed in horror.

A wicked snort from the opposite side of the room announced that Lily's former mother-in-law had heard and found the entire episode vastly amusing.

Lily withdrew her arm from the grip of her new acquaintance. "I assure you marriage has much to recommend it other than material acquisitions, Miss Ryan."

The woman laughed out loud at that, her dark eyes twinkling with mischief. "I daresay it does, at least with regard to Duquesne." She chuckled, a low throaty sound. "And do call me Sara if you like."

Lily bristled. "I shouldn't like that at all."

"Oh, come now. We have gotten off on the wrong foot," Miss Ryan said with a frown. "I do apologize for my presumption. Come, let me show you my aunt's handiwork. The dining room is a wonder."

Lily went for no other reason than to avoid seeing the dowager's smug expression.

The moment they were out of earshot, Sara Ryan turned to her. "Look, I should explain. I owe my life to your husband and I think the world of him. As a *friend*," she added with feeling. "If I gave you the wrong impression, I am truly sorry for it."

Lily regarded her sincere expression. "Duquesne saved you? How so?"

A mixture of emotions animated Miss Ryan's dark, classic features. "I eloped with a young man who promptly discarded me without the promised wedding. When I found myself alone in London, I remembered that Lord Duquesne kept a house there. It was either go to him and beg his assistance, or take to the streets. I knew no one else."

"And he agreed, of course." Lily could see Guy taking Sara Ryan under his protection. What man would not? She was very beautiful.

Then Lily realized that she and Sara had much in common with regard to Guy. She had done virtually the same thing, applying to him for help when stranded in the city. He had not taken advantage of her, had he? She decided to give her husband and Sara the benefit of the doubt. "Thank you for explaining."

"I knew you would understand. I fear my insult to the state of matrimony offended you, but the feeling of betrayal is still quite fresh." She dimpled fetchingly. "I am something of a cynic. And far too outspoken. Say you forgive me."

Lily nodded, but refrained from any other comment.

Instead she changed the topic to their surroundings. "So, have you learned to crochet? All of this looks to be the work of more than two hands."

As the tour of the vicarage progressed, Lily became lost in recollections of a girlhood spent in the place. Indeed, it had changed. Without her mother to guide her hand, Lily had never been able to impart the proper hominess to it. Her father should have remarried.

When they returned to the parlor, she was surprised to see it nearly filled with ladies. Caught up in greeting faces she scarcely remembered and trying to match them with names, Lily felt relieved when tea was served. Her mouth felt incredibly dry and her head had begun to ache. This fete had become a chore she heartily wished to be over.

"These are delicious," Sara said, handing her a porcelain plate with several tiny cakes. "My aunt outdid herself."

Lily nodded her thanks and concentrated on finishing the elaborate little sweets and washing them down with the worst tea ever brewed. The vicar's wife refilled the cup herself. Even as Lily complimented her hostess, she made a note to send over a tin of her best blend as a thank-you. Perhaps some coffee, as well. What she had drunk earlier tasted musty.

The chatter became unnerving, its volume increasing by the minute until Lily thought her head would explode. Even as the number of guests dwindled, the noise did not. Louder and louder it grew until she could hardly bear it.

Lily paced the parlor, desperate to find a quieter spot. It seemed imperative that she do so.

Pictures on the wall swayed from the wires suspending them from the moldings. Furniture appeared where she thought there was empty space. Her eyes would not focus. She wanted to scream for quiet, for stillness, for peace!

Where was Guy? Why wasn't he here? He should be here to take her home.

Suddenly she stumbled against a sofa, barely catching herself as she tumbled to the floor. She was on her knees.

Voices battered her from all sides, bodies closing in around her. Hands, rustling skirts, attacking. Bats swirled, plucking at her hair, her upraised hands. Squeaking and screeching at her. She beat them away, frantic for a breath of air, for safety.

"Thank God you are here!" Lily heard the dowager's exclamation above the horrible sounds and prayed Guy had come to save her.

Then a high keening in her own throat drowned out the frightening noise. She closed her eyes and buried her face in her hands. It was the last thing she knew.

Chapter Eleven

"Where is my wife?" Guy demanded as he stood at the door. The vicar and his wife kept tripping over each other's words, trying to explain. A crowd was gathered outside, everyone abuzz and frowning, none willing to relate what the trouble was. Beau clung to his leg like a spider monkey, his eyes wide and seeking. Guy put a hand on Beau's shoulder to calm him. Lily was obviously not here.

"Lord Duquesne," said a familiar voice, much calmer than the rest. He recognized the person edging her way between the couple in the doorway.

"Sara! Tell me what has happened."

She grasped his elbow and pulled him away from the others. They let her, obviously relieved someone else had taken charge of the telling. "Your wife…became…well, distraught, I suppose you would say. One moment she was fine, but the next she grew terribly disoriented and incoherent. Her brother-in-law arrived just then to collect his mother and was immediately appointed to take her home."

"Clive?" Guy fairly spat the word as he turned to go. Beau clung to his hand, utterly pale and silent. Guy scooped him up in his arms and started out.

"Wait!" Sara said, a warning note in her voice. "I overheard their conversation as they were departing. There was a mention of Plympton." Her dark eyes were knowing. "Let me know if there's any way I can help, will you?"

He gave her a curt nod and hurried to the carriage. If they had taken Lily to that asylum, heads would roll.

All the way back to Sylvana Hall, he struggled for calm, for the patience required to deal with a weeping child who feared the worst. He held the boy close and made promises that probably could not be kept, gave assurances that were likely untrue. He would lie to the Almighty Himself to get Beau through this ordeal. How well Guy remembered this feeling of desolation.

But he knew from experience that terror of the unknown could be far worse than facing up to a real threat, however bad it might be. He should be straight with the boy, enlist his help, give him something positive to do. "We have to be brave for her, Beau. Crying won't help either of us and it won't help your mother," Guy told him.

Beau made a valiant attempt to control himself. The sobs subsided to frequent shudders and sniffs. Guy gave him his handkerchief.

"You must help me plan, lad. I've sent for a special doctor all the way from Edinburgh, but it will be a while before he gets here. In the meantime, we must decide how to handle this."

"What is…dis…traught, sir?" Beau asked, his words wobbly.

"It means upset. Something upset her."

"Mama's…mad…again. Isn't she?"

Guy met the tearful, wide-eyed gaze and released a sigh. What could he say? The child was canny enough to recognize that Guy had been lying and placating him earlier. That hadn't worked. The truth would be best. "I don't know, Beau. If she is, we'll take care of her together. You saw before how quickly she improved after she had that spell at the picnic? I expect this will be no different. By tomorrow, she will seem well again, I don't doubt it."

The blue eyes shone with hope. "Maybe she'll stay well this time?"

"That's the hope, son. But you and I will do everything we can to shield her from anything else upsetting, shall we? Together we'll protect her."

"With our lives," Beau added with a jerky nod. After a moment of quiet he added, "It's people."

"What?" Guy asked, not following the boy's train of thought.

"People upset her, I think. A great lot of 'em all together."

Guy's mouth almost dropped open. "By Zeus, you're on to something there! The musicale, the picnic, this fete today…yes, that could well be a contributing factor." He patted Beau's shoulder. "Brilliant of you, mate."

He was relieved to see the boy light up again. A small fist landed in an open palm. "We'll keep her at home and stand guard. No company," Beau declared with a fierce little frown.

"Excellent plan." Guy glanced out the window of the carriage. "Almost there. Blow your nose and straighten up. If she's not sleeping, she shouldn't see us all disheveled."

Guy knew the moment they rounded the house that Lily was not there. The dowager and Clive would never have left her alone with the servants, and their carriage was not there. With that mention of Plympton Sara Ryan had told him about, he had figured they might have taken her on to the asylum. Sylvana had been on the way there, however, and he had hoped against hope.

"Beau, I have to ask you something that will be very difficult for you, but I need you to do it."

The trusting face peered up at him, waiting for the assignment.

"If your mother is not here, you must stay behind while I go to fetch her. Will you do that for me?"

The trembling little lips formed a circle. "No."

"Please, Beau. If force is called for, I will use it, but I cannot be worrying about your welfare at the same time. Besides, your mother would tear a strip off my hide if I put you in danger."

"Will there be danger?" the boy whispered. "Mama won't be hurt, will she? Where is she if she's not here?"

"A place reserved for…the sick." Guy rushed to add, "I'll bring her away from there as quickly as possible, I promise. Home again, safe and unharmed."

He watched Beau consider, then agree with a nod.

"Good man. Watch over things while I'm gone. You might ask Cook to make some special things, whatever your mama likes best to eat."

"And I'll make her a small picture to mark her place when she reads," Beau said. "She's always trying to make me draw."

Beau looked up at him as the carriage halted with a jerk, and an unspoken message passed between them.

They both loved Lily. It was understood. Until that

moment, Guy had not admitted to himself how much he cared.

A few moments later, after questioning the footman who came out to help with the horses, Guy's worst fears were realized. Lily had not been returned to Sylvana Hall. The Bradshaws had taken her to the madhouse.

He wanted to saddle up and ride like the wind, get there before them and prevent Lily spending so much as a moment in that place, but the carriage would be needed to bring her home. There was nothing for it but to wait for a fresh team.

When he arrived, the Bradshaws had left Plympton. Guy announced who he was and demanded to go to Lily immediately. To his surprise, the proprietor offered no objection.

Mr. Colridge seemed a pleasant enough man of around fifty, heavyset with a kindly smile. "Of course, my lord. This way, please." He led Guy up the stairs of the old mansion to the second floor. "She has one of the best rooms," he assured Guy, "luckily vacated by Lord Blankenship not three days ago. The poor fellow succumbed to a heart problem."

Lily was ensconced in a private chamber outfitted with the barest of necessities, a bed, a heavy chair, a small wardrobe that bore a padlock. Though large, the dreary room was little more than a cell with bars at the windows and heavy locks on the door. He approached the bed where she lay sleeping.

How fragile she looked. Someone had divested her of the beautiful gown she'd worn to the vicar's and replaced it with a simple, unadorned shift of rough gray linen. Her hair, already shorn, lay in awkward curls as if her bonnet had been roughly yanked off. Guy smoothed it with a gentle touch so as not to wake her.

Though he needed to get her out of here, it wouldn't hurt for her to sleep a little while. Perhaps she would wake up well enough to walk out of here on her own, establishing to this Mr. Colridge that she was not afflicted as he must think.

"We should speak in private," the man suggested softly.

Guy left Lily reluctantly, promising himself he would return and be there when she woke up. It wouldn't do for her to awaken alone and frightened. God, how he hated to see her this vulnerable. She would hate it, too, if she knew.

When they reached the corridor outside, he stopped instead of going back down the stairs. "Talk to me here if you must. I don't like to leave her."

"I know, sir. It's often that way, but there's little you can do for her. The doctor will be 'round first thing in the morning to evaluate her."

"Which doctor?"

"Ephriam. He comes every other day."

"How was she when she arrived?" Guy asked.

"Delusional. She believed bats were after her. We gave her something to calm her and she went off to sleep without further incident."

"Opiates?" Guy demanded.

Colridge nodded. "That is the remedy prescribed when a patient is overset to that extent."

Guy knew that well enough. "I'll be taking her home as soon as she wakes," Guy informed him. "She is my wife. So long as she is not a danger to others or charged with a crime, you cannot keep her here without my authorization."

"True, nor would we wish to," Colridge admitted. "However, you might want to consider having her stay at least until Dr. Ephriam has seen her."

"She goes home," Guy insisted.

"As you wish, my lord." He gestured toward Lily's room. "Please feel free to remain with her until she wakes."

Guy glanced up and down the corridor, at the walls and the worn, faded carpet. He recalled the downstairs with its sparse furnishings, all of the horrid gray paint and depressing atmosphere that pervaded every inch of the place that he'd seen thus far. Though the house had once been beautiful, it had become as institutionalized as the patients confined within it. "I've changed my mind," he told Colridge. "I'm taking her now."

Colridge sighed and started down the stairs. "I'll send an attendant to change her and we'll bring a litter."

"No, don't bother," Guy said, reentering the room where Lily lay. He wrapped her carefully in the thick warm blanket someone had left folded at the foot of her bed and lifted her in his arms.

She stirred, mumbled something he could not understand, then snuggled against him and went limp. He prayed she stayed asleep until they reached Sylvana Hall and would never remember being here.

Moments later he was seated in the carriage with Lily resting on his lap. "We will be all right, Lily. You'll be fine," he whispered as he nuzzled the curls that teased his chin. They were wet, he realized, wondering how that had come to pass. It had not rained since early afternoon.

* * *

Lily woke with a seriously debilitating headache. She could scarcely open her eyes. Bright light poured through the windows, telling her it was still day. Somehow, she couldn't figure how she had gotten to bed.

"Good morning," Guy said from across the room. She squinted at his form, limned by the sunlight. "How are you feeling?"

"Dreadful," she admitted as her stomach lurched. He must have read her face since he rushed forward with a basin just in time. She fell back on the pillows when she had finished, her eyes shut tight against the horrible embarrassment.

"It's the laudanum," he said with a resigned sigh. "To be expected."

"You gave me laudanum?" she asked, her voice sounding weak to her own ears.

"Not I," he declared.

She should ask who, but she was too exhausted.

"Beau's beside himself. Can you tolerate a brief visit?" he asked softly.

Lily forced a smile and brief nod. Had she been ill? Of course she had. She still was, she realized. Some sort of ague that had taken her unawares.

Beau tiptoed in when Guy opened the door. He approached and his small fingers pinched at the bedcovers. "Are you better now, Mama?" he whispered.

"All better," she assured him, reaching out to touch his face. "My head hurts a bit, but I expect that will go away very soon."

"You aren't mad anymore?" he asked, desperation clouding his words.

Lily swallowed hard, bile threatening again. "No,

dear. Not to worry." She motioned with one hand for Guy, who quickly scooped Beau up and hauled him out of the room. She heard them talking as the door closed. Within seconds, Guy was back.

"I sent him off with Nurse. He only wanted to see for himself that you were recovered."

But she was not and she knew it. "The last thing I recall is the noisy gaggle at the vicar's house," she told him. "What…what did I do?"

His hesitation lasted too long.

"I had another spell, didn't I?" she guessed.

He sat on the edge of her bed and took her hands in his. "Yes, but you're fine now. Awake and fine."

"Tell me," she insisted.

"Later," he promised. "I'll go down and arrange for tea. You need to eat something."

Tea. The very last thing in the world she wanted. She closed her eyes, hoping to retreat into sleep again.

"Am I insane?" she whispered, feeling tears escape when she tried so hard to contain them.

"No, you're not insane," Guy argued vehemently. "I know insanity when I see it, and you're not insane, Lily, I swear."

She blessed him for the lie, but it was no use.

A soft knock on the door interrupted what he was about to say next. With a huff of impatience, he released her, got up from the bed and went to see who it was.

"Mr. Bradshaw waits in the library, sir," Lochland said.

Guy cursed. Lily could not imagine what would possess Clive to visit Guy.

He returned to her. "Rest, Lily. I'll send up something light for you to eat and I'll be back to join you in a moment."

Lily noted the way his jaw clenched and his strong hands had contracted into white-knuckled fists. Anger rolled off him in waves, but she knew it was not directed at her. She somehow sensed it was on her behalf and to do with her brother-in-law, but Guy left before she could question him.

There wasn't much a bedridden madwoman could do about it anyway, she thought with a scoff. Suddenly determined to exert what control she could over herself, Lily sat up. A slight dizziness and nausea lingered, but she refused to languish here in bed. Her mind had cleared enough that she could tend to herself. Beau must be frantic about her after seeing her this way.

She plucked at the unfamiliar garment scratching her skin and wondered where it had come from and why she was wearing such a thing.

Guy strode toward the library with murder on his mind. He could kill Clive Bradshaw with his bare hands. He flexed them in anticipation. That would surely seal the lid on his jar, however. He'd be locked away and unable to protect Lily and Beau. What would happen to his father? All three would be at risk without him. He took a deep breath before entering the room and reminded himself of the priorities.

"Bradshaw," he said with something approaching calm. "What are you doing here?"

"I came to explain." Clive made a supplicating gesture. "Believe me, I hated having to take Lily to Plympton. I simply didn't know what else to do with her."

"I guess you used up all your favors at Bedlam, eh?" Guy barked.

Clive appeared confused. "That horrid place? Never! Besides, London was too far away and she was in dire need of immediate treatment. I figured Plympton was close by and would be convenient for you to visit her."

"Visit her?" Guy thundered. "Surely to God you didn't believe I would leave her there!" He itched to snap Clive's neck.

"I suppose not since you never committed your father. I merely came to assure you that I only had Lily's best interests at heart."

"So you had her locked in a lunatic asylum?" He approached Clive, purposely threatening.

He backed away, glancing at the door as if to make a run for it. "I—I took her there for help, Duquesne! She was raving mad, I tell you. So much so she had to be restrained." He cuffed his own wrist with shaking fingers and rubbed it. "I hated being responsible for her and no one knew where you had gone. Mother was beside herself in the carriage. Nearly hysterical!"

"But I notice you didn't lock *her* away, more's the pity."

"Please, be reasonable, Duquesne. Lily is truly ill. Surely you can see she needs constant care."

"Which I will provide. Now get out," Guy growled. "I never want to see you here again or I will use that knife I threatened you with, regardless of the consequences."

A wary Clive skirted around him to the door and quickly disappeared. In London, Guy would never have made a threat and not carried it out. He was known for keeping his word to the letter. These were extenuating circumstances, however, and he doubted Bradshaw would spread the news that he had escaped Guy's wrath unharmed.

There was something about Clive's fearfulness and apologetic attitude that gave Guy pause. Why would he risk life and limb doing what he'd done and then come here to face a man who had threatened to kill him? It made no sense. Unless... "Beau!" Guy shouted, and dashed out to find the boy. If Clive had dared take *him,* Guy would do worse than murder.

He almost collapsed with relief when he saw Beau clattering down the stairs.

"Thank God. I thought—" Unable and unwilling to finish the sentence, he joined Beau on the bottom tread where they sat together, out of breath.

"Mama's better," Beau said finally. "I was coming to tell you. She's dressed and taking tea in her room."

"Thank God," Guy said, blowing out a breath of relief. "What say you and I have a spot of..." He halted, realizing belatedly that Beau was too young to have spirits. At least by standards outside the stews. "Milk," he finished. "Milk and perhaps some of those dandy biscuits Cook keeps tucked away for emergencies?"

"Grand idea," Beau said with a smile. "We shall celebrate Mama getting well again."

"Just so," Guy agreed, getting up and offering Beau a hand.

He had never felt less like celebrating, but he must keep up a good front for Beau's sake. And Lily's, too. There seemed nothing else he could do until the physician arrived from Edinburgh.

Even then, there was no guarantee anything could be done to prevent further episodes. His heart ached for

Lily, for Beau and for himself. And he had never prayed fervently or constantly in his life until today.

The remnants of religion in his soul surprised Guy a little. They had lain dormant for a very long time. Lily's father must have had a stronger impact on him in church than he had thought.

"Did you see her? How is she?" Bernadette asked Clive.

He tossed his gloves on the table by the door. "I only spoke with Duquesne. He's so outraged, I was lucky to escape with my face intact."

"He wouldn't dare touch you," Bernadette assured him. She tapped her finger to her lips thoughtfully. "Do you suppose that anger of his could be due to worry? He can hardly help being upset after discovering his wife truly is mad." She smiled. "I was quite beside myself when I first saw her in a fit. Weren't you?" She fanned herself with her hand. "I'm still a bit faint."

Clive snorted inelegantly and smoothed his hair back from his forehead. "Do try to bear up, Mother. Perhaps you should send for the doctor."

Bernadette airily waved away the suggestion and reached for the bell cord. "No need to trouble Augustus today. I'll simply ring for Evan to bring me a sherry."

"Is that my cue to ride out again?"

Bernadette gave him a coy shrug. "You do whatever you like, darling. All I want is for you to be happy."

Chapter Twelve

Guy paced impatiently while Dr. Ephriam made his assessment of Lily's condition. She had insisted on greeting the doctor in the parlor and then asked Guy to await them in the library.

Dressed in a pale blue morning gown, her sunny curls modestly confined in a delicate little halo of lace and ribbon, she had appeared in perfect accord with her role as noble wife and mother.

He remembered her in scruffy, borrowed men's attire and smiled to himself. Her entire personality seemed to change when she had donned skirts. Both Lilys were perfectly fascinating. Whether swaggering about, daring him to marry her or sitting quietly as the most circumspect lady, there was an indefinable quality within Lily that intrigued him. More than one quality, come to think of it, not the least of which was her inner strength.

Today, however, that strength was what mattered most. If she experienced any trepidation at having her sanity closely questioned, she wisely concealed it. Guy felt tremendous pride in her composure under duress.

She showed no outward signs of unease when the doctor arrived, though shadows of exhaustion still lay like small bruises beneath her eyes.

He had been beside her the entire night in the event she woke and needed him. She had slept like the dead, causing him to lay a palm on her chest several times to reassure himself that she still breathed. He'd felt tremendously relieved when she had finally opened her eyes and spoken to him this morning.

He should have discussed with her then what she might expect when Ephriam arrived. Guy wished he had helped her to prepare for it. Now here he was, wringing his hands, seriously considering interrupting.

Just then Ephriam entered the library and carefully closed the door behind him. "I have finished my evaluation," he declared.

"Then you see that my wife has quite recovered," Guy said.

"She appears lucid," Ephriam agreed with a sniff. A short, rotund, balding man of near sixty, nattily dressed, the doctor wore his usual tight-lipped expression of self-importance.

How did one "appear lucid"? Guy wondered. They were either lucid or they were not, and Lily certainly *was*.

Though they had been acquainted almost all Guy's life, he had never really liked Ephriam. Their association was merely one of expedience. Ephriam was the only doctor in the county willing to visit the earl regularly at home. That might bear rethinking.

"Where is Lily?" Guy asked.

"Gone to her room," the doctor assured him. "I gave her something to keep her calm and prescribed plenty of bed rest." He shook his head and sighed. "My guess is that she's not had much of that of late."

The statement gave Guy pause. He remained silent.

Ephriam cleared his throat and avoided Guy's gaze. "It would be wise if you did not trouble her overmuch with marital relations in the future."

Guy stifled the urge to order the pipsqueak out of the house. The reason for Lily's lack of rest had nothing to do with lovemaking. Except for the once, and that had not lasted long enough to tire anyone.

However, something like guilt nibbled at Guy and prevented his lashing out. "So you believe this would exacerbate her condition?"

Ephriam nodded. "I fear so. She's already in a highly excitable state."

Small wonder after enduring an abduction, worrying about her own and Beau's safety and committing to a marriage of desperation. But she had not let that show this morning, had she? No, she had been perfectly calm and in control when he had left her with the doctor.

"You see," Ephriam continued, "conjugal relations most likely bring to mind her...inability to give you an heir." One bushy black eyebrow rose as if to ask whether Guy knew about that. "That deficiency alone could cause hysterical behavior in a woman."

"Deficiency? I would hardly call it that," Guy scoffed. "Lily need not give me an heir. She is fully aware that I already have one."

Ephriam appeared surprised. "Who?"

"Her son."

"But...the lad cannot inherit your title as viscount or the earldom after your father passes it on to you," the doctor reminded him.

Guy shrugged. "The titles will abate at my death, that's true. But the Edgefield estate is not entailed and will double his property. Beau is already a baron in his own right, as you well know."

Silence reigned for a moment, then Ephriam sighed. "Well, do keep in mind your wife's welfare if you will."

"Always. Thank you for coming," he said by way of dismissal.

They were both still standing, so the doctor turned to go. He stopped after he had opened the door. "You have not asked my projections on the eventual state of Lady Lillian's mind and whether she should be confined."

"No, I have not." And Guy did not intend to ask. He would wait for someone with more expertise and more tricks in the bag than a quart of laudanum. "This concludes our discussion, Doctor. Good day."

Ephriam frowned, then left without another word.

Guy immediately went up to Lily, anxious to reassure her that he would make no further demands on her if it troubled her. Perhaps she had been afraid to broach this matter with him and had asked the doctor to intercede for her. She had rather wistfully mentioned her wish to have another child immediately after they had made love.

When he arrived at her room, he found her curled in a chair, engrossed in a book. She looked up as he entered and smiled. "So, what did the esteemed doctor have to say behind my back? Am I to have bars on the window and no knives at table?"

Guy crossed the room and sat on the side of the bed. "You sound chipper. But how are you feeling, really?"

"Much better," she declared, setting the book aside.

"Though I am convinced our doctor is grasping at straws. He believes me weighed down by responsibilities to the extent that it has caused hysterics. Women are so *weak,* you know."

Guy smiled and shook his head. "Women are the stronger gender by far. Any man who refutes that truth is a fool. Anyone who could overpower a guard, escape Bedlam and brave London streets in the middle of the night the way you did is no weakling. You are very strong, Lily. Strong, clever and decisive."

Lily pursed her lips, her fingers tented beneath her chin. "And very probably mad. Until the fete at the vicar's, I believed Clive had given me something in my food to make me behave as I did at the soiree and at the picnic. Something had to be at fault other than a loose connection here." She tapped her temple with her finger. "However, Clive was not present at the vicar's cottage."

"His mother was," Guy reminded her.

Lily inclined her head and blew out a gusty sigh. "Yes, I know, but I never saw her leave her chair before I…"

"Someone else could have tainted your food. You did eat or drink something, didn't you?"

She stood to pace, cradling herself with her own arms as if she needed warming. Her frown told him she was replaying the scene. Then she answered, nodding. "Yes, but so did everyone else. It was not the best fare I've ever had, but they had the same fare that I did and none of *them* collapsed in a fit." She turned and met his gaze with one of intensity. "Did they?"

"None that I know about," Guy admitted, but he wasn't ready to dismiss her former suspicion, one that he had shared, believed in and counted on. "We will get to the root of this, Lily. I've told you that I sent for a doctor, a friend whom I trust, to evaluate you. Unfortunately, he will only have gotten my request today at the earliest. It could be a week or so before he arrives from Edinburgh."

"Has this doctor seen to the earl?"

Guy felt a stab of guilt for not having thought to do that since meeting Thomas Snively. Truth be told, Guy had not seen the need to impose on his friend for a diagnosis that was well established and documented by two physicians. "No, but I had the best out from London a decade ago and they concurred with Ephriam's diagnosis."

"I see. Suppose this doctor validates what Dr. Ephriam says of me?" Her voice trembled a bit as she asked.

He knew her worry. It was his own worst fear for himself. "I will never send you away, Lily. You have my word." He stood and opened his arms. She walked into them and Guy embraced her fiercely, hoping to reassure her that she would never suffer anything alone again.

Her warmth felt so right against him, so necessary. He felt so much more than desire for Lily, more than admiration of her courage, and something far more compelling than his vow to protect her.

He wanted to tell her now that he loved her, but he knew she would think it was sympathy, maybe even pity, that made him say it. What if it was? He had to consider it. God only knew he did sympathize with her.

His embrace grew even more fervent, desire the last thing on his mind. She was his now. His to keep and keep safe.

* * *

Later in the day Lily grew weary of the constant vigil kept on her. "I feel like one of Beau's bugs in a bottle," she complained to Guy when he looked in on her. He returned almost every hour on the hour, probably to see whether she had lapsed into another of her spells.

"A very pretty bug," he said with a smile. "Are you bored?"

She tossed aside her knitting, not caring if the yarn tangled. "This is not how I mean to spend my days, like a…an invalid. I'm fine now," she assured him, meeting his eyes directly. "Do you really think it's necessary for me to remain cooped in my room until this fellow you've sent for arrives?"

"No, of course not. That could be weeks." He walked over, crouched beside her chair and took her hand in his, examining her nails. She had trimmed them all to the quick since she had somehow broken several in her struggles yesterday. "I suppose you've rested sufficiently."

Lily pulled her hand from his. His merest touch unsettled her, incited wicked thoughts, reminded her of more intimate caresses. She clutched her hands together to erase the tingling. "I would like to ride."

"Lily…." He sighed heavily. "I cannot in good conscience allow you to perch on a sidesaddle and risk tumbling off."

She whirled on him, angry. "I have never fallen from a horse in my life!" But she might if she suddenly collapsed as she had done yesterday. As loathsome as she found the possibility, it did exist. "Very well. I shall settle for a stroll in the garden. Surely you can't object to that. If I sprawl witless among the weeds, at least I shan't break my neck."

He looked chastened and she felt awful for spending her fury on him when he had nothing but concern for her. Besides, the woebegone expression did not suit his features.

She forced a bright smile and held out her hand. "Come with me, then. You can hold the basket and supervise me while I cut blooms for the table. Unless you no longer trust me with sharp tools."

His frown deepened. "This is not like you, Lily. This…bitter self-deprecation."

She raised both eyebrows and made a face at him. "Haven't you heard? I am *not* myself. I am the infamous madwoman of Sylvana Hall."

"If I were you, I wouldn't try to act the part. Some people might believe it."

Her mirthless laughter sounded a bit mad, even to herself. "They already do. You, in particular. Beau does, surely. The servants will have heard what happened at the vicar's house and the result of that, and I can't think they would have drawn any other conclusions. News travels this county with the speed of a gale-force wind."

He had drawn himself up to full height, clutching her hand almost painfully tight. "I do *not* believe it."

But he did, or he was extremely worried that it might be so. She could see it in his eyes. Tearing her gaze from his, she yanked her hand free and plopped back down in the chair, suddenly weary and dejected, totally uninterested now in a stroll or anything else that involved leaving the room. She folded her arms across her chest and leaned back. "Go, just go."

"And leave you like this? I can't, Lily. I won't."

She puffed out her cheeks and blew out the breath she was holding. It was unreasonable to hold him to blame. "Go ahead. I promise I will take some of the tonic Dr. Ephriam left and go to sleep, so you needn't worry."

"Tonic?" He glanced around the room and saw the brown bottle on the table by her pitcher of water. "Laudanum," he said.

"I expect so. I haven't taken any yet."

He marched over, took the bottle off the table and opened it. Then he sniffed it, stoppered it again and put it in his pocket.

"What are you doing?" she demanded.

"Preventing your getting caught up in the endless cycle that controls my father," he snapped. His eyes flashed when he turned to her. "If you have any further digressions, we'll weather them without this. I will hold you until you are calm." He gave a sharp pat to his pocket. "Opiates are vile, Lily. I have seen what they can do. If you experience intolerable pain for some reason, this might be worth taking, but I will *not* allow you to dose yourself merely to escape boredom."

"Thank you, *Dr.* Duquesne," she muttered with a roll of her eyes.

"Get your bonnet and scissors," he snapped.

She heaved herself out of the chair and marched over to confront him, hands on her hips. "You, sir, are becoming an overbearing *bully!*"

He grasped her by her shoulders and kissed her soundly on the mouth. Shocked, Lily froze, then thawed immediately when fire zinged through her veins.

His mouth was so hot, encompassing hers, teasing her lips open, plundering shamelessly. She threw herself into the kiss, loving the taste, the feel, the scent of him. If only he would… Suddenly he stopped the kiss and pulled away from her, leaving her breathless and a bit dizzy.

"I'm the bully you chose, remember? Now get your damn bonnet and let's go!"

Furious and not entirely certain why, Lily stalked over to the dressing room and grabbed a wide-brimmed hat, slamming it down on her head with greater force than she'd meant to. "Now would be the time to have a full-blown fit. It would serve you right," she muttered under her breath.

The fear that she might do precisely that, and that he would think she had control over it and would use it purposely, kept her from shouting the words out loud.

"That's quite a temper you have there," he commented as he escorted her down the stairs. She could swear he was amused, though he wasn't smiling. She looked closer. He was *carefully* not smiling.

At least she knew anger didn't trigger her episodes. She would never admit it to Duquesne, but their set-to had energized her. She felt much better, except that she could not forget that kiss. Her ready response to it troubled her. He made her feel wanton, wicked and wild. What did that mean?

A sane woman would have pushed him away and slapped his face for such rough insolence. Or would she?

She had to wonder if Guy would greet every confrontation in that manner. Lily was appalled to find herself searching her brain for reasons to confront him again. Tonight, perhaps.

Chapter Thirteen

As they walked in the garden, neither of them had much to say, both lost in their thoughts. Lily tried hard to conceal how concerned she was about his opinion of her. Despite what he said, she knew he doubted her sanity. She had begun to doubt it herself. At the moment Guy seemed more concerned about the question of what to do with her, rather than in determining whether Clive had a plan afoot to commit her.

Was Dr. Ephriam in collusion with Clive? And was their motive truly Clive's greed to gain control of or eliminate her son? Or did they truly believe her mad and that they were doing the right thing by her and Beau?

Regardless of her own state of mind, Lily knew she could never surrender her care of Beau to the Bradshaws. Even if their intent was not evil, they would ruin him. She shuddered to think he might become the sort of man Clive was, or absorb any values or behavior from his conniving grandmother. Jonathan's only saving grace had been the fact that his father had insisted on his going away to school at the age of seven.

Suddenly she turned and hugged Guy with all her strength. "Promise me you will keep Beau safe from them."

"That vow was made, Lily," he told her gently. "The moment you became my wife."

Though they had not discussed it, Lily knew that Guy worried he might one day succumb to his father's malady and be unable to carry out his promise to her. Suppose they both landed in custody and left Beau vulnerable before he was old enough to manage his own affairs? That possibility must be taken into account.

"Excuse me, my lady, my lord."

Guy released her from the embrace and answered the interruption. "Yes? What is it, Lochland?"

"A messenger, milord, a groom from Edgefield."

"Show him out," Guy said, frowning. Then he addressed her. "Would you like to go upstairs and rest while I see to this? It's undoubtedly something to do with Father. It always is."

"No, I promise you I'm fine today. There is something I'd like to discuss with you afterward."

He nodded as a young lad entered the garden behind Lochland. Nervously shifting from one booted foot to the other and twisting his woolen cap, the hired man from Edgefield looked from Guy to her and back again.

"Well, speak up, Corrie. What's the problem?" Guy asked.

"It…it's his lordship, sir. He's taken poorly this morning. Worse than usual. Mr. Mimms says you must come right away if you can."

"Is he dying?" Guy asked with a sigh, obviously unwilling, in any other circumstance, to go to Edgefield and leave her and Beau here unattended.

"Go on, Guy. We'll be fine," she told him.

"No," he answered simply.

The boy cleared his throat. "Mr. Mimms says he might be. Dying, that is. He's right bad off, sir."

"I'll fetch Beau," Lily announced. "We shall all go."

When Guy looked as if he might protest, she held up a hand to prevent it. "We will accompany you and there's an end to it," she said firmly.

She noted his look of relief as Guy addressed the messenger. "Go to the stables and have them harness the trap. Then ride back and tell Mr. Mimms I am on my way."

Lily rushed upstairs and found Beau at his lessons. By the time they were ready to leave for Edgefield, she discovered that she felt quite herself again. Exhaustion had given way to a sense of purpose. Guy needed her.

"Must we see the old earl again?" Beau whispered as they hurriedly descended the stairs. He grasped her hand as tightly as he could.

"Never fear, darling, you need not see him when we get there," she assured her son. "But Duquesne should not have to face this alone. The earl is his father and the only family he has."

"He has us," Beau declared. "And I'm not afraid."

"There's my brave boy," Lily said with a smile. "I knew we could count on you."

"You are all well again, aren't you, Mama?" he asked, peering up at her with concern too deep for a boy of his age.

"I am," she promised. "And I intend to stay that way." If sheer will could accomplish that, she added to herself.

* * *

As soon as they reached Edgefield Manor, she and Guy left Beau in the care of his housekeeper, Mrs. Sparks, and hurried up the stairs. After only a cursory attempt to prevent her going with him, Guy relented.

"Thank God you've come," said the heavyset older man who greeted them at the door to the master chamber. "He's worse. I've sent for the doctor, but he's not yet here."

"Mr. Mimms, my father's man," he said to Lily, by way of a hasty introduction. "This is my wife, Lady Lillian."

"Ma'am," the man acknowledged, suddenly distracted by a groan from inside the chamber. He immediately left them for the patient. She and Guy followed him inside.

The earl's complexion was ashen. Sweat covered his brow and dampened what she could see of his nightshirt. In spite of that, he was still a handsome old fellow with granite features. His graying hair, thick and unruly, had a familiar texture and the beautifully winged eyebrows and long eyelashes reminded her of Guy.

Lily realized she had unconsciously held out a slender hope that perhaps her husband had been sired by someone else—not unheard of in the upper echelons of society where bored or neglected ladies took their pleasure where they found it—but apparently that was not the case here. There was no mistaking the strong resemblance between father and son. She fully understood Guy's consternation over what he might inherit in addition to the earl's physical characteristics and the title.

Guy had pressed his fingertips to the earl's throat. When he removed them, he addressed the valet. "His heartbeat's uneven and he feels cold."

Indeed, the man had begun to shiver uncontrollably. Guy tucked the covers more securely. Worry suffused his strong features and Lily could well see why. The earl might not be dying, but Guy's father obviously was far from well.

Eyes moved frantically, back and forth beneath the closed lids as if he were dreaming. His lips parted. "Mimms!" he shouted, and began to thrash violently.

Only then did Lily notice that his wrists were bound with lengths of silken cord secured to the bedposts. After a few moments of useless twisting, he quieted again.

Guy ushered the valet a few feet away from the bed and spoke in a low voice. "Did you administer the laudanum?"

"I did, sir, over an hour ago. It seemed to have little effect other than to make him sick."

Mimms grew more agitated, rubbing his own chest with his palm and staring at his master. "I fear to give him more. His tolerance for it has grown so great, it takes a near fatal dose to calm him now. Perhaps if he had more of the herb, that would help, but there is none left."

"Herb? What herb?" Guy demanded. "What else have you given him?"

Mimms blanched at Guy's sharp tone and backed away from him a few steps. "Only herbal tea, sir. It's nothing bad. He's drunk it for years, two, sometimes three times a week."

Guy's eyes narrowed on the man. "Ephriam prescribed this?"

"No, sir, not his idea, though he knows of it. I told him myself." Mimms began to sweat profusely and tug at his high, stiff collar. "Since our time in India, the earl has had a preferred tea, a rather bitter brew. But it is difficult to procure in quantity. Mistress Andolou makes it for him."

Guy placed a firm hand on Mimms's shoulder. "Listen to me, Mimms. Does this tea alter my father's behavior at all? You, above anyone, would know. Tell me the truth."

Mimms swallowed hard. "I believe so, my lord." He shook his head. "Often it gives him dreams of…of your dead mother. Only she is alive to him. He craves those dreams like air, sir."

Guy clenched his eyes and guessed. "That's not all, is it?"

"Once in a while the dreams turn very bad."

Guy turned to his father and peered down at him. "Did he have any today?"

"Early this morning, sir. As I said, I was going out for—"

"Go now," Guy ordered. "Get it from Andolou. I'll stay with him. Say I will be coming to speak with her later about this."

Mimms hurried to obey.

Guy turned to Lily. "I think we must stay here at Edgefield until this matter is settled one way or another. Do you mind?"

"Mind? Of course not. Is there anything else I can do?"

"Make yourself at home," he said with a poor attempt at a smile, brushing a stray curl off her forehead. "I am so sorry this has happened, especially in the midst of all our other trials. I promise this will not interfere with my duty to you and Beau."

Lily grasped his hand between hers. "You are not to worry about anything right now other than your father's welfare, do you hear?" She looked toward the man on the bed. "Do you think this herb tea might have made him worse?"

Guy sighed and ran a hand through his hair as his gaze followed hers. "Who knows?"

"Andolou's potions are quite popular with many in the county," Lily said. The herb woman had been living on the outskirts of the village for as long as Lily could remember. Her father had attempted to befriend the foreigner with no success. Andolou had her own religion, she had avowed, and it did not include churches and such.

Rumors circulated that she dabbled in black magic, but no one took that seriously. Her mysterious origins accounted for the gossip. She was simply an island woman, brought to England from the West Indies and probably abandoned for one reason or another. She made a living the only way she knew how.

Andolou provided useless love potions and the occasional aid to digestion, along with regular herbs for the family cook pot. These were the mainstay of her livelihood. Lily herself had purchased a few of the latter from her when the garden at the vicarage failed to produce them.

"It's probable that your father felt desperate enough to seek a cure on his own," Lily said.

"Or perhaps a cure was not what he sought," Guy muttered, his eyes still trained on his father. "We shall see."

Lily left him to tend the earl while she went down to arrange for moving to Edgefield.

She had few qualms about bringing Beau here to live for a while. The village nearby had been her home for the first eighteen years of her life. The place and its people were familiar to her.

The old manor house seemed comfortable enough even if it did lack the polish and many fine furnishings of her house. She would put her efforts into making it more presentable, more befitting the title of its owner. It was the least she could do for Guy, and indeed, fitted perfectly with their agreement to help one another.

As an added benefit, engaging herself in this would give her purpose and distract her from her current problems.

Also, it would remove her even further, physically and emotionally, from her former in-laws. That could only be a good thing in light of her suspicions. She felt that she and Beau would be safer here where no one in the household could possibly benefit by getting rid of her.

To that end, Lily decided she would not send for Beau's governess or anyone else employed at home. Guy's staff would suffice and she would tutor Beau herself.

Guy set aside the book he was reading and reluctantly welcomed Lily back to the master chamber later that evening. He had not been out of the room all day.

"How is the earl?" Lily whispered as she approached the bed.

She quite naturally rested her palm on Guy's shoulder, a caring gesture he valued. Every touch she offered fueled his need for her, but he now recognized that some needs transcended the physical.

He placed a hand over hers and gave it a fond squeeze. The newness of sharing worry would never grow old for one who had faced it alone these many years the way he had done. If for no other reason than that, he would hold Lily dear. But there were certainly other reasons.

"He's been sleeping peacefully since around noon. Let's have a seat over there," he said when he saw she meant to stay.

He took the chair facing the bed so he could continue to observe his father. "His pulse seems normal now and his color has returned. His heart might be affected, but I believe he will recover."

"You must be so relieved," she said with a sigh. "I've been thinking about the tea."

"So have I. I questioned Mimms further when he brought it and found that father's been ingesting the stuff since shortly after my mother died."

Lily frowned. "You think it's possible that the tea could be producing his fits."

"That's what I first thought, but now I recall there were a couple of incidents before he began taking it."

"Will you tell me about them?"

"Apparently he became violent when told of Mother's death. He was in London when it happened. He destroyed an entire room and put his fist through a window. Cut himself badly and refused to let anyone tend him. He might have bled to death, but a friend knocked him senseless so they could treat his wounds. Saved his life."

Lily shook her head, her eyes sad with sympathy. "Poor man. There was another, you say?"

He swallowed hard. The memory was like a physical blow. "After Mother's burial. I was privy to that one myself. Not a sight for a boy who worshiped his old man."

"Dr. Ephriam came," Lily guessed. "And administered laudanum?"

Guy agreed. "And Mimms has done so ever since. He has been with Father since they served together in India. My uncle was earl then, but he died and Father was called home from his post to assume the title. Mimms went from batman to valet when they left the army."

"A dedicated retainer," Lily remarked.

"Absolutely. I've often wondered why, Lily. Why would he remain loyal to a man who…who was no longer the man he admired so? There have been times when I could not afford to pay him, yet he has stayed on."

Lily smiled as she left her chair and knelt before him, placing a hand on his knee. "Obviously because he is devoted to your father, Guy. And, I would venture to guess, because he admires you."

Guy looked down into the clear blue eyes that held such innocence despite all she had suffered. "Or because there was nowhere else for a former soldier with scant training as a valet to go."

She shrugged. "Perhaps. But back to the tea. Could those two times your father lost his reason immediately after your mother died have been due simply the wildness of his grief for the woman he loved?"

"I don't know, but that's my hope. In any event, I plan to test the tea." He smiled down at her. "The question is *how* to test it."

Lily was about to answer when a brusque voice

sounded from the doorway. "Now this seems a strange honeymoon. Not as strange as your wedding, I'll admit, but—"

Guy laughed softly. "Jelf? What the devil are you doing here?" He rose and gave Lily a hand up.

"Interfering," Jelf said. "Smarky let slip that you've need of a friend and, in my book, he hardly qualifies. He came to tell you that the fellow you asked about— Brinks, was it?—is dead. Drowned in the Thames. Foul play, no doubt."

"Damn!" Guy heaved a gust of disappointment. "He was the one holding Lily in Bedlam when she escaped. I was hoping to question him. Among other things."

"I can well imagine what things. Sorry, old man. Anyway, Smarky's outside, scouting the premises for possible threats." Jelf rolled his eyes. "I'd count the statues in your garden before he leaves if I were you."

"It was very kind of you to come, too," Lily said.

"Ah, Viscountess. You are a sight different than when we met at your wedding. Believe it or not, I was sober enough to realize you were wearing breeches at the time."

"So I was. Unkind of you to remind me of it, but I forgive you." Lily smiled and Guy had the unreasonable urge to order Jelf to leave immediately. Jealousy had been foreign to him until he met her. That must signify something ominous.

Jelf sketched a bow. "Please, do call me Galen, my lady. So few people do."

Lily strode over to him and held out her hand. "And I am Lily to my friends."

"Then may I ever be one of those, since you are wed to the worst scoundrel I know and may have great need of me."

Shoving his jealousy aside, Guy had an idea. "It's I who have need of you at the moment."

A sandy eyebrow shot up as Jelf questioned, "How so?"

Guy looked at Lily who was regarding him with curiosity. "I'll get Mimms. He can make the tea."

Her mouth dropped open. "Guy! You would *not!*"

He laughed at her shocked expression. "No, sweetheart, I wouldn't," he assured her. "It's for me to drink and Galen to observe. I trust him to keep you safe if the stuff happens to do me in."

"No, I won't let you drink it!" she exclaimed, grabbing his forearm. "We…we'll test it on an animal or something."

She cared. Was there another soul in the world who would worry that much about his health? Hell no. Most of his mates, including Jelf, would say he deserved what he got for his daring.

His chest swelled with feeling for her. "An animal would not have the same reaction as a person, Lily. It has to be done."

Jelf was looking from one to the other as they argued. "What must be done? Are we performing experiments?"

"Have a seat and Lily will give you the details while I go and find Mimms."

"Never mind. I'll go. You stay and explain things to…Galen."

Guy tried to ignore the way his friend ogled his wife. It was just Jelf's way. Still Guy did his best to draw Galen's attention away from Lily as she left the room.

"Justice Jelf would not have stirred himself to travel

this far from London simply to see how the marriage he had performed was getting on," Guy observed. "There must be more to the incident at Bedlam than has thus far met the eye. What have you learned?"

Galen, for once entirely sober and looking quite official, leaned forward in his chair, elbows resting on his knees. He got right to the point. "What do you have a mind to do with her?"

"The primary objective," Guy said, choosing his words carefully, "is to find out whether there is or was a plot afoot to confine Lily and take charge of her son and his property."

"The brother-in-law?" Galen asked.

Guy nodded. "We believe he was responsible for drugging her and carting her to London, to St. Mary's."

"He must have known her presence there would have been reported within a day or so. It's the law."

Guy scoffed. "Yes, but if she had not escaped, who would have questioned it? Her son is seven years old. She's lived a fairly secluded life here after her marriage to Bradshaw. Her father and the rest of her relatives are dead. Conveniently, there were witnesses to her behavior at a soiree who might have supported any claim he would have made that Lily is insane."

"Is she?" Galen asked, taking a sip of his brandy and regarding Guy with an inquisitive lift of the brow.

The blunt question gave Guy pause, but he quickly recovered and shook his head vehemently. "No, of course not."

"But?" Galen insisted.

Guy sighed and propped wearily against the front of the desk, tossing back his own drink. "There have been three episodes of erratic acts on her part."

"Caused by?"

"I haven't determined that as yet, but Lily is perfectly lucid except for those occurrences."

"Some sort of drug, you're thinking?"

Guy nodded. "Perhaps the very thing I intend to test when she returns with Mimms. I am almost convinced it is what has affected my father all these years."

"Something he is taking voluntarily?" Galen asked thoughtfully.

"Yes, unfortunately," Guy answered. "The local herb woman, whom I suspect is his mistress, furnishes it according to Mimms."

"You think it affects the mind? Have you questioned her?"

"Not yet. Suppose it is only tea after all? Let's see what happens first. If it hasn't done in Father after drinking it for so many years, I'm confident I'll survive one cup."

Lily pleaded with all three men as they prepared the tea at Mimms's instruction. She hovered around them, feeling totally shut out. They refused to pay any attention to her protests whatsoever.

Mimms heated a small amount of water in a little long-handled pot at the fireplace, apparently accustomed to doing so a number of times over the years. That accomplished, Guy dropped in two spoons of grayish, dusty-looking tea leaves and stirred. Lily sniffed the air. "Very little scent to it." Mimms covered it.

"It should steep until it's lukewarm," he declared, "else it will burn his mouth." Mimms looked over at the earl. "You should wait several days, you know. Even if he demanded this, I believe it's too soon. His heart, you know…"

"Not to worry," Guy said. "Father will be fine."

Mimms had not been told the tea was for other than the earl and simply believed Guy wanted to see how it was prepared and help administer it to his father. When the brew had steeped long enough, the valet strained it from the pot into a heavy porcelain mug.

"That will be all, Mimms," Guy said. "You may retire now."

He clasped a large, gnarled hand to his chest. "But I should be the one to stay here and see to his lordship."

"Not tonight. You deserve a good sleep," Guy said evenly. "That will be *all*."

Mimms moved hesitantly toward the spacious dressing room adjacent to the master chamber where his cot was located.

"Not in there, Mimms," Guy said. "Go belowstairs and find a room."

"Guy," Lily whispered, tugging at his sleeve. "That's not done." It was a horrid come-down for an upper servant to be sent to stay belowstairs. A valet to the servants' quarters? Mimms would never forgive it.

But the man did not object to that. What he did question was the welfare of his old commander. "Sir, I beg you. Caution him to wait. He is too weak."

Guy paused as if thinking it over, then nodded. "You're right, Mimms. I promise on my honor that I won't give it to him. Not a drop. Do you trust my word, Mimms?"

"Yes, my lord, of course." Then he promptly left as he'd been ordered.

"Now then," Guy said, turning back to the small serving table where Galen Jelf stood, licking his lips and making a face.

"That is a foul-tasting bit of deviltry, Guy. Whew!"

"Jelf! What have you done?" Guy knocked the cup from his hand.

"Now look at that mess," Galen scolded. "There were a couple of swallows left. How shall we get the full effect?"

"Damn you, man! That was for *me!*"

"Trust me, it was no treat you missed." Galen grinned and held out the lengths of silken cord Guy had collected for the purpose of restraining himself. "Would you like to do the honors, Lily?" He wiggled his eyebrows up and down. "I am feeling rather ravenous already. Are we certain that nasty brew wasn't aphrodisiacal?"

Guy snatched up the ropes and roughly bound his friend hand and foot, while Galen shook with laughter.

Lily thanked the man with all her heart. If he sickened from this wicked dose of tea, she might feel guilty, but Guy was safe from its possible effects and that was all that mattered. As for it making Galen Jelf lose his wits, he had seemed a bit lacking at the outset.

The old earl slept on, blissfully unaware of what they were doing on the opposite side of the room. Lily kept watch, both on the patient and on Galen Jelf.

Guy had lowered him to the soft, thick carpet, well away from the fireplace. And they waited.

At first he appeared to be falling asleep, his eyelids at half-mast and a faint smile curling his lips. She glanced at Guy and he shrugged. Neither knew what to expect next. This could be the extent of the effects.

The earl's soft snore, the crackle of the dwindling fire and the ticking of the clock on the mantel were the only sounds in the room.

Soon Galen began to hum intermittently. A wider smile graced his handsome features. Lily could almost imagine him languishing in the arms of a woman, so sensuous was his expression, the sounds he made and the subtle shifting of his body.

Those sounds brought to mind her night in bed with Guy. When she darted a glance his way, she knew his thoughts had also flown in that direction.

He cleared his throat and looked away. She, too, felt uncomfortable. And warm, very warm.

"He seems all right thus far," she whispered, hoping to dispel the sudden tension between them.

Galen's eyes opened fully and he looked at her and Guy. Or perhaps through them. His voice grew even more sultry, the words disjointed and indistinct. But he did not exhibit behavior beyond that of being pleasantly inebriated.

"Perhaps he didn't drink enough of it?" Lily ventured. "Since some was spilled."

"This is not working," Guy grumbled, his disappointment evident because he thought the test had failed. "He's only foxed and was probably that way when he arrived. Let's bring him around and put him to bed on Mimms's cot."

"I don't believe so, Guy," Lily argued. "He didn't seem drunk when—"

"With Galen it's often difficult to tell. He wears his liquor exceptionally well most of the time. God knows he's had enough practice at it."

With that, he knelt beside Galen and shook his arm, tapping him lightly on the face. "C'mon, old boy. Sober up now."

Suddenly, Galen issued a howl and came alive with a

vengeance. Guy tried to cover his mouth to keep him from waking the earl and narrowly missed getting bitten.

Horrified, hand over her own mouth, Lily watched with morbid fascination as Galen Jelf evolved into a snarling, snapping beast, struggling to snap his bonds. His sharp cries chilled her soul.

Guy managed to hold him nearly immobile, but Galen fought all the harder, twisting and groaning, obviously terrified and wild in his fear. They inched closer to the fireplace.

"Watch out! Do not let him hurt you!" she warned Guy.

"This explains giving laudanum!" he snapped back, but she knew he wouldn't give it.

Were Galen not bound, Lily hated to think what damage he might be doing. The struggle seemed to go on forever and Guy was tiring. She dropped to her knees beside Galen's feet and helped hold him down.

Guy's eyes met hers as he pinned Galen's upper body flat to the floor. They remained in that uncomfortable and strained tableau until they were fairly certain the worst was over. Then Guy walked on his knees over to Lily and she fell into his arms. He almost crushed her.

She realized she was weeping. "Oh, Guy, that was so…awful."

He took in a deep breath and when he spoke his voice sounded thick. "It is the tea, Lily. Thank God in heaven. It is the tea."

They sat there on the worn carpet beside Galen for another hour and more, fearing he would wake up and resume his thrashing. Guy leaned against the front of the heavy armchair and Lily reclined against him, sheltered in his arms.

The clock ticked on as the earl snored in his bed. Galen remained silent and still as death. His chest hardly rose and fell at all.

Finally, Guy moved her away from him and went to kneel over Galen. "I think it's probably safe to untie him now and put him to bed."

"Try waking him again first," she suggested.

Guy managed to rouse his friend enough to sit him upright, though the heavy shoulders slumped forward as if he were extremely exhausted.

Tears leaked from the corners of Jelf's eyes as he raised his head slightly to peer at her. He bit his full lips together and slowly shook his head back and forth.

The poor man badly needed comfort. She leaned forward and placed her hand on his arm. He caught back a sob and closed his eyes. Gone was the cheerful, rakehell lord justice. Galen seemed broken and totally defenseless.

"I am forever in your debt, sir," she whispered sincerely, knowing that if not for Galen's interference, Guy could be this ravaged soul sitting beside her on the floor.

Chapter Fourteen

Lily waited impatiently in the study for Guy to come downstairs the next morning. He had spent the night in his father's chamber, keeping watch over both Galen and his father.

Beau had been fed earlier and was playing in Guy's old nursery with one of the two maids still employed here.

Lily had learned this morning that the entire staff consisted of Mr. Mimms, the housekeeper she had met on her first visit, one stable lad and two maids. She would have to remedy that soon. There was work here for twice that number.

Lily sipped her third cup of coffee and nibbled on a cold scone as she waited, but hunger eluded her. She knew she would never be able to drink tea again.

Guy entered, holding the door for a lethargic Galen Jelf to enter. He placed a hand on his friend's shoulder and guided him to a chair. "We smelled the coffee," he told Lily with a wry half smile.

"How are you, Galen?" she asked, leaning over to pat his hand.

He gave a one-shoulder shrug and even that seemed a great effort. "Tired to death. Guy tells me I delivered quite a show."

Lily exchanged a glance with her husband. "Not one I'd care to see again, but I've probably given that same performance a time or two."

He nodded. "The tea was drugged. The question is, with what?"

Guy filled two cups with coffee and set one in front of Galen. "Was there anything familiar about the sensations you experienced?"

"Like nothing I've encountered," Galen admitted, nodding to her as he accepted the plate she had prepared at the sideboard. He attacked the scones and preserved pears with more energy than she had seen him exhibit thus far.

He chewed rapidly and swallowed, then washed it down with the entire cup of coffee before he continued. "The effects were not akin to overimbibing spirits of any sort. Or even with smoking hemp." He winced at what was probably a particularly bad memory. "More in line with eating opium, I should say, only much worse. There is a queasiness and residual head-pounding that smacks of a gin hangover."

"You banged your head on the floor, in case you don't recall," Guy reminded him.

"Oh. Well, I suppose that could account for it. My stomach's settling now that I've eaten." He gratefully accepted more coffee. "I should feel quite the thing after this," he said, lifting his cup in parody of a toast. "Thank you."

"No, it is we who should thank you," Lily said sincerely. "You have no idea what might have been added to the tea?"

He shook his head, but carefully, as though it still ached. "None."

Guy issued a mirthless laugh. "And he should know."

Lily shushed him.

"No, he has it right," Galen admitted ruefully. "My misspent youth stretched several years into my adulthood, if I'm to be perfectly honest, Lily. I wonder at times how I survived it with any sort of mind intact."

"That question goes begging," Guy quipped, softening his words with a smile. "But you have provided us with evidence of what has likely affected Father all these years, and what might possibly be the cause of Lily's supposed affliction."

"Nothing *supposed* about it," she retorted. "Whatever caused it, my condition was still very real and horribly frightening, both to me and those around me."

"But we can now be almost certain it was induced," Guy assured her. "The trick remains to prove that and to punish the one responsible."

"Clive," Lily stated.

"Probably," Guy said, wearing a thoughtful look.

"You doubt it?" Lily asked. "Who else has reason to do such a thing?"

His long agile fingers toyed with the handle of his cup. "Dr. Ephriam seems to be the one connection you and my father have in common." He paused, thinking. "But what would be his motive? Then there's Bernadette. She's certainly capable."

Galen leaned forward, his elbows on the table, hands spread in an encompassing gesture. "A conspiracy," he suggested. "Say the doctor is hired by one of them. He profits only if they succeed in having you put out of their way and gain control of your money."

"My *son's* money," Lily corrected. "And my son himself."

"Control of him and his inheritance, then," Galen said. He sat back in his chair and crossed his arms over his chest. "A dastardly plan. All the pickpockets aren't in rags it seems."

"So what do we do now?" Lily asked, turning to Guy for the answer.

He smiled. "Go to the source of this tea and ask a few questions. That should settle it once and for all."

Galen stood. "Well, I came because I thought you might be up against some dark force you couldn't handle. Since it's only a doddering old doctor and greedy in-laws, I'm off to London. Unless you need me for another dose of humiliation?"

Guy laughed and rose, too. He rounded the table and reached out to shake hands. "You've endured quite enough, Jelf. I don't quite know how we're to thank you."

Galen released Guy's hand, stepped away, quickly leaned down and kissed Lily full on the mouth. She gasped, flummoxed that he would dare such a thing. It had been hasty, yet definitely not a brotherly buss. Her lips tingled.

He chucked her under the chin. "There. All thanked."

Guy spun him around and clenched a fist in the front of his shirt, raising Galen to his toes. He growled through gritted teeth, his brow lowered. "By God, if you weren't a friend…"

"You would kill me. I know." Galen bumped him lightly on the shoulder with a fist. "Apologies, old son. Mark it up to an addled brain if you like. But you know I never pass up the opportunity to kiss a beauty."

"Henceforth, leave *this* beauty alone," Guy ordered.

"Noted." Galen winked down at Lily. "Send Smarky to London if you need me." With that, he waited for Guy to release him, smoothed down his shirtfront with an open hand and executed a slight bow to each of them. "I bid you good day."

"I'll walk you out," Guy grumbled, shooting Lily a dark look. "You stay here."

Lily hid a smile behind her fingertips and met Galen's gaze of amusement with one of her own. "Safe trip," she murmured, unable to contain her delight.

Men were extremely territorial, she knew. That could account for Guy's angry reaction to the kiss. But she liked to think it was more a personal thing, that he wanted all of her kisses for himself.

Childish and foolishly romantic of her, but there it was. She wanted Guy to love her.

He had once sworn never to marry, never to love anyone. He had forgone the first. Why not the second? Was the only impediment to loving a woman his father's illness and the worry that it might occur in him, as well?

Guy had borne such great responsibility from such an early age. She ached to take some of that from him, to help him and to show him he need not shoulder it all alone. Did she have the right to have him love her or would it only cause more heartbreak for him later?

The future would indeed prove much brighter for both of them if his father's madness, as well as her own, had been induced by a substance they had ingested. Easily remedied, easily banished. There was hope.

She rose, went to the windows and pushed the draperies wide open to let in the sunlight. Her soul felt as sunny as all outdoors.

But when her gaze drifted to the graveled drive below, her fingers clutched the damask fabric of the drape. Clive's barouche sat near the front entry.

What wickedness was he up to now? More than she dreaded what that might be, Lily feared that after what they had learned last night, Guy might kill him on the spot.

She tore out of the morning room and rushed down to the foyer. Like it or not, she must intervene.

Given her husband's reputation and his dire threats against her former brother-in-law, there could very well be bloodshed.

Guy sent the little housemaid Gretchen out to the stables to have Corrie saddle Galen's mount. "One drink for the road while I give you a lesson in manners," he told his friend.

"Oh, for heaven's sake, spare me your outrage, Guy. It was only a kiss between friends. No tongues involved, I promise."

"Excuse me, Guy…uh, milord," Mrs. Sparks interrupted from behind them before they reached the library. "Mr. Bradshaw is in the parlor." She paused and looked around, lowering her voice to a gruff whisper, "Along with the constable. What have you done now?"

Guy slipped an arm around her hefty shoulders and gave her a hug. "Nothing at all and you're not to worry. Go along now, I'll take care of it."

He marched up the hallway and into the shabby parlor. So Clive had brought protection along this time, had he? Constable Frick was no friend, but neither was he much of a threat. What did Clive have up his sleeve now?

He regarded them with a glare, the slick-haired, would-be baron and the pudgy, pug-nosed extension of the law. "Mr. Bradshaw, Mr. Frick, to what do I owe this unexpected visit?"

Clive deferred to the constable with a nod, as if encouraging him to speak up. Frick took a deep breath and proceeded to do so. "Milord, you are in violation of the ordinance preventing the operation of a non-licensed facility for housing the insane. I believe you have two patients on the premises?"

Guy laughed in disbelief. "I have *what?*"

"You have two patients with the aforementioned affliction. Fully documented, I believe, by a reputable physician. This is against the law. We shall have to remove these unfortunates to a proper place of confinement and take you into custody, sir. Charges have been filed. There will be a fine of five hundred pounds."

"But he *is* licensed," said a deep voice from behind him. Damn, but Galen could sound authoritative when need be. And, lord, could he lie with a straight face. Guy only prayed the lie would hold up to legal scrutiny.

All eyes focused on Galen who lounged in the doorway, arms crossed as he leaned indolently against the jamb.

"I would see the license then," Frick said. His eyes darted to Clive and back again.

"It is with Lord Havington at the moment, being further validated as we speak," Galen said. "He's on the High Council."

"Who are you?" Clive demanded.

"Lord Justice Jelf of London, at your service. Chairman of the committee formed to investigate Lord Duquesne's petition, which I have approved. All it lacks is the final signature. That is currently being remedied."

Guy simply nodded and offered Frick a questioning look. What would he say to that?

"Charges have been filed," Frick insisted, "and I must do my duty. As soon as the presence of a license has been verified—and if it is adjudged to predate the formal complaint—the patients shall be promptly released into Lord Duquesne's care. In light of this new information, I believe I might forgo his lordship's arrest."

"And the patients will remain here," Jelf insisted.

"No, my lord, I cannot agree to that. We have attendants without who are to transport them to Plympton Sanitarium immediately."

"No!" Guy protested, but Galen had come forward and now clutched his arm. Guy realized he would be fighting a losing battle. If he attacked either Clive or Frick physically, they would have good cause to arrest him then and there. But he could not allow them to take Lily away. Nor his father. God, the earl had not left the estate for fifteen years. A change like this would sorely confuse him. If it was a drug he had been taking, who would help him through the after-effects when it was no longer available? And who knew what would happen to Lily there without his protection?

Clive shot him a smug look and Guy tensed. It would almost be worth a week in jail to bash in that aquiline nose. Instead he held his peace.

"Take the earl," Jelf suggested, giving Guy's muscle a warning squeeze as he made the untenable decision for him. "Keeping one patient in residence violates no ordinance."

"No, he should take Lady Lillian," Clive argued.

"Over my dead body," Guy announced, jerking away from Galen's hold. "She is my wife!"

Clive retreated behind a chair, gripping it with white-knuckled hands.

Frick cleared his throat. "That also has come into question, my lord. You see, I've been informed that the lady was in no state of mind to make the decision to marry when you were wed. For all intent and purpose, sir, the marriage could be invalid."

"Prove it in the courts," Galen challenged. "Until then, the marriage stands. I have it on excellent authority she was quite sane when their vows were spoken."

"On whose *excellent* authority?" Clive demanded.

"My own," Galen replied without rancor. "I attended the ceremony myself. Five weeks ago," he added with an inclination of his head. "Earls Kendale and Hammersley were present as witnesses to the event." He smiled sweetly. "A good time was had by all."

Frick turned his glare on Bradshaw as if damning him for false information. Then he heaved a weary sigh. "Very well, that will be easy enough to prove or disprove. But the other patient must go to satisfy the requirement. If the license proves valid, you may fetch him from Plympton and bring him home." He strode past Guy and Galen, his head down and lips pursed. "I will summon the attendants to collect the earl."

Guy focused on Clive Bradshaw who was now in the room alone with him and Galen. "You will pay dearly for this, Bradshaw. I should have employed that butter knife as I promised. Now you may expect worse. *Much* worse."

"Touch me and you'll be arrested!" Clive warned, his voice a full octave higher than usual.

"Leave it," Galen said, his voice low and even. "Everything to its season, Guy. Go and see to your father."

Lily stepped into the room. "I overheard," she said simply, her eyes narrowed on Bradshaw. "You greedy wretch!"

Galen held up a hand to silence her. "Enough. Bradshaw, I would advise you to leave while you are still physically able." When Clive glanced from one to the other, obviously unwilling to give up the relative safety of the shielding chair, Galen added a sharp, *"Now!"*

Clive skittered around them and hurried out of the parlor. His hasty footsteps clicked against the old tiles of the foyer and a door slammed.

"Now go prepare your father," Galen said. "I'll watch over Lily." He made a placating gesture when Guy started to protest. "And I promise to behave myself. Go!"

"Yes, go on, Guy," Lily encouraged. "He needs you now."

Guy went, very reluctantly, torn by the urge to remain at Lily's side and the necessity of trying to explain things to his father in a way he might understand.

God, this had begun as such a hopeful day. Probable relief from the threat of going mad himself as the years progressed, the near certainty that Lily's spells were also the result of drugged tea, the knowledge that she cared about him and that the feeling might deepen into something even more wonderful.

He heard a second crack of thunder that promised a sudden storm. It seemed a bit late for a warning.

Lily gave in to Beau's pleading to go out of doors for a while. Guy had gone off to find and speak with Andolou, but it wasn't as if he had left them alone. Smarky, the little man he had hired to keep watch, was there by the stables. What harm could there be to a walk in the gardens, other than perhaps getting tangled in the overgrown vegetation? Clive was well away now and Guy had not ordered them to remain inside.

"Half an hour and then we must come back in. I have things to do," she said, taking her boy by the hand as they went out through the kitchens.

He had grown so rambunctious, the young maid who had been keeping him company in Guy's old nursery had complained she was at a loss to keep him calm. Lily figured Beau had sensed the unrest within the household, even though he had not been privy to any of the conversations between the adults.

"Where is Duquesne?" he demanded. "I want to ride."

"Not today, darling. Your pony is at Sylvana Hall, remember?"

Lily surveyed the wooded area just north of the gardens. What should have been a pleasant view sent a frisson of concern through her. With her free hand she rubbed her forearm where goose bumps prickled her skin. The urge to rush Beau back inside suddenly overtook her. Silly, she knew, but still she couldn't shake the notion that they were watched from within the copse of trees.

"I want to go and get her," Beau argued, his brow furrowed as he looked up at Lily. "Now!" His small hand rested on his hip and his stance reminded her of Guy's. So did the tilt of his head. How quickly children assumed the posture and attitudes of those around them. She thanked her stars that Beau was now removed from the influence of his grandmother and uncle.

"Not today, Beau," she repeated with emphasis. "We'll speak with Guy when he returns about having your mount delivered here. Perhaps tomorrow."

"Are we to stay in this place long? What of Sylvana Hall? Who will take care of everyone there?"

Lily smiled. "It's good of you to worry since it is our responsibility, but Guy will see to it for us for the time being. We'll go home soon."

That seemed to satisfy him. He let go of her hand and skipped off to chase a large grasshopper.

Lily found a seat on an old stone bench and watched him play. She continued scanning the tree line. Was someone there? After a tense quarter hour, she ordered Beau inside.

Guy worried about leaving Lily and Beau, even for the hour or so it might take to question Andolou, but Smarky was there keeping vigil. Still he wished now that he had sent word for Andolou to come to him.

Smoke rose from the chimney of the small stone cottage in the northernmost reach of Edgefield. Obviously, Andolou was at home.

The herb woman's cottage was a quaint little stone structure with a steeply sloped, thatched roof. Charming, really. Before his time, he thought it had once been a hunting lodge. Now it looked rather feminine with colorful flowers blooming in profusion all around it. Not at all like a place where dark deeds and potions were concocted.

He intended to find out what it was that she had added to that tea, why she had done it and what possessed her to continue. And whether the same thing had been purchased from her to give to Lily. More to the point, he needed to know *who* had bought it.

Guy did not know Andolou except on sight, had never spoken with her, though she had lived on the Edgefield property for as long as he could remember. He realized only now that he had taken his cue from his mother who, for as long as she lived, had refused to acknowledge the woman's existence.

Andolou kept to herself. Though the villagers visited her to buy potions and herbs, few in the community called her friend. He had been surprised to hear that Lily knew of her at all, even though the cottage was as near to Sylvana Hall as it was to Edgefield.

Guy suspected that his father had known Andolou better than anyone, most likely in the biblical sense. Why else would she have been given a house on the Edgefield estate if she hadn't been mistress to the earl? However, that was not a thing to be discussed then, and he would not mention it today.

He reached the front of the cottage, dismounted, strode down the flat paving stones that led to the front door and knocked as he called, "Madam Andolou? It is Duquesne."

Guy waited a bit and knocked harder. "Come out. I would speak with you." He tried the door and found it unlocked.

Perhaps she was hard of hearing. Or ill and unable to answer, he thought, knowing he invented excuses to enter her home uninvited. At this point, he was too desperate and in too much of a hurry to care about her sensibilities. He pushed the door open and stepped inside.

The little cottage was dark except for glowing embers in the fireplace and the bit of light seeping in around the window shutters.

Guy made his way over to a table that held a large

mortar and pestle and a foot-long slab of marble. He noted a number of glass jars and bottles, some clear, some dark, all labeled in a neat hand. He found a tin of lucifers beside an oil lamp and quickly lit it.

An ornately carved, tightly lidded box rested near the mixing area. Guy opened it and sniffed the contents. It smelled of plain tea leaves. Did this already contain the substance that had so altered his father, and probably Lily, as well? He replaced the lid and set the box aside.

As he did so, his hand brushed a small glass jar filled with gray-brown powder. No identifying label on that one. He sniffed it, too, but couldn't identify the musty odor. It was the only other ingredient on the table. Everything else Andolou had prepared for sale or use set upon shelves, clearly marked.

He lifted the lamp and looked around more closely. Clothes hung on pegs. No cabinets in which to conceal anything.

The place appeared clean and very neatly kept. In one corner sat a rather large bed with an expensive-looking damask coverlet and fluffy pillows. On this side of the bed was a small table supporting a china basin and water pitcher. A twin table stood on the far side, holding a silver-backed brush, comb and hand mirror. Gifts from his father or purchases made with profits from her trade? Guy wondered.

There was also an upholstered chair and footstool, mate to the two in the library at Edgefield. No question about who had provided those.

He noted the aromatic herbs and dried flowers hung in rows from the sturdy rafters. A plush Oriental carpet softened the worn flagstone floor. An array of gleaming copper pots hung near the fireplace.

He walked out the back door that led to a well-tended garden and looked around. "Andolou?" he called.

Then he saw her. She lay in a crimson heap at the foot of a rowan tree beyond the herb plots of her garden. Though her face was not visible, he knew it was Andolou because of the bright fabric. None of the locals would wear that purplish scarlet color. And no one else was likely to be lying on her property.

Heedless of the plants he trampled in his haste, Guy ran to her by the most direct route. He dropped to his knees beside her and pressed his fingertips to her neck, praying for a pulse. If she were dead, he might never find out what he needed to know.

There, he felt it, a slight flutter. Quickly he lifted her and carried her back into her home and placed her on the bed.

She didn't stir. It might be her heart. Or perhaps she had merely overexerted herself working in the garden and fainted. Andolou looked rather young for heart problems.

It was hard to tell her age, Guy noted. Her face and neck, the color of coffee with heavy cream, betrayed few wrinkles. Her graceful, long-fingered hands were scarred with burns, the nails clipped to the quick. Her high-breasted, slim-hipped figure was still that of a girl.

He could well understand the appeal she might have held for one of his father's station. She was wildly exotic, mysterious and as far removed from a cool, English beauty as a man could find.

Guy had seen too much of the exotic and mysterious during his life in London to deem that attractive. There were hundreds of Andolous in the brothels there, wretched souls abandoned by men who had brought them to England then tired of them.

Lily was the anomaly in his world and the only woman Guy had ever met who could stir his blood to boiling the way she did.

But what was he to do with Andolou? He hated to leave her unconscious while he summoned help. And what help would that be? Old Dr. Ephriam who probably saw her as a threat to his own profession? If it was her heart, a dose of laudanum wouldn't do her much good and that seemed to be the extent of Ephriam's treatment.

Perhaps if he could revive her, she might suggest her own remedy. He poured tepid water from the pitcher into the basin, wet a cloth he found and tried to cool her face. He spoke softly to her, called her name and encouraged her to wake up.

Eventually, when he had almost given up, she groaned and squinted up at him, her dark eyes a cloudy brown. A pained smile formed. "G'iford? You don' send de liddle mon?"

Little man? Then he realized she wasn't referring to size, but status. His father's man had fetched the tea. "Mimms? No, not this time."

The woman had never met Guy, so he figured she must think he was his father. How long had it been since the earl ceased to visit here? Guy wondered. He decided not to correct her thinking.

"Andolou? Have you been ill?" He mopped her brow again, dislodging the turban. Her hair was clipped very close to her scalp. Traces of silver mottled the tight black curls.

Her fingers plucked at his sleeve as she frowned up at him. "You come to see me die, G'iford?"

"No, Andolou." He inclined his head toward the

shelves across the room. "Tell me what you need to feel better."

"De shroom dust," she gasped, glancing at the table. "Take no more. All de time he promise me. He say you come here, all well, soon." She winced, grasping the folds of the fabric draped over her chest. "You fine now."

Guy had no clue what she was talking about, but he wanted to soothe her, to reassure her and above all, to get the information he sought before she lapsed back into unconsciousness. "Yes. Fine, I promise. Tell me what you put in that tea, Andolou. I must know. It's very important."

"Shroom." She repeated the strange word, dragging it out in a sibilant sigh as she clenched her eyes shut. "You finish now. No more." Her long sigh sounded weary. "I finish…"

Guy tried to wake her again, this time without success. Her breath became a rattle, then ceased altogether.

"Andolou?" He shook her gently, then more firmly, but she remained limp and lifeless. He placed his fingers on her neck and felt nothing. He moved her hands away and pressed his ear to her chest. She had gone without a whimper or a goodbye.

Guy bowed his head, feeling defeat as he sat there with his father's dead mistress, wondering what the hell he was to do now.

After a bit, he folded her long slender hands across her body. As he pulled the embroidered satin up to cover her, he felt something sharp snag the skin of his own hand.

He ripped aside the fabric of the dark red paisley garment she wore and saw the metal embedded just below her left breast. How had he not seen that or at least felt it before?

Guy cursed. Someone had stabbed her and the handle of the weapon must have snapped off, leaving a rough edge of steel protruding a fraction of an inch above the surface of her skin. She had not bled much, at least not on the outside. Her garment was darker than the color of the blood and had concealed what had seeped through.

He covered her completely and stood. He would go for the constable. Murder had been done here and he felt in his gut it had to do with the business of the tea and what it contained. Why else would anyone do such a thing?

If someone had murdered Andolou to keep her silent, then even Mimms might be at risk. He had to get home and arrange more protection.

After a quick, final glance at the body, Guy hurried across the room and picked up the carved tea box and the bottle of what appeared to be ashes.

He had a feeling whatever it contained was the source of his father's, and possibly Lily's, problems.

Chapter Fifteen

It had been a long, long day and it was not over yet. Lily joined Guy and the constable in Edgefield's parlor where the earlier confrontation had taken place.

Beau had been put to bed in the nursery where Guy had spent his early youth. Smarky had sworn to sleep across the threshold outside the door with a weapon in his hand.

All afternoon, the scrawny little man had entertained Beau with wildly inventive tales of highwaymen and seagoing pirates, told in the cant of dockside London. While she might fear for her son's sensibilities, Lily knew she need not fear for his safety so long as Smarky was around.

Now she listened for the second time as Guy related what he had found at Andolou's cottage. He explained what he knew of the herb woman's death and the possible motive for it.

"I believe that ingesting this powdered matter, whatever it is, must be the cause of my father's behavior through the years. Lord Justice Jelf certainly was convinced. Someone learned of its effect, acquired a supply and used it upon my wife. I believe Andolou was murdered to keep her from revealing who purchased it," Guy concluded.

Mr. Frick wore a tolerant expression, but Lily could see he believed not a word. "I am loath to arrest you, Lord Duquesne, but I see no alternative. There are no other suspects in this murder. You were at the scene. I'll wager you stay armed. And you can't deny you're certainly capable of committing the deed."

"Why would you think so?" Guy asked carefully.

"Your feats are legend even among the rustics, that's why. You're feared above any by the riffraff of London as well as our enemies of state. It's rumored you balk at nothing."

Guy did not deny it. "It would be good of you to remember which side of the law I've been working, Frick."

"That's precisely why you aren't bound and on your way to a cell already. You say you believe the culprit to be Mr. Bradshaw, but he has the most ironclad alibi possible. Until an hour ago, he was with me. All day."

Lily interceded. "Sir, if you would keep an open mind and consider, Dr. Ephriam could well be involved in this."

Frick frowned. "Ephriam? He's an old fellow, hardly with strength enough to overpower a woman of Andolou's size."

Lily persisted, trying to keep from wringing her hands in frustration. "Any ruffian could have stabbed Andolou. Her death might not be related to this at all. What if it was some man disappointed when one of her love philters failed to bring the desired results?"

Frick looked thoughtful, brushing his fat mustache with the tips of his fingers.

"Give us time to sort this out," Guy said. "You know where you can find me."

"In London?" Frick said with a mirthless chuckle. "Not if you don't wish to be found."

"I give you my word I will be available to you and I will share any information we uncover about this crime or the other."

"Other?" Frick asked, his frown deepening. "What other?"

"The kidnapping and unlawful imprisonment of Lady Lillian," Guy announced. "I *will* bring charges when I find proof of who took her to Bedlam that night. I should file suit against Clive Bradshaw for hauling her off to Plympton's from the vicar's."

"I would think twice about that," Frick advised. "He had good cause to take her away, so I hear, and there are plenty of witnesses to verify her state at the time."

He raked Lily with a narrow-eyed gaze, as if assessing whether she truly was mad and hiding it well. She met his look with one she hoped appeared challenging and, above all, sane.

Frick looked away first, then suddenly rose from his chair, dusting the crown of his stovepipe hat as he made his way to the door. A heavyset, self-aggrandizing bully, Lily thought.

There, he turned to them. "Three days seems sufficient for you to discover something in the way of proof. In the meantime, I won't be idle. I believe you might have killed that woman, Lord Duquesne. If I find one jot of evidence that you were involved, you will be arrested and brought to justice by your peers." He plopped his hat on his head and grumbled, "For all the good *that* would do. Half of London's in your pocket, so I hear." He stalked across the foyer to the front door and saw himself out.

Guy's eyes met hers. "Three days."

"That isn't much time," she said.

"It will have to do." For the first time Lily saw real doubt in his eyes. Doubt that he could accomplish what needed doing. Doubt that he had let no one else see but her.

She went to him, hoping to share the confidence he continually inspired in her and restore his own. He opened his arms, welcoming her as if she were cherished. Lily rested her face against his chest, her fingers toying with the lapel of his riding coat. "Together, we will think of something," she promised.

"Of course we will," he replied softly. His embrace tightened around her, his large palms caressing her back and her waist. Was he thinking, if not for her, he would not be at risk?

Lily snuggled closer and slid her arms around him. Guy's reassuring words held neither desperation nor cynicism, but she did detect serious concern. He sincerely needed her now as much as she needed him. It was as if no other comfort would do for either of them. In view of all the troubles they faced, it was a wonder that seemed so terribly important to her, but it did.

She sighed as he embraced her, reveling in his nearness. "A part of me wishes to run away," she murmured. "Simply make a dash for the coast with you and Beau and begin a new life in a place where no one knows us." Tantalizing as the thought of escape was, she knew very well that Guy could never take the coward's way out.

Neither could she, really. "That says little for my courage."

He made a lazy sound of contentment, almost a chuckle. "Don't think I haven't considered that, too. But you know we have to see this through."

"I know," she whispered, pressing her fingers into his back, the length of her body against his, trying to hint at what she dared not ask for. "But not tonight."

He stood very still and after a moment of silence, he lifted her into his arms and gazed into her eyes with a heat she could never have imagined. "Tonight we escape in our own way."

She smiled. "Spirit us away to a place with no cares," she said, linking her hands behind his neck. "Will you?"

He grinned the devilish grin she expected. "Indeed."

The stairs creaked under their combined weight as he carried her up to a bedroom she had not seen before. At the opposite end of the corridor from the earl's chamber, this was another of like size. The furnishings were as much in need of refurbishing, but it possessed a homier quality than the master suite.

He placed her on the edge of the high tester bed and kissed her gently on the lips. "I never apologized properly for the night we made love."

"Apologize? Whyever should you have? It was... quite nice." Lily's face heated with a blush.

"*Nice* could be improved upon," he growled as his fingers traced the hooks and eyes that fastened her gown at the back. "And so could brief. Did you like brief?"

Lily hardly knew what to say to that. "Brief is relative," she ventured, her voice faltering a bit as he carefully tugged her gown from her shoulders and pressed his lips to the curve of her neck. "For instance, I feel a need to rush…now," she admitted.

His lazy chuckle vibrated against her skin as he exposed her breasts. Instead of kissing them as she expected—no, wanted him to do—he stood away, his hands playing with the loosened straps of her chemise. "What a picture you are." He breathed the words and slid his palms down her arms and up again to cup her gently. For what seemed an eternity, he brushed his thumbs over her hardened nipples, creating a flood of warmth in the nether regions of her body.

She watched as he began to fiddle almost idly with the laces of her corset, to pull them free, slowly and surely, while she bit back the urge to hurry his efforts with her own.

Oddly enough, instead of feeling embarrassed, Lily experienced a rush of power. The way he looked at her, with that hot and hungry gaze, made her feel lush and provocative and somehow in control. She had not moved, but did so then, raising her hand to his foulard. Anticipation begged her to hurry, but she took her time, as he was doing.

His smile was one of pleasure. And also a wordless challenge. Who would be first to give in to eagerness? Not her, she decided. One glance down assured her that his need was at least as fierce, perhaps more urgent than her own. And he couldn't see hers. She grinned, plying her advantage, slipping the studs from his shirt one by one.

"A quick study, I see," he muttered beneath his breath.

"Lassitude is my friend," she crooned. "Take your time, my lord."

"Provoking baggage," he accused, his laugh a near groan. "You want me to fall upon you like a starving wolf."

"Do I?" she drawled, sighing as he slipped her corset off and tossed it aside. "Will you?"

He answered by shrugging off his coat and shirt together and dropping them to the floor as his lips met hers, a mere caress of moist warmth. She wanted devouring, longed for it, almost pleaded.

Again he moved away, lifting her to stand on her feet, then peeling away her gown and chemise, leaving her in only her pantalettes, stockings and shoes. He certainly looked wolfish with that grin, with his member straining against the tight nankeens. She risked a pointed look, abandoning every residue of modesty.

He waited, apparently to see what she would do. The game was on.

This was Devil Duquesne, a born rakehell. There was probably little he had not seen or done during his wild years in London. Why should she play the fainthearted maiden with him?

Lily realized now that, since her return from London, she had reverted to that same young woman who had married Jonathan Bradshaw. She was behaving exactly like that new baroness who had feared that as a mere vicar's daughter she was without the proper deportment to become a baron's wife.

True, now she was wed to a viscount, but what a viscount he was! Definitely not a man confined by Society's rigid code of gentlemanly behavior. Lily could be herself with him. How freeing.

She felt emboldened, more uninhibited than ever before in her life. With a lift of her chin, she eyed him from beneath her lashes and slipped the button at the waist of her pantalettes. The garment slid over her hips and landed around her ankles. Coyly, she stepped out of them and kicked them aside.

His breath had caught in his throat. She watched him swallow hard and shake his head once. "Point to you."

"Giving up?" she asked.

"Not yet." He undid his trousers and peeled them down his narrow hips. They caught at the top of his boots.

Lily lifted a brow. "A problem? Shall I assist?" She slowly knelt and reached for one boot, fully aware of his view of her, naked and kneeling at his feet.

With another laughing groan, he stepped back until he bumped into the chair and sat down. In a trice, he had off his boots, stockings and the trapped trousers.

How enticing he looked then, broad chest and muscled arms and legs exposed. He knew it, too, the wanton rascal. The white silk smalls he wore only accentuated the breadth of him elsewhere and barely contained what they concealed.

Lily sat on the carpet and enjoyed the view. There was much to be said for the joys of anticipation. Now it was her turn to wait him out.

"Come here," he invited, beckoning with a curl of one finger and a devastating expression of desire.

She smiled and shook her head. If she approached him now, she would betray the full extent of her need in a heartbeat. And as for heartbeats, hers had accelerated to what must be a dangerous level. Her breath came fast, but she struggled to control it.

She stood, slowly uncurling from her kneeling position and straightening to full height.

Lily drew a middle finger slowly up the center of her body, trailing between her breasts, up the side of her neck and over her right ear, then lazily raked her hand through her hair. His eyes followed the path of her hand, then met her daring gaze with one of sizzling heat.

He left the chair and came to her—unhurriedly, though she could see that was an effort for him—stopping just out of arm's reach. With a daring grin, he released the button on his smalls and raked them down his hips. "Your move."

The sight of his blatant arousal fascinated her, so much so, she forgot to speak. Never had she seen such a thing in that state. Never before would she have thought to want to see one.

"Well?" he prompted, shifting his weight from one foot to the other, obviously impatient though still trying not to show it.

Lily cleared her throat and, for the moment, totally neglected her ploy to entice him to hurry. "You...you are doing precious little to make your case for a leisurely coupling," she remarked.

He laughed out loud and came swiftly to her, taking her in his arms. She felt the hardness of him pulse against her belly. "Ah, Lily," he said, embracing her fiercely, "you win, game, set and match, you minx."

She yelped softly with surprise as he lifted her to the edge of the mattress. Her legs parted and he pressed between them, entering her without so much as a word.

His eyes met hers as he began to move, his palms pressing her closer in time with each thrust.

Tension built within her, a sensuous swell of intense pleasure that threatened to burst at any second.

"Lie back," he whispered, his palms supporting her

as he lowered her upper body to the bed. His hands slid around her ribs and cupped her breasts, those magic thumbs abrading her unmercifully.

Lily gave herself up to feeling, closing her eyes with a moan of encouragement. She wished it could last forever. She wished to end it now, to reach the ultimate explosion. Her inner war did nothing to diminish the indescribable sensations that grew ever more keen.

"This," he murmured next to her ear, "is taking my time. Do you like it?"

Surely her sounds of encouragement and the reaction of her body gave him answer enough. She wanted to tantalize him as he did her, but he was the one who knew where and how to touch, to stroke, to circle just so, and drive her wild with urgency. For a glorious and astonishing length of time, he held the promise of that keenest of pleasures just out of reach.

Feelings she never knew existed swept through her, waves of them, heady and, unbelievably, even more arousing. Overpowering. Each breath drew in the erotic scent of their loving. Each caress awakened a new, an undiscovered path to bliss. And every hot, wet kiss lifted her to a higher plane of rapture. But not the very height. Not yet.

His rhythm changed, exciting her anticipation, then quieted to a slow and deliberate torment she both welcomed and fought. The strong beat of his heart thundered, his sweat-slick skin sliding sensually over hers. Moving, ever moving. Faster now. Lily grasped his hips, insisting, demanding. "Damn you, Guy!"

"Now," he growled, his voice rough with emotion. And then he touched her where they joined. Lily lost herself in him, crying out with joy, gratitude and, yes, not a little fear.

She opened her eyes and saw his face as he plunged one last time, claiming his own measure of ecstasy. Claiming her forever as surely as if he had burned a brand on her flesh. His features pulled tight. His huge hands gripped her just below her waist, almost encompassing her completely. His eyes met hers in the throes of his release. A final ripple of sweetness shook her when his warmth flooded her body.

"At last," she whispered, more to herself than to him.

How had she been wed for so long and never experienced this bliss? Why had she been denied? Surely, Jonathan had reached the pinnacle each time.

Anger suffused her, then melted away. Maybe he had not known how, or even that she wished it. Perhaps she had denied herself unknowingly in her attempt to be the lady she thought her husband needed her to be.

Guy lifted her legs onto the bed and gently rolled her over to make room for himself. When he lay beside her, pulled her back against his body and encircled her with his arms, Lily forgave everyone everything. Replete and secure, she only wished to fall asleep and wake later within his embrace. She never wanted to be without him again.

"I shall win next time," he murmured against her ear.

"I thought you *did* win," she answered, her voice slurred with fatigue. "You took your time, after all."

"Oh no, love," he argued halfheartedly, a smile in his voice. "Less than a quarter of an hour shames me."

Lily giggled, giving the hand clutching her breast a little pinch. "Redeem yourself tomorrow night, then."

"Must I wait so long?" he growled. "Think of my pride, woman."

He pressed that pride against her backside and uttered a heartfelt groan.

Lily sighed, enjoying the feel of him, hot and damp and eager. "Well, since you put it that way…"

Chapter Sixteen

The old clock on his mantel softly chimed eight. Guy knew he must drag his weary body from the bed, but he delayed anyway. His delicious little wife lay dead to the world, snuggled in his arms as if born to be there. He could hardly make himself release her after such a night.

If he was not in love with her, he was as near as no matter. His desire for her outstripped anything he had ever felt for a woman. His admiration for her knew no bounds. Every aspect of her did and would continue to fascinate him, he knew. Her happiness was more important to him than his own would ever be. Did all that constitute love? What else could he call it but that?

He, who had sworn he'd never let himself fall prey to that lovely trap, had stumbled directly into it. His friends had succumbed, of course. All but Jelf, who like himself lacked the resources to support a wife properly. Guy's reason to avoid love and marriage, beyond the financial, had been the stain of family madness that must not be passed on to any children he might father, or endured by a woman who might love him. That reason would prove invalid if what they suspected was true.

At the moment he felt blessedly content, happy to be caught, decidedly charmed and determined to make a good husband. "Yes, I do love you," he whispered, and brushed her forehead with his lips.

She stirred, smiling in her sleep, inadvertently brushing against him in a way that made him ache to have her again. If he did not get up right now, he might well make hash of any tender feelings she might have of him after last night's loving. She must be exhausted.

Gently he extricated himself from the arm she had slipped around his neck and left her there, naked as a nymph and twice as enticing. He pulled the covers up to her neck and began to collect his clothes.

He had just pulled on his trousers when a soft knock rent the silence. Guy tiptoed to the door barefoot and opened it a crack. "Yes, what is it?"

"A visitor's come," Mrs. Sparks whispered. "All the way from Scotland, so he says. Sounds like it, too." She tried to peek around Guy's shoulder into the room.

"Where is the boy?" he asked, realizing he had not given a thought to Beau since he woke up.

"He's with that London bloke Lord Jelf brought with him. They are at the stables. Someone brought the little pony over from Sylvana Hall and they're seeing to it."

"Excellent. Her ladyship's still asleep should he ask for her. I'll be dressed in a moment. See that the doctor's made comfortable until I come down." He closed the door in her face.

When he turned, Lily was sitting up, rubbing the sleep from her eyes. A more fetching sight, Guy swore he had never seen.

"Who was that?"

"Mrs. Sparks. I'm needed below, but you needn't get up now. I know you must be tired."

She grinned, brushing the bedcovers flat against her stomach, causing her small, perfect breasts to rise above the fabric in invitation. "Hurry back," she said.

He grinned and sat down to put on his stockings and shoes. "You're determined to win the last round, aren't you?" With a grimace, he stood. "Sorry, darling, but our contest will have to wait for tonight to continue. The doctor's arrived."

She scoffed. "Ephriam?"

"No, Snively from Scotland, the one I told you about. Never expected him this soon. He must have taken the first ship down the coast after receiving my letter."

Guy frowned at the stricken look on her face. He went to her immediately. "You're not to worry, Lily. This is a trustworthy man who will exhaust every method he knows to discover what has been happening, both with you and with Father. Trust me on this. I'd not have sent for him otherwise."

"He is our last resort, isn't he?" she asked quietly.

Guy kissed her palm. "There is *no* last resort, love. Merely the next step in proving what we know is true."

She scrambled past him and got off the bed, oblivious of her nudity. "I'm coming with you."

"No," he argued, clasping her arm and pulling her to him. "Let me see him first."

She glared up at him. Then she raised both hands to her tousled locks. "Perhaps I should brush my hair first."

Guy tapped her lightly on one cheek. "And put on some clothes. Else you might drive *him* to madness. You're doing a fair job on me as it is."

That brought a smile. "You're joking about it. That's reassuring, you know. If I were insane, you'd be serious."

"Right as rain. I'd be desperate never to mention the word in your presence," he told her, not daring to admit that he had lived with his father's madness and the prospect of his own for so long that making jests about it was his one defense.

"Thank you," she said, her smile one of infinite gratitude. "Go on then, see what he has to say. I shall be down to join you in half an hour."

When he reached the door and had it open to leave, she called to him. "Guy?"

He turned. "Yes?"

"If we're wrong, I release you from your promise not to send me away. Beau shouldn't have to endure the painful vigil you have had these past years with your father. But I expect you to honor your vow to protect my son at all costs. I demand it of you."

How could he not love this woman? Guy met her determined gaze. "We are not wrong, Lily. I'd stake my life on it."

"All I ask is that you don't stake his on it," she replied.

Guy refused to answer. He had promised to keep her by him no matter what and he would. Beau could jolly well deal with it if he had to. Didn't Lily realize the quickest way for him to lose her son's regard was to give up on her?

When she came downstairs to join the men, Lily found that she quite liked Guy's friend the doctor immediately. He appeared younger than her husband and yet his eyes seemed old. They must have seen too much suffering, she supposed.

He wore a long coat of black superfine to match his trousers. Though wrinkled from his travels and obviously tired, Thomas Snively's manner and obvious self-confidence left no doubt he was a gentleman of substance. Also one who believed in getting to his point straightaway.

"I have told Lord Duquesne that in all probability you were dosed with the same substance as his father. However, before I state that conclusively, I should like to examine the matter in more depth," he told her.

"Examine *me,* you mean to say. Ask me questions and determine whether I exhibit any other odd quirks my husband might be concealing to spare me embarrassment?" she asked, smiling as she accepted a glass of sherry from Guy.

He inclined his head, admitting she was right. "True. But I also need to see the earl and evaluate his condition."

"We plan to ride over to Plympton first thing in the morning," Guy told her. "For now, perhaps you wouldn't mind if Thomas got on with interviewing you." He turned to his friend. "Shall I leave or stay?"

"Leave," the doctor said frankly. "It is standard procedure with me to conduct this sort of thing with the patient in private."

Guy nodded, almost concealing his frown. Lily gave his arm a reassuring pat. "We shall get on fine here. Go and play with Beau."

When Guy had gone out and closed the door, Snively turned to her. "You spoke to him as though he were a boy himself. Do you usually?"

Lily laughed. "He *is* a boy at times. You should see the antics those two get up to. But no, the suggestion was meant as an affectionate jest. You mustn't think I'm one of those women who rules the roost. If you know Duquesne at all, you know better than that."

Snively pursed his lips and paced, hands clasped behind his back. He stopped and cocked his head thoughtfully. "How do you get on with him? Is he harsh with you? Tender?"

Lily paused. Guy had been both at times. She felt she must answer carefully. "He treats me as he would a friend, I suppose. He raises his voice when I do something that worries him and he wishes I would not. But tender, mostly. I feel…very cared for."

Snively nodded noncommittally. "Then your marriage to him is what you might consider normal? As was your first marriage to the baron?"

"Oh, there's normal and then there is normal," Lily quipped before she thought how it might sound.

"What do you mean by that?"

Had she put a foot wrong already? Lily sighed and sat down, hoping the doctor would do the same. Her nerves were beginning to fray. "Bradshaw was a wonderful husband, though much older than I," she began. "We got on famously, right from the outset. But he was not…not as active as Duquesne."

"Sexually?" the doctor added, again with total frankness.

Lily decided to answer in kind. "Yes, that is precisely what I mean. He was older, you must understand."

"Does it trouble you, Duquesne's demands?"

She felt her face heat and knew it was bright red.

With a hand to one cheek, she looked away, out the window, hardly able to speak above a whisper about such things. "No. No, it does not trouble me at all."

Snively clapped his hands once. "Well done of you. Now that we have that matter settled, we might as well get on with the important issue."

"If it is not important, why did you introduce it?" Lily snapped. "Have you a prurient interest in this, sir?"

"Not at all!" It was his turn to blush. "Duquesne merely mentioned that Dr. Ephriam had cautioned him not to bother you in that regard because it was what had upset you."

"He what?" Lily jumped to her feet. "That weasley little worm! I could twist off his ears! How dare he…"

She halted in midtirade when she noticed him observing her too closely. She took a deep breath and released it slowly. "I am not about to go into a tear, Dr. Snively. If that is what you intended to cause, you might as well try again. It's true I have a temper at times, but I promise you I never lose my senses." But she had. Several times now. Quietly she added, "Hardly ever, at any rate, and certainly do not intend to at this moment."

Instead of appalled or even relieved, he only looked interested. "Excellent. Now tell me everything you recall from each incident. Not what others have told you, but the actual sensations you personally experienced. Be as honest as you have been thus far and as detailed as you are able."

Lily found she trusted this man, even if he had delved into what should have been an unapproachable subject. She still liked him. More than that, she liked the way nothing she said seemed to outrage him or even rattle his composure.

He came and sat across from her in a chair and listened to her every word as the entire story spilled out.

Just as she was relating her concern about her son's witnessing any future aberrant behavior on her part, Guy strode in, followed by Galen Jelf.

Both she and the doctor rose as they entered.

"The commission's been formed and will arrive this afternoon," Guy informed them, his voice gruff with worry. "Galen has managed to get himself assigned as justicier. The hearing is to take place at Sylvana Hall."

"You're the justicier, Galen. That's good, isn't it?" Lily asked, looking from one to the other. It did not appear they thought so. "Can't you simply—"

"No," Galen interrupted. "I was able to order the location of the inquiry and preside over it, but I do not have the final decision-making authority."

"Then we must convince the commissioners?" she asked.

Guy slid an arm around her shoulders. "They cannot dismiss this out of hand. It is the accuser who must be convinced to drop the allegations. Even as your husband, I could not forestall your committal unless we could prove beyond doubt to everyone that you are indeed sane."

"And Clive Bradshaw has witnesses to the contrary," the doctor declared. "A veritable hoard of them, I understand." He addressed Guy. "Your denial would be considered that of a husband who selfishly desires the continued services of his wife rather than having her treated for her own betterment."

Lily coughed with disbelief. "You are telling me this matter is left to Clive Bradshaw to decide?"

Galen blew out a breath of frustration and waved an

impatient hand. "No, of course not. Constable Frick will determine whether taking you into custody for committal is the proper course. The commission will create the writ to do so if at least four of them agree it's necessary. My only part in this will be to keep order as the evidence is presented and to summarize for them when it is done. Vagaries of the law, I'm afraid."

"If we can't convince them, there is no recourse?" she murmured, the horror of it all but striking her mute.

He inclined his head and pursed his lips. "Well, there is one. Assuming we cannot prevent the writ, we will of course take it to the courts. Cases are back-logged a thousandfold. However, it could well be over a year before yours is heard. Meanwhile, you'll be sent to Plympton or somewhere similar to await the trial."

"I can't let that happen." Guy began ushering her to the door. "Go and pack for you and the boy, Lily. We can make the coast by midnight and secure passage."

"Bound for where?" she demanded, anger replacing her fear. "Where would you take me that word of this would not follow?" She snatched her arm from his hand. "I will stand and fight! I will prove to them Clive has cooked up this scheme to get his hands on my funds and Beau's. Perhaps he even did the murder of Andolou to keep his plan secret." She stamped her foot. "He'll not get away with this. As you told Frick, we will accuse *him!*"

"Counter and put him on the defensive. Galen, might that work?" Guy asked.

"Not without some basis in fact. He has witnesses to validate his claim. As far as I know, you haven't a one, have you?"

Lily could feel Guy's excitement growing by leaps as he rubbed her hand between his. "We will. I'll see to it."

Galen snorted. "If what you're hatching is illegal, don't tell me."

"As if that would bother you," Guy muttered off-handedly, and turned to the doctor. "What we need to do now is to put a name to that damned gray powder that's caused all this trouble. Find out precisely what it is. Could you do that, Thomas?"

Snively shrugged. "I have a fair idea already, but presenting that to Mr. Frick and the commission would only establish your father's problem and perhaps get him released to your custody for recovery. You have said he took the substance voluntarily, that his man, Mimms, went to Madam Andolou for it and then prepared it for the earl. We haven't a shred of evidence that it was ever given to your wife."

"I might have what you need," Lily said.

They all turned to her, waiting.

"I have a bottle with a dose of something that Brinks was to give me when I was at Bedlam. It might be the same thing."

"I thought you said you gave it to him in order to escape," the doctor said.

"There were two different concoctions prescribed for me, apparently. One was to keep me sedated, which I poured down Brinks's throat. The other was to ensure that I put on a proper show when they came to certify me. I still have it."

"That might help," Galen said, shrugging. "Or it might not. It will depend on whether the constable and the commissioners believe your story about being taken to Bedlam in the first place. There are no witnesses to that, either. Only your word."

"I will convince them," Lily vowed.

"Bring the bottle to me and I shall compare it to what was given the earl," Dr. Snively suggested. "Though I haven't any of my equipment here to analyze it, perhaps the smell, taste and consistency will be enough to determine if it is the same."

"You'll have to do that on the way to Sylvana Hall," Galen said. "There isn't much time."

"We leave Beau here with Smarky," Guy said. "No sense in having him involved."

"But he already is." Galen sighed and ran a hand over his face. "He is listed as one of Clive's witnesses. A primary one, in fact."

"No!" Lily cried, wringing her hands and shaking her head furiously. "He cannot require such a thing of my own son! He would make a child give testimony that his mother is mad? I won't have it!"

Thomas Snively stepped closer. "Lady Lillian, stop and think. There is no way anyone can give you anything to cause a display of madness before the commission. Therefore, it seems obvious to me that this detail has been added to destroy your composure and perhaps cause you to appear distraught. You must, at all costs, remain calm about this. Hysterics won't serve."

"Oh, for goodness' sake, I am not hysterical! I'm angry!" Lily grasped Guy's hands and leaned into his embrace, hoping to draw strength from him. His nearness calmed and reassured her. He was so strong. He would think of something, even if as a last resort, he had to steal her and Beau away and take them somewhere safe.

Perhaps she was wrong to insist on fighting Clive's charge. How could she hope to win?

Guy gave her hands a comforting squeeze. "Beau will survive this and he'll be the stronger for it, you'll see." Then he smiled down at her. "Besides, if we leave him here, he'll find a way to follow us. Remember when they locked you in your chamber and he used the key so he could keep watch over you?"

"He's my baby," Lily said, hardly able to keep her tears confined.

Guy raised her hands to his lips and kissed them. "He is your son and full of spirit, a lad who has reached his age of reason, Lily. Give him full credit."

Her shoulders slumped in defeat. "He is seven years old and afraid for his mother. He will either fight or lie for me. I do not want him forced to do either."

"The choice is not ours. If he is not produced, the constable has the right to fetch him," Galen said, his words rife with worry. "We should be going now. We have very little time to get to Sylvana Hall and set up for the hearing. The commissioners are all local and will congregate there in two hours' time."

"Local?" Lily could not believe it. "How is this so? Local men might be friends with Clive and will surely support him. Some might even have witnessed what happened at the soiree. Why aren't they from London, appointed from the courts there?"

"Because this is still considered a local matter. The only reason I may act as justice for it is because I am a lord and I own property within the county." He looked meaningfully at Guy. "Though there are a number of gentlemen landholders about, the only other peers in this area are the earl, Guy and your seven-year-old, all of whom have a personal stake in the outcome and are not eligible to serve."

"You own property here, in this county?" Lily asked, surprised. She had never heard of Galen Jelf until he had married them in London.

He nodded. "A recent purchase. I own three acres with a cottage on it, thanks to your husband. Now if you will collect your son, we really must be on our way."

"Come, Lily," Guy urged. "Time is not on our side. Go and do what you must to get ready. Find that vial you acquired at the asylum and give it to me. I'll bring it down to Thomas while you dress."

No, she wouldn't forget that, though she doubted it would help. How could she prove it was the cause of her temporary madness when she was not even certain of it herself? She could take some of it again, she supposed, but how would they know whether she feigned the madness this time?

It seemed she was destined to endure this unfair trial and its results, whatever they might be. There was little hope that Clive's fear of Guy might prompt him to withdraw his charges. Thus far it had not. With the backing of so many witnesses against her and the protection of six gentlemen of the commission who were his neighbors, it seemed very likely that Clive would prevail.

This entire scheme had brought her to Guy and caused her to find a happiness she had not known was lacking in her life. Now the same scheme would snatch her away from it, unmercifully. She would lose her son and all that was dear to her.

Not if she could help it, Lily decided, her lips firming with determination as she hurried up the stairs.

Chapter Seventeen

The large ballroom on the first floor of Sylvana Hall had been readied for the hearing. Almost every chair in the house had been placed there so that those attending could be seated for the event.

Though he would have preferred to keep it as private as possible, there was already a crowd. The witnesses against Lily were limited to fifteen, counting Beau. Then there were the six commissioners, the constable and his two enforcers. All totaled, there would be at least thirty people involved, directly or indirectly.

At Guy's instruction, a table laden with tea, coffee and spirits stood to one side. Mrs. Prine, Lily's housekeeper and two footmen were already dispensing refreshments to those who had arrived. The makings of a party, Guy thought as he surveyed the room.

Lily stood beside him dressed in dark blue merino with a demure lace collar at her throat. Her hair, brushed severely back from her smooth forehead, was confined by a proper morning cap of white linen and lace. How young she looked and how innocent. She had schooled her sweet face to betray no emotion, but he knew her mind must be swirling with the dire possibilities in store for her. He was no better off, though he thought he might have a bit more hope than she did.

How much wiser it would have been not to fall in love with her. He might be able to defend her better if his blood did not run so hot when she was threatened.

The strange thing for him was that these feelings had burgeoned even before he and Lily had become lovers. The emotion was so foreign to him, it had taken a while to recognize it. Now he wished he had known sooner, that he had at least told her of it. But if he confessed that he loved her now, she would only believe he was saying it to bolster her confidence for the hearing.

His gaze then fastened on her son, the brave lad standing beside them, ready to use every ounce of his power to negate what was about to happen, while fearing it would not be enough. Guy realized he loved the boy, too. This was the son he had wished for, or the closest to one that he was ever likely to have. He placed a hand on Beau's shoulder and smiled down into the solemn blue eyes.

Guy glanced at the huge ring on Beau's hand, a keepsake from Guy's long dead uncle, the former earl. Candle wax filled in nearly half the opening so the trinket fit the boy's thumb. "Take heart, Bradshaw. We're in this together, come what may."

"Yes, sir," Beau replied, "I know."

"There are Clive and Bernadette," Lily whispered as her former in-laws entered the room.

"I should have throttled him when I had the chance," Guy muttered.

"I suppose it's too late now?" Beau asked.

Lily shot the boy a look of concern. "Guy…?"

Guy cleared his throat. "Yes, I'm afraid it is." But he would get around to it if this debacle went the wrong way. "Now we must do right by the relatives and make them welcome, eh? See that they are served personally?"

Beau nodded, still very solemn, and immediately headed over to the table where Mrs. Prine welcomed him with a sad smile. Beau shook his head at the woman and brushed past her. He made a show of stuffing a small biscuit into his mouth. When Mrs. Prine's attention wandered back to the arriving company, Beau unstoppered one of the decanters, poured two glasses of sherry and marched dutifully toward his uncle and grandmother. He tread carefully so as not to spill any.

"There's a good lad," Guy muttered to himself.

Lily frowned. "Whatever is he doing?"

"His duty," Guy replied. "We had a talk about it while you were seeing to refreshments. It will go much better if Clive and his mother are made comfortable at the beginning. They might be more inclined to show mercy, don't you think?"

She scoffed without changing expressions, but said nothing.

"Oh, I believe they will," he assured her as he noted the slight nod Beau sent him from across the room. He beckoned to the boy to come back and sit with him.

At Galen's insistent signal, the tapping of a heavy paperweight against the long table set up at the front of the room to serve as the bench, the attendees began to take their seats. He motioned Lily to one of the chairs directly in front so that she faced him, the commissioners and the constable. Clive and Bernadette came forward, as well, and took seats on the front row.

Galen rapped the paperweight again. "This hearing will come to order. I am Lord Justice Galen Jelf and will preside. The six commissioners present and Constable Frick will hear testimony in this matter and come to a decision that shall be accepted as final." He paused, then added, "Unless the defendant later elects to pursue the matter of criminal conduct by her accuser before the King's Bench."

Guy heard a collective indrawn breath from those behind him. Clive Bradshaw's mouth dropped open. Guy smiled. That provision had set up the idea that Clive's motives were not at all altruistic.

Galen continued. "This will be a relatively informal proceeding but I will brook no interference, either with the testimony or after the decision is made. Anyone seeking to disrupt this hearing shall be summarily arrested as would occur in the courts."

He paused again. "We are here to determine the condition and disposition of Lady Lillian Upchurch Bradshaw Bollings, Viscountess Duquesne." He looked up from the papers in front of him and fastened his dark, penetrating gaze on Clive. "The allegation of insanity by reason of mental disease is brought against the Viscountess by Mr. Clivedon Bradshaw, the brother of her first husband, Baron Bradshaw. He seeks to have her confined to an asylum for treatment and possible cure. Is this correct, Mr. Bradshaw?"

Clive set his glass on the floor and stood. "Yes."

Galen looked down again and shuffled the papers. "Mr. Bradshaw, please advise us why you have taken it upon yourself to act in what you term Lady Lillian's best interests when she has a perfectly good husband who surely would have noticed if she needs help."

A titter of laughter sounded from the back of the room, which Galen, despite his prior warning, ignored.

The wide-eyed Clive glanced down at his mother.

"We are waiting, Mr. Bradshaw, if you please," Galen prompted.

Clive cleared his throat and stood straighter. "He—he is most likely too affected himself. After all, his father is—"

"Is not the subject of this hearing, Mr. Bradshaw. Please confine yourself to one allegation per day, if you don't mind."

More laughter, this time, heartier. Galen remained straight-faced. Guy tried not to smile.

"You have not answered the question, sir," Galen admonished. "What would you hope to gain by having Lady Lillian incarcerated."

"Hardly *incarcerated,* my lord. Merely confined for her own personal safety and those around her until she recovers, if she ever does." Clive began to shift nervously from one foot to the other.

Galen nodded. "I see. Very commendable of you, I'm certain. But tell us, Mr. Bradshaw, who would then have charge of her son, the young baron, and his estate and fortune?"

Clive swallowed audibly. "Lord Duquesne, her husband, I would assume."

"Whose marriage to her you were unaware existed when you bound her and took her to an asylum in London on the twenty-ninth of last month, is that not true?"

"No! I did no such thing, my lord. The only time I escorted the lady to an asylum was when my mother and I took her from the vicar's house to Plympton."

Guy had to admit, Clive's answer rang true. How-

ever, Bernadette was wringing her handkerchief and
her profile looked pinched. Could it be that she was the
one who had arranged all of this? Guy watched her
closely as Galen kept firing questions and Clive grew
more restive by the minute.

Dr. Ephriam came next, declaring Lillian had indeed
undergone periodic episodes of wild hysteria in keeping with the diagnosis of insanity.

Witness after witness was called to describe Lily's
actions, both at the soiree to which Clive had accompa-
nied her and at the vicar's house during the afternoon
tea.

Lily would not be allowed to speak for herself, but
Guy was prepared to speak for her. At last Galen called
him to the fore and Guy stood.

"Lord Duquesne, as you have heard, your wife, Lady
Lillian, is supposed by Mr. Clivedon Bradshaw to suffer mental disease. Have you any information that might
refute that allegation?"

"I do," Guy stated. "I believe my wife was given a
substance provided to someone by Madam Andolou, the
local herb woman. This particular powder, mixed with
tea, has been proven to initiate visions and behavior that
mimics madness."

"And how do you know this?" Galen asked.

Guy turned to look at his father's valet. "Because Mr.
Mimms, my father's man, has acquired this same powder for my father these last fifteen years and it has had
precisely the same effect."

The crowd began to buzz until Galen quieted them
by banging the paperweight sharply on the tabletop. Silence fell.

"How can you be certain it is the same potion? And

how do you know Lady Lillian received such doses to cause her odd behavior?" Galen demanded.

Guy looked around, meeting as many eyes as he could while he paused for effect. "Because, my lord, during her imprisonment at St. Mary's Asylum after she was abducted, she overheard the guard being ordered to dispense this to her immediately before the commission arrived to judge her mental state the next day." Guy held up the half-full vial of powder for everyone to see. "I have it on authority this is exactly the same as that which Mr. Mimms purchased regularly from Madam Andolou."

"Simple enough to verify, I would think," Galen said. "We shall call to witness Madam Andolou."

"You cannot, my lord justice," Guy said, his voice gruff. "The woman is dead. Murdered at her own home, obviously by someone wishing to keep her silent."

The commissioners looked at one another in horror. The room fell to deadly silence. Constable Frick watched with growing interest. Guy could well understand. If not for Lily's freedom being in peril, he would be enjoying every minute of this drama himself, but things could go so very wrong.

Again Galen silenced the mutterings. "A tragedy, to be sure. But upon what authority have you declared these substances to be similar, Lord Duquesne?"

"Not similar, my lord justice. Identical," Guy declared. "An expert on matters of the mind and the causes of aberrant behavior, Dr. Thomas Snively from the University at Edinburgh, will confirm this if you would hear him."

Galen held up a finger. "In a moment. First, relate how your wife received this…what would you call it? An intoxicant?"

Guy shrugged. "Yes, of sorts. She believes she was given it in a glass of sherry before her abduction." He looked pointedly at Clive who was sweating profusely. "Poured for her by Mr. Bradshaw. The next time, it was administered to her somehow during a tea held at the vicar's."

"By whom?" Galen asked, though Guy knew he did so reluctantly.

"That is yet to be determined, my lord. There were many present. However, the effects were precisely the same. My wife did recover completely and is as you see her now, composed and as sane as anyone in this room. Perhaps more so than some," he couldn't help adding.

"Thank you, Lord Duquesne. That will be all," Galen said dryly. "Will Dr. Thomas Snively please come forward?"

Snively rose and approached the bench.

"Is it your conclusion that the substance in the vial acquired by Lady Lillian during her abduction is the same as that administered to Earl Edgemont, the one ostensibly causing impairment of his senses?"

"It is, my lord. The consistency, odor and color are exactly the same. The bottles containing the intoxicant are similar, as well, probably purchased as a lot by whoever prepared the intoxicant."

"So it is an intoxicant," Galen said. "An opiate of some sort?"

"Not an opiate, but dried mushrooms of a special sort crushed to powder. These have been used for many centuries in certain pagan ceremonies to induce a peculiar state of mind. If ingested with anything but water, they are usually undetectable. Within half to three-quarters of an hour, the subject begins to hallucinate."

"See things that do not exist?" Galen clarified in the event that some in the room did not know what it meant.

Thomas nodded. "Also ordinary things often take on strange and frightening proportions and movement. If one is prepared for the experience and welcomes it, the results can prove euphoric. If not, it can induce unbearable fear." He sighed. "And if given in too great a dose, it can be quite lethal, as you know certain species of mushrooms *are*."

"Oh, no!"

Everyone turned to the sharp outcry. Beau stood, his hands clasped over his mouth. His blue eyes wide and frightened.

Galen patiently regarded Lily's son. "What is the matter, Beau?"

"I hope it wasn't too much, Uncle Clive! I only meant to give you a bit in the wine to make you sleep, not kill you!" He held up the oversize poison ring, its hinged compartment open and empty. "But it *was* a lot."

"My God!" Bernadette Bradshaw leaped to her feet, oversetting her chair. "What have you done, you wicked child!"

Beau shrugged, looking guilty as hell. Guy almost laughed. The boy was a natural actor. "I'm ever so sorry, Grandmother. But he gave some to my mother. I thought it would only make him sleep. He was going to say bad things about her here and I didn't want him to."

"Ephriam!" Bernadette cried, searching the room frantically for the older doctor. "Augustus! Come here! Hurry!"

"Hurry!" Beau echoed. "Come quick, before he dies!" Guy motioned for him to be quiet now. He had done quite enough and his contrition was slipping.

Clive promptly fainted, falling forward out of his chair. His mother dropped to her knees beside him, rolling him over, slapping his face repeatedly. "Clive! Clive! Oh, darling!" she cried hysterically. "I wish I'd never learned of the cursed stuff!" She searched wildly for Ephriam. "Augustus, come here! Hurry! You know he can't abide this! The antidote!"

A stillness fell over the room.

Ephriam stayed in his chair, frantically shaking his head in wordless denial.

"*How* did you learn of the 'cursed stuff,' as you call it? And *when?*" Galen insisted, his words like cannon shot aimed at Bernadette. "And how do you know there *is* an antidote? Dr. Ephriam?"

"N-no! There is no known—" the doctor stuttered. "Only laudanum to calm… But he's already—" He dropped his face to his hands.

Bernadette realized she had given herself away. Everyone was staring at her. She cast about frantically for something to say.

"Did you kill or have killed the herb woman known as Andolou?" Galen shouted, standing and pointing an accusing finger at Bernadette. "Did you stab her in the breast so deeply you broke off the knife's hilt?"

"No! No, she tried to… She wouldn't give… It was an accident! We struggled and…" Her eyes wildly searched for someone to believe her. But all eyes were fixed on her, disbelieving, damning. She cringed. "I only wanted to…"

"Imprison the baroness? Secure her property for yourselves?" Galen demanded loudly. "Take charge of the young baron and his holding?"

Bernadette swung his way and screeched. "My son

should have it! He should have from the start, not that milksop Jon. Then she…she had that…that…" She pointed at Beau, her face a fiery red, apoplectic.

Suddenly she leaped at Lily. "You witch!" she screamed. "This is your fault! See what you've *done!*"

Lily dodged just in time to miss catching Bernadette's full weight on top of her, but the woman snagged Lily's sleeve and they both fell.

Guy rushed forward to separate the two, but Bernadette had clasped Lily in a bear hug as she rolled, wrestled and screamed obscenities. Lily's arms were trapped.

Guy feared the woman would crush her. He leaned over the two, grasped Bernadette's hair and yanked. It came off in his hand.

Dumbfounded for a second, he stared at the wiglet. Bernadette grabbed for it. Lily pulled back a fist. Guy watched as she planted Bernadette a facer old Gentleman Jack would have applauded. The older woman collapsed backward and Lily staggered up, rubbing her fist and wincing at the pain.

Guy quickly whisked her away from the woman who was rolling on the floor, grasping her bloody nose and weeping maniacally.

The constable smiled and crooked a finger at the two heavily muscled helpers he had brought with him. They assisted Bernadette to her feet while she struggled between them. "Lady Bernadette Bradshaw, you are under arrest," Frick announced. "Take her away."

Bernadette was screaming to high heaven, audible even after they had exited the front door with her.

"A moment more, Constable," Galen said, stacking the papers in front of him as he sat down again. "We still have the question of Lady Lillian's disposal to adjudicate."

"Send her home with her husband," Frick advised with a negligent wave of his hand. He turned to the commissioners. "Unless one of you has a different notion."

"And the earl? Shall you have him released, as well?" Galen persisted.

"Into the custody of Lord Duquesne, of course," Frick said.

"Any votes of nay on either course of action?" Galen asked the commissioners. There were none. The men serving on the council sat wide-eyed, mouths slack, too shocked by events to speak. They simply shook heads in unison.

Guy already had Lily in his embrace and rested one hand on Beau's shoulder.

"What of Uncle Clive?" the boy asked, pointing to the prone figure that had not stirred.

The beefy constable went over and picked the man up with one hand by his collar, setting him on his feet. "You have quite a few questions to answer before I lock you away."

"I did nothing!" Clive protested, his words slurred. "I am innocent, I swear!"

"Let's see you prove it," Guy said with a smile.

He noted Dr. Ephriam had disappeared during Bernadette's fracas with Lily. He wouldn't get far. Frick would see to that.

Lily brushed back her tousled curls and knelt to hug her son. "Beau, I am so sorry about your grandmother. She is obviously—"

"Mad," Beau finished, nodding emphatically. "I gave her the wrong sherry, I think."

Guy shook his head, marveling at the resilience of youth. Lily, judging by the look she shot him, was about to take Guy to task for involving the boy in his scheme to force a confession out of the Bradshaws. Guy expected the reprimand, but doubted she would issue it in public. Maybe there were advantages to marrying a lady of propriety, after all.

Who knew? Perhaps she would. Propriety hadn't stopped her from knocking Bernadette to hell and gone. He tried not to smile.

"Wait until I get you alone," she warned him through gritted teeth. Her eyes snapped blue fire. He was damn glad she wasn't wearing those riding boots she had crowned her guard with that night. Her little fists were lethal enough.

"I'm waiting," he said, deciding to take his dressing down with good grace. Quite looked forward to it, in fact. Here was the Lily he loved best. What spirit! He could kiss her senseless, right here in front of everyone.

She was within her rights to object to what he had done. He'd be the first to admit that his manner of dealing with children probably left a lot to be desired. All the reference he had for that lay in his own boyhood and how he would have liked things to go.

In his experience, adults invariably underestimated children. At least he wasn't guilty of that. He knew the mischief boys could get up to and figured they might as well do something constructive with all that energy. He'd had a veritable army of pint-size informants in the streets of Whitechapel.

He had felt it was important to include Beau in the plot to resolve Lily's problem. There was nothing more frustrating for a lad than to be left out of things and not able to help his own mother.

"Why involve Beau?" she rasped, her whisper vehement. "Tell me why!"

He shrugged. "Clive and Bernadette would never have accepted a glass of sherry from *me,* and their drinking it was crucial to the outcome."

"Just you wait," she warned again, her voice shaking.

Guy rocked back and forth, impatient to have done with all this and take her home.

Galen adjourned the inquiry. The commissioners and witnesses began to disperse, gossip over the events, buzzing loudly as bees in a hive disturbed.

Galen came from behind the bench and slapped him on the shoulder. "That was a masterful twist you provided, but how could you be certain the old lady would react that way?"

Guy hadn't known what Bernadette would do. "Well, the revelation was pure luck," he admitted. "At the very least, I thought a practical demonstration of the effects of the substance in question were necessary. Thomas's verbal description seemed too tame. Who better than the guilty party as the subject? I was fairly certain you wouldn't volunteer to ingest it again."

Galen laughed heartily, bade them a speedy goodbye and wished them luck. Smarky would accompany him back to Town now that he was no longer needed.

Dr. Thomas Snively congratulated Lily on her release. He was to stay on several days to see what he could do for the earl and to interview Bernadette and Clive for his research.

Others broke away from the crowd to speak with them. Sara Ryan added her congratulations. "It was the coffee, Lily!" she said excitedly. "Lady Bradshaw had the opportunity to slip something in it, remember?" She had been summoned as a witness to Lily's hysterics at the vicarage, though she had not been included in the limited number actually allowed to speak.

Guy noted Lily's keen attention on Sara as she agreed and thanked her. So she was a bit jealous, was she? That boded well.

Before he knew it, the crowd was gone. Not daring to smile, Guy winked at his coconspirator and Beau winked back. Guy's heart lifted like a hot-air balloon soaring through a sun-filled sky. Pride filled it. *His boy.* Or as near as could be.

Mrs. Prine approached when the servants had cleared away the table of refreshments. "Could I interest any of you in biscuits and milk in the kitchen?" She was looking directly at Beau and smiling. He nodded and scampered off, leaving Guy to his fate.

Lily closed the door and turned the key. They were alone at last.

"Ah, poor little chick," Guy said, taunting her just a bit. "You must have been terrified. That old bat didn't hurt you, did she?"

"Hurt *me?* I should say not!" Lily cried, planting her fisted hands on her hips, shaking with rage. "That beastly cow should be hanged, drawn and quartered along with her stupid calf! How dare they…" She began to pace, gesturing angrily, letting loose with invective Guy would never have expected to hear from her lips. Not exactly profane, but extremely colorful and quite inventive. High marks for that, he thought.

He drew his eyebrows down and forced a frown, nodding in absolute agreement with it all. He locked his hands behind him because it was all he could do not to grab her, swing her around and kiss her till she begged for mercy. That would be forever. His Lily would never beg.

Here was her passion erupting. Here was that nine-year-old churchman's imp who had risked life and limb to see life from the top of an oak. Lily was a woman who took fate in her hands, forcing it in the directions she would take. He loved her so much he wanted to shout it to the world.

When she ran out of words and energy, she simply stopped and turned, apparently confused by her sudden outburst.

Guy held open his arms then and she ran to him, grasped him around his waist and buried her face in his chest.

How had he lived with solitude for so long? Why had he not found her years ago? All this was enough to overwhelm a bachelor so set in his ways.

Lily and Beau had shown him what joys were to be had as a husband and father. He would never have guessed at those. And Galen had underscored the value of friendship. Guy had taken his old friends for granted or not believed in them quite enough. He had mending to do on that front. God, he felt so aware of things, of people, of hope, and especially of Lily at the moment. Warming his heart and heating his blood.

"Are you still angry with me?" he asked.

"No," she whispered. "It wasn't you. It was… everything."

He tipped up her chin. "You are magnificent," he said, kissing her with all the desperation he had been suppressing.

When he broke the kiss to let her breathe, he couldn't stop the words. "I love you, Lily. I think I've loved you from the moment you walked into my study in London."

She nuzzled his neck where she had torn away his tie and collar. "Remember you thought I was a man at first."

He laughed. "Did I? Didn't seem to matter at the time."

He had coaxed a laugh out of her with that.

"You are far too wicked, you know?" She sighed, releasing some of the pent-up tension of the day. "Devil Duquesne. Now I know how you got the name."

"Oh, no, you don't. But if you'll let me carry you upstairs, I'll show you."

She met his eyes with a half-lidded look of daring. "All the way upstairs? There's a perfectly good divan by the window there."

He studied her face. Her expression had grown softer after their kiss, sweeter, less combative. "Is this another surrender on your part, Lily?" he teased.

She laughed again, more easily this time. "A surrender on *my* part? Hardly, Duquesne. I rather meant it as a demand on yours."

Chapter Eighteen

"The truffles are excellent!" Galen remarked with a sly wink and attacked the dish with enthusiasm.

"If I never see another mushroom of any sort, it will be too soon," Lily remarked with a shudder.

Almost two months had passed since the hearing at Sylvana Hall and they had come to London for Bernadette's trial. The sumptuous dining room of the Regent's Hotel provided a welcome retreat after the long day in court.

Neither Galen's bachelor town house, nor Guy's shambles of a mansion on the fringe of Mayfair was adequate for a supper of celebration. Instead, they had gathered here at the Regent's where Thomas Snively resided until his return to Scotland.

The doctor sighed, sitting back in his chair and smoothing the edge of his linen napkin. He looked up and smiled at Lily. "Now that everthing's come right, your lives can begin." He raised his glass. "Happy days to you both."

Lily laughed and raised her own. "If we waited for a perfect future, sir, we should never get on with it."

"True enough," Guy agreed, gesturing to the waiter to refill their glasses. "Even so, dearest, I'm relieved your erstwhile mother-in-law is out of our picture. Broadhurst will be the perfect place for her. I would be happier if her pup were there in an adjacent padded cell, but I suppose we can't have everything."

"She swore Clive was innocent. So did Ephriam, and he had no reason to lie," Lily reminded him. "At least they are gone."

Bernadette had been adjudged criminally insane and would spend the rest of her days under guard. Clive had escaped and disappeared before the trial. Guy's contacts had traced him to the docks and learned he had taken ship for New South Wales. Dr. Ephriam would languish for years in Newgate for his part in the conspiracy.

"You know, I well understand a mother's love. But how could a woman go to such lengths, simply to advance her son to a title? Kidnapping, unlawful imprisonment, even murder?" She shook her head sadly.

Guy hummed his agreement. "I am just glad to discover Clive was her only issue and that she's in no way related to Beau, after all. The poor little fellow would have to suffer the same worry I've had all these years."

"I wonder why Jonathan never mentioned to me that his mother died in childbirth and his father married again while he was still an infant," Lily said. They had investigated birth and marriage records after Bernadette's ravings about her *only son*.

"Perhaps he didn't know it himself," Galen suggested. "He was sent away to school at seven and never lived at home again until he inherited. Bernadette might have feared to tell him at that time. She and Clive were dependent on his generosity. His death probably instigated her plot."

"So she really planned to do away with Beau?" Lily asked Galen.

He nodded. "And have it seem that he died naturally. As for you, she simply needed you out of the way. There might have been an inquiry if both you and Beau were eliminated."

Guy took her hand and gave it a comforting rub. "Let's not dwell on it any longer," he suggested. "It's over and done."

"So it is. Well, if you will all excuse me, I shall forgo dessert and coffee and retire so that I may get an early start for home tomorrow," Snively said as he rose. He nodded to Guy and Galen, who also stood. "I bid you adieu and thank you for the opportunity of furthering my research."

"It is we who thank you, Thomas," Guy answered sincerely. "We owe you more than we can ever say."

Thomas smiled and bowed to Lily, taking her hand. "Lady Lillian, I wish you all the best. Perhaps a daughter as bonny as you, or a son as delightful as little Lord Bradshaw."

"Thank you," Lily whispered, tears in her eyes.

"I'm off, as well," Galen announced without resuming his seat. "See you tomorrow?"

"No, we plan to leave for Edgefield at first light," Guy said, sounding too distracted to take proper leave of their friend.

"You'll come for the wedding?" Lily asked, smiling up at him. She and Guy were taking vows at the church in Edgefield to augment their civil ceremony. Neither of them was entirely certain it was legal anyway.

"I made the first one, didn't I?" Galen said, laughing. "Be well, both of you."

When he had gone, Guy took her hand. With his free one, he brushed away a tear that slid down her cheek. "Forgive Thomas. He had no way of knowing."

Lily toyed with her fork. "Knowing what? About children in our future?"

He nodded.

"But he does," she said, placing the utensil on the table and facing him fully. "You see, we discussed it at length while you and Galen were out investigating Clive's disappearance."

"Then why would he say such a thing about babies to you. He's made you cry!" Guy's face darkened with anger as he glanced at the door where Thomas had exited, as if he might follow.

"Can't you guess why he said it?" Lily asked, rolling her eyes and pretending impatience. "For goodness' sake, Duquesne! Thomas is first of all a physician."

His dark eyes widened, his words a mere whisper. "You are not…?"

She grinned, nodded and grasped his hands. "I am."

"But you were told…"

"By Ephriam," she reminded him, "who was under the spell of Bernadette who definitely did not want me to conceive again."

"But suppose you had? How would he ever have explained?" Guy asked.

Lily shrugged. "A miracle, perhaps? But that was highly unlikely to happen since Jonathan was of the opinion that lovemaking was created solely to produce heirs."

Guy wore a look of disbelief. "After that you sim-ply...stopped?"

Lily nodded, then cocked an eyebrow at him. "So, are you game for this little adventure? If not, you're in trouble, sir, because it's already under way." She brushed a hand tenderly over her soon-to-increase waist.

His gaze followed the motion. Then his mouth snapped shut and he shook his head as if to clear it. When he looked back at her, his dark eyes were shin-ing.

"We have to go immediately," he said, his words sounding a bit choked as he pushed back his chair and rose. "Before I cause a scandal. Whoever heard of a vis-count kissing his wife in a public dining room?"

Lily smiled. "And you can't wait to tell Beau, can you?"

He grinned his famous grin. "True, but I'm even more eager to thank his mother properly for turning my life around."

"Then kiss me, Duquesne," Lily suggested, leveling her most seductive smile at him.

He raised an eyebrow, his reluctance an obvious sham. "My lady! What would that sort of behavior do to our reputation?"

She pushed her plate away, folded her arms on the table and leaned forward to give him better access. "En-hance yours, I expect. As for mine, rumor has it I'm al-ready mad."

He tipped up her chin with one long finger and pressed his lips to hers, parting them just enough to impart the taste of wine. The kiss proved lengthy, teasing and so inviting. "I'm the one who's mad, you know. Mad for you."

She smiled and sat back away from him. "Then I should lock you away for a while. Perhaps in a bed-chamber, until you come to your senses. I would tend you constantly, of course."

"There are rooms above stairs here that would do. A long, slow attempt at a cure might be just the thing," he suggested with an enthusiastic nod.

Lily stood and took his arm, ignoring the pointed stares from other patrons. "I rather thought a hasty shock to the system might suffice."

He laughed, his eyes full of deviltry he was known for. "We'll try that first if you like. Then we shall see."

Epilogue

Edgefield—January 1860

"Is she still sleeping?"

"Yes and it's no wonder."

Lily lay in the darkened room, her limbs almost too weak to move. She could do no more than listen as voices outside the door spoke in low tones.

"Give her this when she wakes."

The words chilled her briefly, bringing back the memory of another dark room in what seemed another life. She had been so alone then, so terrified and uncertain. Perhaps that marked the moment when she began to become her true self, the woman she was meant to be.

A faint mew nearby drew her back to the present. This time she was not alone. Even if she were, the threat she had faced was a thing of the past. She had met her fear head-on and was extremely proud of that.

Light poured in as Guy entered silently and approached the bed.

She looked up and smiled. "Aren't you lucky? No boot to the head for you. I'm too weary."

Guy laughed softly, set down the lighted lamp he carried and took her hand. "I probably deserve it after what I've put you through."

A sound from the opposite side of the bed seemed to agree. Lily turned her head to look at the high-standing cradle with its lace-frilled canopy.

"Will you bring her to me?" Lily asked.

Guy hurried around the bed and gently lifted their daughter, cradling her in his large, capable hands. "Isn't she beautiful?" he whispered with awe in his voice. "Our Katherine. Our miracle. Wide blue eyes and that nimbus of gold curls. So like you." He chuckled when the baby yawned.

He settled the child in the crook of Lily's waiting arm, then lay down, too, propping his head on one hand so that he could look down at them. He touched the baby's hand and she grasped his finger. "Four hours old. She's growing up too fast."

Lily laughed. "Where is Beau?"

"Camped outside the door with Father, both eager to come in as soon as you feel up to it."

"Now is fine," Lily said, and Guy called out to them.

The door opened wider and the old earl entered, ushering her son with a hand on Beau's shoulder.

The two had become fast friends in the months since her father-in-law had recovered. Guy's father was a quiet man, one given to melancholia at times, but with less evidence of that as the weeks progressed. It seemed that Beau offered him the chance to correct all the missteps he had made with Guy when he was a boy. But wasn't that the natural order of things for grandparents?

Lily smiled up at the earl and he returned it full measure, obviously very proud of his new granddaughter, and perhaps of Lily, as well, she thought. He frequently thanked her for loving his son and for helping to restore an old fellow to reality.

They had restored Edgefield Manor, too, and lived here with him now that it was as it should be. Though they visited Sylvana Hall regularly and managed the property for Beau, this was home.

Lily beckoned to Beau. He looked very serious. The confident swagger he affected looked so like Guy's, she had to laugh.

He peered over her at the baby, his eyes narrowed. "It's very small to cause so much trouble and make you so ill."

Guy frowned. "Beau, this is your sister, not an *it*. And I daresay your mother thinks the trouble was worth it, just as she did when you were born." The reprimand was mild and Beau merely shrugged it off.

"How long will you stay sick?" Beau asked Lily.

"I'm not ill, darling, only tired. In a day or so, I shall be good as new."

Beau continued assessing the new addition. "All right, but I believe this one will be enough."

"Kick off your shoes and come up here with us," Lily told him.

He did as she asked, crawling up on the bed and kneeling between them. He cocked his head and looked at Guy. "Will she learn to talk soon?"

"Within the year, I expect she will know some words," Guy replied. "Why? Do you need to ask her something?"

Beau rolled his eyes. "No, but we can't have her

calling you Duquesne when she hears me do so. It's not the thing at all."

"What shall we do about that? I wonder," Lily said.

Beau considered carefully, staring at the baby as he thought. "Though it is common, Da is easy to say, I should think. Father would be too hard. Later perhaps she could learn that, but I believe I should call you *Da* when she's likely to overhear. Would you mind so much?" he asked Guy.

"Not at all." Guy's voice sounded thick. Lily suspected there were tears behind those lowered lids as he spoke. "Thank you, Beau."

Her son shrugged, reached out and touched the baby's foot, tracing the tiny toes with a tentative finger. He smiled. "We have to think what's best for her, I suppose."

For a long moment a comfortable silence reigned, the four of them there on the bed, the earl standing at the foot of it, observing. But life moved on, consigning the moment to a memory.

"Enough dawdling here," Beau announced, and scrambled backward off the bed. "Grandfather has promised a game of chess when I've done with my Latin." He shot the earl a saucy grin. "I shall trounce you soundly today, sir."

"We'll see about that," the earl replied with a wink at Lily and Guy.

When the door closed, Lily turned her attention to Guy. "Wishes do come true, don't they?"

He traced the line of her cheek with his finger and leaned over to kiss her lips. "I hadn't even sense enough to wish for this. You came into my life after I had accepted solitude as the only way to live."

"And you into mine, when I needed someone to show me my own strengths. We seem a mad pairing indeed," Lily said. "Do you think people will ever accept that we're really sane? I suppose there will always be rumors to the contrary."

He kissed her again. "I am mad about you and that's no rumor, it's a fact."

"And I, you. We're good for each other."

He laughed quietly and brushed her lips with his again. "The vicar's daughter and Devil Duquesne. A match made in hell. You know, that's what Londoners call Galen's neighborhood where we were wed."

"And it's led us to heaven," she replied. "You know, that's what I call this." She kissed him back as their little angel lay sleeping between them.

* * * * *

Harlequin Historicals®
Historical Romantic Adventure!

FOR RIVETING TALES OF RUGGED MEN AND THE WOMEN WHO LOVE THEM CHECK OUT HARLEQUIN HISTORICALS!

ON SALE MARCH 2005

THE BACHELOR
by Kate Bridges

At the town harvest festival, dashing bachelor Mitchell Reid is raffled off for charity—and lands in the unlikely arms of no-nonsense, hardworking Diana Campbell. Ever since the Canadian Mountie mistakenly tried to arrest her brothers, she's attempted to deny her attraction to the roguish Mitch. Twenty-four hours spent in his company just might change her mind....

TURNER'S WOMAN
by Jenna Kernan

Rugged mountain man Jake Turner rescues Emma Lancing, the sole survivor of an Indian massacre. Burned by love in the past, he's vowed to steer clear of women. But the young woman in his care is strong and capable— and oh, so beautiful. Can this lonely trapper survive a journey west with his heart intact?

If you enjoyed what you just read,
then we've got an offer you can't resist!

Take 2 bestselling
love stories FREE!

Plus get a FREE surprise gift!

Harlequin Historicals®
Historical Romantic Adventure!

CRAVING STORIES OF LOVE AND ADVENTURE SET IN THE WILD WEST? CHECK OUT THESE THRILLING TALES FROM HARLEQUIN HISTORICALS!

ON SALE APRIL 2005

THE RANGER'S WOMAN
by Carol Finch

On the run from an unwanted wedding, Piper Sullivan runs smack into the arms of Texas Ranger Quinn Callahan. On a mission to track outlaws who killed his best friend, Quinn hasn't got time to spare with the feisty lady. But he can't help but be charmed by Piper's adventurous spirit and uncommon beauty....

ABBIE'S OUTLAW
by Victoria Bylin

All hell is about to break loose when former gunslinger turned preacher John Leaf finds himself face-to-face with old love Abbie Moore. Years ago, John took her innocence and left her pregnant and alone. Now Abbie's back and needs his help. Will a marriage of convenience redeem John's tainted soul and bring love into their lives once more?